A LONG PADDLE HOME

R. G. WRIGHT

A Long Paddle Home
Copyright © 2019 by R. G. Wright

Cover Photography - Liam P. Wright
Literary Consultant - Shannen R. Wright

Tellwell Talent
www.tellwell.ca

ISBN
978-0-2288-0816-9 (Paperback)

For Patty, the woman who married this forest boy thirty two years ago and has never stopped me from putting on my moccassins.

And to the wild ones; it is in their foot prints that I walk.

FOREWORD

A PAGE FROM THE LOG BOOK OF STEVEN STILES.

S hadows had texture; hiding amongst the trees which stood guard on the rocky shore as my canoe slid past. Sound rebounded out onto the lake as my paddle hit the hull of the sleek boat; nothing stirred in the forest, yet I knew I was being followed by something unseen. I wondered what it saw and felt. Did it hear the thumping of my heart that was undoubtedly sending pulses through the hull into the water? Most importantly, did it see me as a threat, or was I a creature which merited only a cursory glance?

As I pushed my paddle into the dark water of a remote lake that has existed within its banks longer than human memory, my eyes wandered the shoreline relaying images of mystery and wonder. I left the entrapments of modern life, shedding them in the wake of my canoe. I was free to examine the world without expectations; my mind was open, allowing it to accept the possibility of a world which is far beyond the reach of logic and social engineering.

As the light faded from the landscape, the shadows disappeared and darkness filled the unseen forest trails my canoe was paralleling. The sense of being watched intensified, and I felt a pressure building deep within, whispering of danger and personal survival. Pushing through the curtain of uncertainty, I set my canoe onto the shore and walked inland to become acquainted with my fear.

Sitting with my back against a large pine in the primal darkness of the forest, I closed my eyes and immersed myself in the raw uncompromising power of the wilderness — the same power that has been haunting humans from the time of the first fire. This power pushed its way into my soul and challenged every preconceived idea I have of this place we call Earth.

THE CITY

The venue was packed with people; aisles between vendors were filled with meandering lanes of congested human traffic. People jockeyed for position and pushed their way to various booths, hunting for the pamphlets and trinkets which would become lost in their loot bags. The digitized calls of loons, wolves, and all things wilderness, broadcast throughout the space by loudspeakers, collided with the cacophony of human language to create a kaleidoscope of noise, thereby challenging the ability for anyone to engage in internal dialogue.

Steven Stiles sat on a chair in complete submission. With his elbows propped on a table and his fists pressed against his cheeks, he watched the throngs as they meandered and pushed their way past his booth. The pamphlets promoting the Sherborne Lake Canoe Trails were snatched up by people who barely took the time to examine them before they vanished into the piles of other pamphlets they carried. No one noticed the earplugs in Steven's ears.

His mind travelled back to two a.m. when his alarm clock had invaded his dreams. He had showered and put on a pressed grey shirt to which a crest was affixed denoting him as a Park warden. The shirt was followed by his favourite pants, unwashed and adorned with various offerings of the forest such as pine sap and mud stains. He had walked out to a wide dock which floated on the water of

St. Nora Lake and stood quietly on the aged planks, drawing the silence of the lake and forest deep into his core.

He had made the trip to Toronto before the sun had crested the horizon. By the time his vehicle merged into the never-ending parade of traffic on Highway 404, he was depressed and wanted to turn around.

Steven closed his eyes and tried to feel what he had experienced that very morning on the old dock, but the hell surrounding him precluded success.

"Hey mister, are you awake?"

Steven lifted his head and stared into the eyes of a young boy who was holding a book in his hand.

"I am, what's up?" Steven replied as he pulled an earplug out of his left ear.

"Can you tell me what this is?" The boy opened his book to a page which displayed a picture of a mammal.

"That's a fisher; he's part of the weasel clan. He's a carnivore and he hunts squirrels, mice, porcupines, and birds."

"Is he bad?" the boy asked.

"No way; this guy's important to the forest. He's part of a chain which keeps the forest healthy. Why did you ask if he's bad?"

"He kills things, so he's mean and bad."

Steven looked up at the boy's mother and asked her if she agreed. She nodded.

"What's your name?" Steven focused on the boy.

"Ryan."

"Ryan, I want you to pretend that your left hand is a rabbit and your right hand is a hawk. Can you do that?"

"Yes."

"Good. What does the rabbit eat?"

"Carrots!"

"Let's say green stuff, ok?"

"Ok."

Steven placed his left hand on the table and manipulated his fingers to mimic a rabbit foraging, next, he floated his right hand high above the table and told Ryan it was a hawk. Ryan's left hand nibbled at the table, mimicking Steven's hand.

"The green that the rabbit eats becomes the rabbit. Just like the food you eat will make you grow."

"Ya." Ryan's eyes were wide with anticipation.

Steven circled his right hand over his left hand and then covered it. Ryan watched closely.

"The hawk eats the rabbit." Steven monitored Ryan's mother for any signs of a negative reaction.

"The rabbit becomes the hawk," Steven continued.

"Really?" Ryan's smooth face wrinkled as he replied.

"One day, the hawk dies and falls to the ground." Steven placed his right hand on the table, palm side up.

"Why does he die?" Ryan frowned with wonder.

"Bad rabbit! I'm just kidding. All creatures die, Ryan." Steven looked at Ryan's mom, who appeared concerned.

"The hawk melts into the ground to eventually form soil. You were taught this in school, right?"

"Right!"

"What grows from soil, buddy?"

Ryan looked puzzled for a few seconds, and then he pointed to a grass stain on Steven's pants. "Green plants!" he yelled out.

"What eats green plants?" Steven pointed to his left hand which was still formed into a fist.

"Rabbits!" Little Ryan jumped up as he made the statement.

"The rabbit eats the hawk." Steven smiled as he said it.

"Wow! Can I tell my friends?"

Steven looked at Ryan's mother again; she was smiling.

"That would make me happy, Ryan." Steven drew a circle on the back of a pamphlet. "Everything is part of everything else, Ryan. Try to find all the circles you can." Steven handed the young boy the pamphlet.

"That's cool!" Ryan gave Steven a high five.

Ryan's mother walked over to Steven and spoke in his ear. "You made his day, and mine. Thank you so much." She hugged Steven lightly.

Steven smiled for the first time that day. As little Ryan and his mother blended back into the crowd, he pushed the earplug back into his ear and resumed his position at the table. He waited for the next question which would either make his day worthwhile or push him to the limits of his tolerance. Second by miserable second he observed the hands of his watch. This helped him to visualize where the sun sat in the sky. He paced in circles, staying within the taped-off confines of his booth and avoiding contact with as many people as possible.

"Are you ok?" a woman from the booth to his left called out in a voice loud enough to cut through the surrounding din.

Steven turned. "No, this place is driving me crazy; I can't hear myself think!"

"You should learn to meditate and do yoga," the lady advised as she handed Steven a brochure from her booth.

Steven looked at the brochure which sported a photoshopped picture, taken in a wooded setting, of a group of people sitting cross-legged around a man wearing a bandanna.

"Holy Fuck; try this in a real forest and you yogis would run screaming."

"Pardon? I couldn't hear you."

"I said that's a great group of people you have there. Where is this forest?" Steven pointed at the photo.

"I don't remember that particular park. We hold sessions in many different natural settings around the city. Would you like to join us?" The lady handed Steven a price list.

"You seriously think that this park is a natural setting?" Steven again pointed at the brochure.

"Of course, nature is awesome!" The woman threw her hands up in a gesture of rejoicing.

"God, we're doomed."

"Pardon?"

"Sorry, I said I agree." Steven placed the brochure in a bag which was already pregnant with other brochures.

He folded his arms across his chest and watched as the cheerful woman blissfully explained the virtues of combining yoga and nature to a group of young women. They happily inked their names onto a form, passed along their credit card information, and strode away chattering about enlightenment.

Steven's mind was bending, trying to hide deep within itself where it could not be discovered by or exposed to the rampant narcissism surrounding him.

Grabbing his backpack, he left his booth and pushed his way through the crowd to the Swift Canoe display. He ran his hand along the smooth, sleek hull of a prospector canoe. He instantly calmed and pictured himself plying his paddle while his canoe sang its quiet song as it slid across the water. Steven looked up from his reverie when he heard a familiar voice. An acquaintance from Algonquin Outfitters was engaged in explaining the virtues of a Kipawa canoe to a wealthy couple who were more concerned with the colour of the canoe than its functionality. Steven slipped through the crowd back to his booth and spent the rest of the day hoping it would end.

The moon was sliding down the western arc of the sky, pushing shadows from the trees and illuminating the forest. Steven opened the driver's door and stepped onto the gravel parking lot at the Canoe Trails main cabin. He picked up a handful of the stones.

Man, it's good to be home. That sucked!

He walked to the end of the wide dock and lay on his back. The sky overhead was a mass of stars, covering the entirety of his vision. After breathing in deeply, he exhaled the tension of the day and smiled.

There is not enough of this wilderness left for all the people who want a piece of it. What chance does this Earth have against all of them? As the wavelets lapped at the dock, Steven hoped that they had an answer to his question.

He stood up, stretched, and walked back to the pickup where he retrieved his knapsack and the bag of pamphlets. He walked to the fire pit where a rusted-out fire barrel stood waiting for an offering. With his flint and steel, he lit a ball of pine pitch which he had placed on a stick. This he placed in the bottom of the barrel. Next, he tossed in some dry kindling and then he added brochures. One by one, he watched as the fire consumed the printed paper. Larger pieces of wood were added, and soon a healthy fire licked at the top of the barrel. Steven sat in silence as he watched the flames consume the wood like a predator consuming its prey. The last brochure in his hand was the one the lady from the yoga booth had given him.

Yogis is probably not the best choice of words. It's a good thing she didn't hear me.

He looked at the paper and wondered if the people pictured could handle the reality of the bush.

Do you teach them or do you hide from them? Everyone wants a piece of the wilderness but without the wildness. Yet they can't be separated. Steven spoke the words to the barrel as he placed the yoga advertisement on the fire.

The barrel shot light out into the forest from the multiple holes in its metal jacket to create crimson stars on the leaves and trunks of trees. As the fire subsided, Steven rose and walked back to the building which he called home.

The last gasps of the fire highlighted a pair of luminescent green eyes which hovered within the darkness of the surrounding forest.

CAMP

The fire pushed its flickering light throughout the camp area, creating dancing shadows which moved in concert with the orange glow. A short distance away, a Coleman lantern chased the darkness from a rock which presently served as a table. The faint aroma of coffee, beer, and beef stew filled Ralph's nostrils with enticing comfort. He stirred the meal which simmered in a metal pot on top of a propane stove. Every few minutes, he tilted his head skywards to glance at the stars. For Ralph, site 17A was as near to paradise as life gets.

Rusty, a two-year-old black Lab, dashed around the camp area filling his nostrils with the aromas of the wilderness. Anything that he found of interest was picked up in his mouth and then dropped as soon as he discovered something else to pick up. He too was in paradise.

Tom sat close to the water which was invisible in the darkness. Small ripples tickled the sterns of the canoes as if coaxing them to leave the shore. The inky blackness engulfed him and stirred ancient fears into existence. Reaching into his jacket's left pocket, he pulled out a cigarette and put it between his lips. The flame from his lighter blinded him momentarily. Drawing lustily on the cigarette, he stood and quickly returned to the embrace of the fire.

Bill was new at camping. His back hurt from the weight of the canoe which he had carried two thousand metres to reach the campsite. Massaging his neck, he stared into the fire as it licked its way up the sacrificial wood and sent sparks into the cold embrace of the night. He wondered why he had ever signed on in the first place. Rusty raced up and pushed his way into Bill's embrace, an encounter which made Bill's pain dissipate for the duration of the hug. Realizing his feet were extremely hot, he pulled back from the fire only to see that his new rubber Crocs had become seriously misshapen. Kicking off the melting footwear, he wondered what might go wrong next.

Larry gagged; the smell emanating from the wooden box which sufficed as a toilet was horrendous. His headlight pushed the darkness back slightly, and his mind conjured up images of zombies and monsters lurking just beyond its reach. He pulled his pants up and fastened his metal belt buckle which clanged, causing a ripple in the stillness surrounding him. He walked down the pine needle path back to the camp at a hurried pace, nervously following the light from his headlight while feeling the darkness close in behind him. The closer he got to the fire, the quieter his heart became.

Ralph called the guys to the table rock. They came with bowls, cutlery, and well-earned appetites. Armed with food and beer, they returned to the warmth of the fire. Laughter and deep voices filled the night air and eddied throughout the surrounding wilderness.

"Well boys, welcome to Sherborne Lake." Ralph raised his beer to the sky and drank a long swig of the warm liquid. Bill pointed at the melted shoes on his feet and made a face which elicited an immediate response from the other three who, in unison, burst out with a laughter only a campfire can conjure up.

"What the hell, Bill! Didn't you feel the rubber melting to your foot?" Ralph tried to hide his amusement.

"Ya, I guess my shoulder hurt more than my burning foot, and I was too busy counting bug bites to notice anything else. What was wrong with any of those other campsites? You know, the ones we passed before the portage?"

"Come on, other than the bugs and the ankle-breaking terrain on the portage, it really wasn't that bad," Ralph retorted, trying to keep the stew from escaping his mouth. "I asked you what kind of camp you wanted and you voted for adventure. I mean, take a look around you, man! What else could you ask for? This place is so far removed from our everyday lives it's awesome."

Tom stood, sucked on his cigarette, and canted his head slightly to the left. "Relax and get with the program or I'll have to shoot your head clean off." His imitation of Clint Eastwood was lost on Bill.

Bill shot Tom the finger and laughed hard enough that he farted. Another loud round of laughter pushed its way into the surrounding darkness. After several hours of nursing their beers and gazing at the fire, silence engulfed the camp. Each man began to settle into site 17A in his own way. Rusty, lying on the ground with his head resting awkwardly on a log, sighed with contentment.

Smoke from the spent fire drifted toward the stars. Embers twinkled, desperately clinging to life. Beer cans, some crushed, others whole, gave audience to the sputtering last gasps of the fire. The men had retired to their tents, each happily wrapped up in his sleeping bag. Rusty had curled up beside Bill. His ears twitched and his nose was animated, but even he had fallen asleep.

WATCHED

GREEN ORBS MOVING JUST BEYOND THE REACH OF LIGHT.

The slight breeze on the night air carried information to its keen nose from the humans' shelters as its paws glided over pine needles. Its ears continuously probed the area for any sound, no matter how slight. The smell of humans was overpowering, yet it could discern the individual scent of each man. All were asleep, including the canine.

It passed below a perched raccoon which clung to the tree as if trying to disappear. It glanced at the raccoon, which averted his gaze. Stopping a few feet from the nearest tent, it moulded its body to the ground. Barely breathing, it scanned the camp area and noted where the food was. The lid of the container was still partially open. The men had tied their gear to four trees, and plastic bags had been placed over the packs. The smell of canine feces came from its left, beside the large rock with utensils adorning its top. It spotted a flashlight by the fire pit which had been left on. The flashlight cast an annoying light into the area. Rising, it moved silently through the camp. Unsheathing one of the claws on its left front paw, it depressed the button and turned the offending unit off. The dog awoke. Moving into the deeper shadows, it listened intently to the shelter in which the dog lay.

Bill stretched in his sleeping bag and pulled it up closer to his neck. The night was cool and he wished he had worn his hooded shirt. Feeling around in the tent, he realized his flashlight was missing. Pushing himself down deeper into the sleeping bag, he listened to the forest just beyond the tent wall. The weight of the dog pushing against his legs infused him with a feeling of comfort which helped him to fall back into a fitful sleep. Rusty lay with his head on Bill's leg and used his ears to search the forest.

Lying prone on the spent pine needles, it pulled the cool night air deep into its lungs and released the breath slowly. Standing, it observed the camp one more time, committing every detail to memory. With only a whisper of noise, it walked into the lake.

Rusty bolted up and barked loudly. He pawed at the door and ripped the thin nylon. Bill yelled out. Confused and swearing, he rolled over and searched for the zipper on the door, but before he managed to release the links, Rusty had ripped a Lab-sized hole through the screen. "What the hell is wrong with you?" Bill yelled at the black banshee that had just left his tent.

"Shut up, Bill!" Tom's voice was gruff from sleep.

"This fucking dog's insane! He just tore up my tent! Fuck!"

"Rusty!" Ralph's voice boomed from the tent farthest from the fire pit.

The sounds of sleeping bag zippers being opened and bodies crawling around in nylon tents filled the site. The light from flashlights bounced around the camp, eventually centring on the fire pit and highlighting the wisps of smoke rising from the cooling ashes. Rusty's barking echoed off the ancient granite walls.

Ralph ignited the Coleman lantern. Within moments a comforting yellow glow filled the area with light and shadow. The men scanned the site as if they were on a C.S.I. episode. Rusty refocused and began barking at the tree upon which the raccoon was still securely fastened. Four beams of light converged on the terrified omnivore.

"Jesus, all this for a goddamned raccoon? I could have stayed in the city and seen this right in my backyard!" Bill frowned.

The four men looked at each other and burst into laughter.

"This calls for a beer!" Larry pointed his light toward the fire pit. The lantern light was soon augmented by the light of the campfire. The men took their places next to it and their shadows stood guard around them.

WILD

"HOLD FAST TO THE ONE LAW. HERS."
STEVEN STILES

It climbed from the water and shook. Crouching low to the ground, it looked toward the humans' camp where firelight once again danced on the trees and the shadows had returned. Turning to the surrounding forest, it ran. The trees flashed past and the ground blurred. Gaining a ridge due east of the men's camp, it broke into more open terrain and dropped to its belly. Stunted birch trees grew in small isolated clumps. Rock outcrops poked through the sparse ground cover and stared at the sky with glittering quartzite and mica eyes. Two white-tailed deer moved slowly along the tree line to its left. In a flash, it was moving, covering the ground with lightning speed. It called out to the surrounding darkness. The call echoed off the Precambrian cliffs and resonated throughout the surrounding wilderness. It ran straight at the terrified deer who realized their predicament far too late. It brushed one deer with its paw as it flashed by the terrified animal. Standing in the shadows of the trees, it closed its eyes and voiced its thoughts into the night.

FEAR

SAME TASTE AS ANGER.

The men were transfixed by the fire; the soft sounds of the night forest lulled them into deep meditation. Tom slowly drew cigarette smoke into his lungs and blew it out where it met with the wood smoke and mingled within the rising column of heat. Bill's chest rose and fell slowly. Any pain he felt from the day's adventures had dissipated. Ralph stared into the fire. Lost in deep thought, he felt as if he were drifting in a space where nothing of consequence could ever manifest itself. Larry had a queasy feeling in his stomach. He stood up to head to the toilet and let off a hurricane of a fart. The men fell out of the reverie they were enjoying and laughed until their eyes were blinded by tears. Larry knew he had soiled himself and extricated himself quickly from the warmth of the fire and chiding of his companions.

Trudging his way to the privy box, Larry tried to point his flashlight in all directions at once, hating the darkness which moved beside him as relentlessly as a predator stalking him. Reaching the box just in time, his bowels let go with the force of a mudslide. He buried his head in his hands and hoped that someone had brought medicine.

The banshee-like sound that broke the stillness threw Bill off his seat and sent Rusty flying to the nearest tent where he collided with the guy wire and ripped the peg out of the ground. Tom instantly swore. Ralph jumped from his folding chair and tripped over the pot which had been left beside him.

Larry's bowels responded to the impossible sound by erupting like a split-open water bag. Barely taking the time to clean himself, he ran back to the safety of the fire.

"What the fuck was that!" he yelled at the guys.

"How the hell should I know?" Bill retorted, trying to pull his head into his sweater.

"In all my years of doing this, I've never heard anything like that!" Ralph tried to maintain a calm that he definitely did not feel.

Tom said nothing as he squatted on the ground in a vain attempt at making himself disappear.

"What the hell stinks? Did someone shit themselves?" Bill grabbed his shirt and pulled it up over his nose to block the offending odour.

"I did, asshole!" Larry confessed.

"Oh my god, man, that's brutal!" Ralph imitated Bill's shirt filter.

"Holy shit!" Tom exclaimed with zeal.

The men expelled their recent fright by laughing so hard, breathing became a chore.

"Hey guys, what was that?" a disembodied woman's voice drifted into the camp from somewhere across the lake.

Ralph cupped his hand around his mouth and replied through the darkness.

"I have no idea what that was!"

"We're freaking out! Why are you guys laughing?" the voice from the darkness drifted into the camp.

Tom stood, cupped his hands around his mouth, and shouted back, "Larry shit himself!"

Laughter filled the lake as everyone used the moment to mitigate the terror which had just recently broken the tranquility and peace of the wilderness.

ORLEY LAKE

Mist rose from the lake in a splendour of silver tendrils rising toward the red-hued sky. Softly the lake tickled the shoreline, calling campers to glide their canoes along its silky-smooth skin. The plaintive call of loons echoed through the mist, pushing the music of the wilderness deep into the souls of those who were up early enough to catch a glimpse of the ethereal beauty surrounding them.

Tom floated on the lake. A fishing rod, slightly angled and mostly ignored, lay on the gunwale of the canoe. He watched the mist as it danced upon the water and was completely at peace with where he was. The occurrences of the previous night were still fresh in his head and he chuckled at his buddies' reactions to what he believed was a normal night in the wilderness. Tom wanted to know what type of creature could have made that ball-breaking sound, but he assumed it would probably forever remain a mystery. Solving the mystery by not solving it was good enough for him. He lit a cigarette and continued to watch the mist as it coalesced and formed strange apparitions upon the lake.

"Good morning," a woman's voice beckoned from behind him. Tom dropped both his paddle and his cigarette. The butt fell into the canoe while the paddle fell into the water.

"Holy shit, you scared the hell out of me!"

"I am so sorry; I didn't mean to intrude, but we are on our way to the portage point right there." The woman tried not to laugh as she pointed toward the shoreline barely visible in the mist.

Laughing, Tom replied, "It's okay, I guess I was in some kind of trance or something. How the hell can you see where you're going?"

"GPS," the male in the stern of the canoe chimed in.

"Christ, I thought we came up here to get away from that." Tom tried to hide his obvious objection to the young man's attitude. "I just want to know where the beer and the outhouse are," he continued, while trying to figure out how to slip away from the couple.

The female smiled and the male in the stern made some kind of snide remark.

"Did you hear that noise last night?" she asked with some concern.

"We did and it startled the shit out of us. What was it, any idea?" Tom was happy to have a real topic to discuss.

"We camp here all the time and we have never heard anything like it. Must have been some jerk trying to scare people," the guy stated with an obvious lack of conviction.

"No chance that someone could have made that call. It was probably an animal being killed or something," the girl replied.

"Who knows? A raccoon's enough to stir our guys up, but I would hate to meet whatever made that call," Tom said with an obvious grin on his face. "I have to go wake the crew up and start breakfast. Have a great day." Tom was hoping his lie would end the conversation.

"Ok, take care." The girl smiled.

The couple moved into the mist toward the shore which apparently held a portage trail. Tom repositioned himself in the canoe and went back to watching the lake as it awoke.

Cassie was annoyed with her boyfriend. She felt he was too intense and it was wrecking her vacation.

"Brad, can't we just cruise for once, like that guy? We can make the campsite any time today."

"Come on, Cassie, that was an old guy. His idea of canoeing is totally different than ours; and besides, Bob and Carol could show up early. I want the camp set up before they arrive." Brad was looking at the GPS unit which was in a pouch attached to the kneeling thwart in front of him.

"Brad, the portage is straight ahead."

Brad smiled a smug grin and patted himself on the back for a great navigation job.

"We have been here before, you know." Cassie was annoyed.

A gentle splash of water hit her in the back, the complement of a well-aimed paddle splash.

Cassie searched for a suitable landing. Two logs lay in the water pointing out from shore, angled away from each other to form a funnel shape which the canoe would fit into perfectly. Then she noted a darker shape on the shore.

"Is that a rock, Brad?"

"It's just a boulder. Shit, it just moved!" Brad's reaction caused the canoe to wobble.

Cassie watched as the *rock* lifted itself and drifted into the surrounding woods.

"We are staying out here until the mist burns off, Brad! I don't give a shit about your itinerary, and I am not going through a portage if whatever that was is in there!" Her statement was louder than what was necessary and totally not negotiable.

"No problem, we'll paddle around here until the mist has burned off." Brad acted as if he truly was concerned about his girlfriend's wishes. Campsite number 50 could wait a little while.

The mist on the lake slowly coiled into the air and dissipated under the relentless gaze of the sun.

HIDE AND SEEK

A PREDATORY GAME.

Brad steered the canoe into a natural dock formed by two logs which jutted out into the lake. Cassie climbed out into ankle-deep water and held the boat for Brad as he slid the gear toward the bow of the canoe. One food barrel, two forty-litre canoe packs, and the paddles were soon on dry ground and the canoe was pulled up out of the water. Cassie felt as if she were being watched; it was an eerie sensation and she wanted to remove herself from this leg of the trip as fast as possible. Her feet were wet and the mosquitoes were thirsty, all of them looking for a donation to their offspring.

"Brad, you're leading; I am not going up this trail alone. How do we know that animal is not here watching us right now?"

"Relax, that thing is long gone and this is a short portage. We will be on Orley Lake in twenty minutes," he countered, not feeling very confident in what he was saying.

"Well, let's move; these bugs are crazy!" Cassie swatted the pesky insects. Hoisting one of the packs and grabbing the paddles, she waited until Brad had the food barrel and a canoe pack mounted on his person. Without a word exchanged, the couple made their way along the narrow and rocky portage. The trail followed a small stream which wound its way down from Orley Lake to Sherborne Lake. The trail was inclined and had many places where a misplaced foot could cause a person to lose their balance and end up in a lot of pain. Rock outcrops rose vertically along the passage and the light was dim due to the cover of evergreens which lined the trail's edge. Cassie used her bandanna to mop the sweat from her forehead as she navigated this uneven trail which felt like a walk through a haunted forest. The pair emerged from the trail to a sun-filled lake glittering with sun diamonds; bugs were nonexistent and life was great again. Cassie placed the pack on the ground and sat on it. Taking her shoes off, she started counting the number of bug welts that adorned her ankles. Brad placed the barrel and his canoe pack on the ground.

"I won't be long." He headed back down the trail toward the canoe.

Cassie arranged the pack as a pillow and sprawled out.

This is living. The warmth of the sun on her face and body helped her to shed the last traces of her unease.

Brad made good time down the trail now that he was unencumbered. He was able to look at the rocks and tenacious moss which clung to them. Boulders the size of trucks lay scattered down the trail, evidence of erosion and glacial bulldozing. He noticed the marks left by other people on trees and in the mud on the trail. Large and small animal tracks were also imprinted on the muddy sections of the portage. Upon reaching the south end of the portage and his canoe, Brad was instantly aware of the difference between the two lakes. The Sherborne Lake side of the portage was still in shadow and the bugs were fierce. Hoisting the forty-pound boat onto his shoulders, he turned and began to retrace his steps. Sweat dripped into his eyes and the bugs were relentless. Due to the incline of the portage, the canoe's bow was only four feet off the ground; this limited Brad's vision. Beside a small waterfall which noisily announced the water's journey to Sherborne Lake, the trail levelled out, freeing Brad's eyes to wander the trail to the next bend. Within three paces he froze. Directly in the centre of the path was a nightmarish animal which stood on two legs and exuded primal power unlike anything he had ever seen or felt. Its eyes bored a hole into his soul, suffocating his civilized brain. A deep vibrating growl emerged from its slightly opened mouth, in which ripping teeth were clearly visible.

Brad stood transfixed. He tried to scream but no sound came from his constricted vocal cords. Urine soaked his shorts as panic took hold of his body. Just as fast as it had appeared, the animal vanished. Brad dropped the canoe and screamed. He ran as fast as he could toward Cassie. Arriving at Orley Lake, he collapsed in a grovelling heap at her feet. Tears streamed down his face and sweat dripped from every pore of his skin. Visibly shaken, he told her of his encounter.

"I'm telling you, Cassie, the fucking thing just vanished! I saw it. It growled and vanished, I mean what the fuck!" Brad was trying to come to terms with the last five minutes of his life.

"Maybe the combination of bug spray and your allergy medicine is affecting you. It had to be a bear, in which case we should get on the water!" Cassie was freaking out yet trying to remain as calm as possible.

"I know what a bear looks like. That was no fucking bear, Cassie; where the hell did it go!"

"Let's take the bear spray and get our canoe; we need to get off of this portage!" She pointed to the campsite on the opposite shore which would be their home for the next few nights. Her shaky hands fumbled with one of the packs' buckles and she released the can of bear spray from its nylon prison. With spray and knife in hand, Brad and Cassie summoned the courage to recover their canoe.

It lay as it was dropped, slightly on its right side and completely helpless. Brad grabbed the gunwales and hoisted the canoe onto his tense shoulders. Cassie held the bear spray in a vice-like grip in her right hand; the knife was clenched in her left hand. She resisted the urge to run as she moved back toward the safety of the lake while cringing at every little noise the forest had to offer. Reaching the end of the portage, the pair threw their gear into the canoe without care and launched the boat quickly into the embrace of Orley Lake. The canoe bounced off rocks as Brad pushed hard to leave the confines of the small inlet. Once they were a sufficient distance from shore, he stopped paddling and slumped over the thwart in front of him. Cassie slipped into the bow of the canoe and lay her head on the seat.

"You scared the shit out of me, Brad!" She closed her eyes to focus on her pulse which was out of control.

"I saw it! It was there! I don't know what it was, but it was there!"

"Let's get to that island and relax, and then we can paddle to our site and set up," Cassie pointed toward a small island which was adorned by three gnarled white pines.

"Ok, we will hang out on the island for a bit and then head back to our site. Does that sign say fifty on it?" Brad slipped his paddle into the lake and headed toward the little rocky island that would offer some sanctuary.

"Yes, Bradley, it is our site. You've been here before. Are you losing your memory or something?"

"No, I just got confused, if that's ok with you?" he replied defensively.

Cassie rolled her eyes and tightened her grip on her paddle, resisting the anger which Brad seemed always able to conjure up within her.

CUSTOMERS

Susan stood looking at the map pinned to the bulletin board next to the desk. Pins of various colours showed which sites were occupied and which were designated as rejuvenation sites. Susan's eyes travelled over the map while memories played movies in her mind.

The argument she had with her boyfriend the night prior kept playing back in her head like a skipping record. She absolutely knew he was wrong and she was determined to prove the point. She sipped her coffee and felt the warm liquid slide into her stomach.

The telephone sitting idle in its cradle rang. Breaking out of her daydream, she placed her cup down. Picking up the handset, she spoke with the automation that comes with time served.

"Sherborne Lake Canoe Trails, Susan speaking. How can I help you?" She gazed out of the cabin's window at the cars in the parking lot.

"I would like to report a wild animal incident!" a woman's voice electronically replicated itself in Susan's ear. "My name is Mary Jenson and I am on site number 19 on Sherborne Lake. Last night and early this morning we heard terrible screaming coming from the forest! My husband was fishing this morning and saw a large creature stalking him from the shoreline!"

Susan wanted to scream and throw the phone against the wall. "Mrs. Jenson, you probably saw a black bear. They won't harm you as long as you keep your distance and keep your site clean. Bears are not interested in people except for the food they carry."

"I want you to send someone out here right now!" Mary countered, not believing for a minute that Susan knew of what she spoke.

"Steven Stiles is on the lake; he is our Park warden. I will contact him and have him meet you." Susan tried to maintain control of her emotions.

"Fine, I'll wait. We were going to do some sightseeing, but this animal has all but ruined our trip!" Mary countered.

"I will call Mr. Stiles and then get back to you to let you know when to expect him."

"Hopefully it is sooner rather than later!"

The connection went silent.

"Damn bitch!" Susan yelled at the walls. She depressed the call button on the two-way radio. "Steve, it's Sue."

"Hi Sue, go ahead," Steven's voice burst into the room.

"Can you talk?"

"Ya, what's up?"

"Some lady by the name of Mary Jenson on site 19 wants you to go and hold her hand; she thinks a bear is stalking her and wants us to deal with it."

Steven's voice filled the room again, "Sue, did they see it, or did they imagine they saw it?"

"They saw it, apparently; it was allegedly stalking the husband while he was fishing from his canoe."

"Sue, I'm just putting into Sherborne across from 25; tell them I will be there within thirty minutes. Stay cool; I will update you in a bit." Steven hoped the radio would stay mute.

"Thanks, Steve. Watch your ass on this one; Mary Jenson is a first-class bitch," Sue stated while looking out the window at a young guy who had just climbed out of a jeep.

"Thanks," Steve's voice filled the room again.

The guy from the jeep smiled at Sue and caught her off guard; she smiled and retreated to her desk while desperately trying to fix her hair.

The wind was steady from the northwest, pushing the waves directly at him. Steven swung the canoe west and dug his paddle deep into the cool lake. The sleek green fifteen-foot prospector lurched forward and slid across the water. Steven pushed hard into the wind which seemed determined to place him back where he started. By keeping to the shoreline, he was able to mitigate some of the wind's force. Reaching a point of land which jutted out into the lake, he aimed the canoe northeast and paddled hard until he reached the opposite shore. This sheltered him from the wind. Rounding the bend, he slid past a pair of beavers who were busy chewing on some plants. Startled, they slapped the water hard and submerged. Steven smiled. A dozen paddle strokes later, he rounded the point and spotted site 19.

As he approached, he saw a woman in a red tank top waving him in. She had blond hair and looked as if she had just come from a salon; she also had the attitude of a person who gets everything they want.

"Good morning," he called out to her.

"Are you Steven?" the woman countered.

"Yes, how can I help?" He slid his canoe into a sideways landing.

Without a preamble, the woman told Steven of her encounter with a bear and complained about the customer service she had received from the office. Steven tied his canoe to a small tree and climbed out of the boat.

"I will have a look around for tracks or anything that will help identify the animal you saw," he replied while trying to ignore the woman's glare.

A man sat on a camp chair cleaning a fish.

"Sir, never clean fish within your camp area. Animals such as bears and raccoons are attracted to the smell and you will be visited!" Steven blurted out. "Do you have a valid fishing license?" he added.

"Yes, I do, and I rented this site so I may do as I wish!" the man shot back.

Reaching into his pocket, Steven turned on his voice recorder as a precaution. He also pulled his small camera from a case on his belt; this elicited a response from Mary.

"This is an invasion of privacy; how dare you take pictures of our camp!"

"Mrs. Jenson, I am here to help. I see nothing here to show that you were threatened in any way, but I do see that you have nailed your clothesline to that pine tree and that's in violation of our rules." He pulled out the Park's bylaw pamphlet and handed it to her.

"Is this what you call helping people?" Mary yelled at him.

"This is what I call doing my job, Mrs. Jenson; a job I take very seriously. I hope you realize that I do have the authority to evict you from this site immediately. This is a wilderness park: bear, wolf, fox, marten, fisher, and a host of other animals call this place home. If you can't handle that, I would highly recommend you go to a place where all your expectations can be fulfilled." Steven used a deep and authoritative voice.

"Don't you dare talk to my wife like that!" the man said while attempting to look tough in his expensive Dockers shoes and Tilley clothing.

"I am the Park warden, and you are?"

"Harvey Jenson. I'm an attorney," the man stated, obviously trying to intimidate Steven.

"The animal that is causing you concern is a permanent resident, and you are visiting. Camp in the proper fashion and there will be no issues. Unfortunately, you have already spoiled this site due to your lack of knowledge. Now I am going to ask you to leave before nightfall for your own safety."

"Just shoot the damn bear; this is our site!" Mary shouted.

Steven pulled out his radio. Pushing the button, he called Susan.

"Go ahead, Steven," Susan's voice spilled into the campsite.

"Susan, is site 25 available for tonight?"

"No, a group from Montreal is using it. The Sherborne access sites are open," Susan offered.

"Hold on, Sue." Steven turned to Mary. "Where did you park your vehicle?"

"At the Sherborne access, why?"

"Perfect. You have a choice: pack up your gear and move to any one of the sites at the access, or leave the Park." He held down the radio button, hoping that Susan was listening.

"This is bullshit! I will report you, I promise!" Mary had a fire burning in her eyes.

"My responsibility is to protect the Park and keep you safe from yourselves. I'm doing just that. Please be off this site by dusk; I'm closing it for safety reasons. Try to enjoy the rest of your stay."

He wanted to say a hell of a lot more but resisted the urge. Sliding his boat into the water, he climbed in and did not look back. The feel of the craft under him calmed him; however, he pulled on his paddle with more vigour than was needed. Steven looked at the sun. *It's not quite noon*, he thought as he put distance between the Jensons and his canoe. He never got used to dealing with people like the Jensons. He imagined ways in which he could deal with them. Throwing them into the water was the gentlest of all the thoughts which clamoured for attention in his crowded brain.

DESTINY OR CIRCUMSTANCE

L arry stood knee-deep in the water on a sandbar; the water felt great on his legs and feet. Dipping his hands into the lake, he played with the suspended particles of pyrite which had been stirred up from the sediment.

If only this were real gold.

Voicing the thought which flickered in his mind for a second was followed immediately by the realization of the destruction it would bring.

"What the hell!" Bill shouted as something unseen managed to make its way into his swim trunks as he lay in the water facing upwards. He jumped up and pulled his shorts off, exposing himself to the world.

"Holy shit; the moon's huge today!" Tom yelled out from his position on the shore while throwing a stone at the naked man ten feet from him.

"Something got into my trunks; a guy can't even swim here in peace!"

"You really are meant for a condo, Bill," Larry said, laughing.

"Ok, Grizzly Adams." Bill pulled his shorts back on.

"Bill, did that thing chew your dick off!" Ralph asked with tears streaming down his cheeks.

"Shut up, guys!"

"I've got the evidence." Ralph held the camera for all to see.

"You will never sell it!" Tom laughingly shouted back.

Bill splashed Tom as he passed him, farting in the process.

"Shit!" Tom dove into the lake to escape the lethal gas. Larry bent over, trying to regain his breath from the exertion of laughing.

"Great show; how long did you rehearse?" Steven said while holding the canoe steady with his paddle. All four men stared incredulously at the person in the canoe who seemed to appear from out of thin air.

"This stuff's gone on all night!" Larry answered.

"It usually does. Name's Steven, I'm with the Canoe Trails. Do you mind if I come in?"

"Sure," Ralph replied.

Tom had already made it to the campfire area and was cleaning up the cans from the previous night. Steven saw him from the water and grinned.

The same response I get from everyone, he thought to himself as he aimed the canoe to shore.

"How's it going, guys?" Steven pulled his prospector up on the sand.

"It's a great spot and very few bugs," Bill said, sounding like a used car salesman.

"Relax; I am not here to bust you. I'm just checking on you." Steven felt slightly guilty for his intrusion.

"That's a relief. Don't worry about Bill. Come on and have a beer, man; you've got to be thirsty," Tom said while he pulled the tab off of a Molson can.

"Doesn't do it for me, but thanks. I drink only the hard stuff out here, see." Steven pulled a Nalgene water bottle from a pocket in his cargo pants.

A steady breeze was flowing through the lot and keeping the vampire bugs at bay as the five men took their places around the nonexistent fire. Rusty ran up to Steven and put his left paw on Steven's leg.

"I got a complaint from a lady just over there." Steven pointed toward site 19.

"Sorry, man," Bill responded instantly.

"Relax, it's not about you. The complaint was about a large animal and I want to make sure you're not going to gut fish or do anything stupid to attract it in." Steven ran his fingers through Rusty's fur.

"Last night some freakish noise came from over there." Ralph pointed northward. "It woke the entire area up sometime around one or two in the morning."

"That's what the woman told me. She also said that she saw something stalking her husband while he was fishing. Have you seen anything strange, guys?" Steven pulled out his notebook.

"Ya, just a few minutes ago, you must have seen it too!" Tom replied. This elicited a round of laughter from all the men present, including Bill.

"Last night, Rusty went crazy and all hell broke loose. I felt as if I were being watched while I sat on the box," Larry stated as he squished his beer can.

"Let me look around." Steven stood and the men followed.

He told the guys to hold onto Rusty and not to follow him. He walked to the privy box and noticed where the pine needles had been disturbed by the men's feet. Beyond the box was a slight trail to the northeast which led to a bay. Steven followed the trail. Kneeling down, he noticed depressions in the layers of pine needles; he could discern only two depressions. Walking to the bay he scanned the mud on the shore. Clearly visible was a print which showed four two-inch-long toes, a vestigial toe, and a heel pad which was unlike any he had come across. No claw marks were visible. He placed his pencil beside the track and took several pictures of the print from various angles. He looked over to the opposite shore which was twenty feet away. A path from the waterline led into the forest. Steven walked into the water fully clothed, swam across the bay, and went straight to the path.

"That guy's nuts!" Bill said to the others as they stood on a rock outcrop facing the bay.

"What's he after?" Ralph replied, while trying to hold onto Rusty.

Steven appeared from the bush on the opposite shoreline and called back, "Hey guys, I found a track over here. I am going to follow it for a bit; you can tag along if you want."

"Nope, we're all good, buddy. You go right ahead and do your Davie Crockett thing; we'll watch your canoe and stuff," Tom said while pulling out a broken cigarette from the deck in his back pocket.

"If you don't mind, I could use your dog for a bit. He has a better nose than I do." Steven held his hand over a fresh track he had just found.

"Sure, his name's Rusty, but don't eat him." Ralph let go of the Lab's collar. Rusty shot forward, clearing the dead falls and rocks with the agility that only a dog possesses. With his tongue draping out of the left side of his mouth, he dove into the shallow bay and swam as if he had flippers rather than paws. Reaching the opposite bank, Rusty shook violently and dove on Steven, who promptly fell over and ruined the good print. The men laughed until their vision was blurred by tears.

"That's how we chase wardens off!" Larry shouted.

"What the hell do you feed this dog?" Steven yelled out.

"Wardens!" Tom said, sitting down to catch his breath. Bill, Larry, and Ralph joined Tom on the rock and watched as Steven and the dog disappeared into the forest.

SPOOR

INFORMATION LEFT BEHIND.

The forest was warm and humid. Steven pulled his collar up around his neck to preclude the mosquitoes from an easy target. The trail led up an incline which passed through an open area that sat high up in the centre of a spit of land. Rusty flew up the trail with his nose flat on the ground. Steven was sure the dog was tracking whatever it was that had made the mark in the mud. The dog was ahead and out of sight in no time at all. Steven kept a good pace, negotiating the terrain as best he could while listening for Rusty. The dog came back into view. *That's one awesome dog,* he thought as he reached the clearing. Rusty nosed the ground, completely absorbed in his canine world. Steven knelt down beside the Lab and looked at the spot that Rusty was examining. Moss and lichen had been dislodged and the plants had been forced back toward the direction of the trail Steven had just vacated. Claw marks were visible, scratched into the rock by one hell of a powerful animal. *I wonder if this is a cougar?* he said aloud while looking at Rusty. Walking to the north, Steven stood in the centre of the clearing and called out, imitating the howl of a wolf. He took a few more photos and retraced his steps back to the camp.

Rusty jumped into the water and started to swim in circles. Steven crossed the small bay and joined the men.

"Fuck, man, what the hell was that sound?" Bill asked, clearly worried.

"It was me; I wanted to see if that was the direction the sound came from last night."

"That is exactly where it came from, give or take a bit," Larry responded while the other three men verified his answer with nods of their heads.

"I figured it was. I think what everyone heard last night was a cougar. I have never seen or heard one, but they are in the area. No worries though; they are not interested in you, but keep a watch on Rusty there. He's no match for a cat, though somehow I think he knows that anyway."

"There are cougars out there? Where are they, let's go, guys!" Tom said in his usual joking tone.

"Not the human type, idiot!" Ralph blurted out.

"Christ, that makes me feel so much better, a huge freaking cat prowling around the campsite at night, no worries." Bill's eyes grew wider by the second.

"Bill, honestly, you're ok; that cat doesn't see you as food," Steven said, trying to allay the man's fear.

"No, it just wants to play with your balls," Tom replied, smiling. Ralph and Larry were also enjoying the moment.

"Fuck off! This is one hell of a great time. I have open wounds all over me, my muscles are killing me, I haven't slept in twenty-four hours, and now there is some huge fucking cat stalking us, great!" Bill was seriously annoyed.

"What muscles?" Larry shot back. Four of the five men, standing on the raised outcrop of Canadian Shield rock, broke out in laughter. The sound echoed off the surrounding rock walls and reverberated across the lake. Ravens lifted into the air, adding their conversations to the echoes bouncing from shoreline to shoreline.

TENSIONS

Steven paddled the canoe around a smooth rock face and aimed it toward site 17. Reaching the site, he pulled the canoe up, took his notebook out of his day pack, and headed for a dome-shaped rock outcrop on the south side of the island which seemed designed for contemplation. Sitting, resting his back against a pine, he closed his eyes. Images of animals drifted through his consciousness, but none of the images matched the information he had obtained from his investigation. He reached for the notebook and jotted down some points about this animal.

One: No real image, just large. Compared to what?

Two: Damage to campers' equipment nonexistent.

Three: Tracks are sketchy at best, long toes, four. No claws within the track.

Four: Sound of the animal is unknown, no imitation heard.

He placed the book into his leg pocket and scanned the lake. A canoe poked its nose out from the channel and was heading east toward the landing. Steven picked up his monocular and rested his elbows on his knees. He worked the focus ring, bringing the canoe and its occupants into a sharp focus. The woman in the bow was

Mary Jenson. Harvey was piloting the craft, attempting to keep it moving in one direction. Steven could hear Mary from where he was sitting. Some words were lost in the faint current of wind but the tone was more than audible. *The poor bastard doesn't know any different; he just can't see it,* Steven said out loud to the ants which crossed the granite he sat upon. He was glad to see that the Jensons had taken his advice and were heading to the landing. He stood and stretched, scratched behind his ears where the bugs had found his skin, and retraced his steps to his canoe. Steven lifted the boat into the water, taking notice of the many paint marks on the rocks where others had not been careful with their boats. He took up position within the canoe and turned its bow toward the Orley Lake portage trail.

The campsite was open bedrock. Dense forests backed against it and the sites that were level enough for tents were few and far between. Their tent was relatively small, yet finding a suitable footprint for it was difficult. Brad and Cassie searched around for two suitable places: one for them and one for their friends. Cassie found a small moss-covered area close to the trail leading to the privy. Brad found a relatively flat site five yards from Cassie's site. His site was high and dry and the lake could be seen clearly from the open door of the tent.

"Cassie, let's set up here; there may even be room for the other tent." Brad was already clearing sticks from the area.

"I'll get the tent," she stated while feeling somewhat usurped by his choice. Walking toward the canoe, she found herself lost in the beauty of the lake and its privacy. The deer flies were bad and insect repellent did nothing to deter the pesky dive bombers from their intended target. Donning her trusty camp hat with its cloth towel draped over her neck, she grabbed the canoe pack which contained the tent. "This site is great. The fire pit is perfect and the view of the stars will be awesome," Cassie said as she walked back to Brad.

He greeted her with a hug and a kiss. Cassie pulled the tent bag from the pack and placed the bag on the ground. Then, grabbing her camera, she took a few shots of Brad and the site. Small and fast to set up, the tent was totally waterproof and windproof; she was proud of this tent as it had been her decision to buy it. The pair set up the tent and discovered there was room for a second tent in the same area. She was glad and hoped that their friends would set up beside them. Brad busied himself by setting up the kitchen area. He placed the Primus stove beside a rock which would act as a windshield and then he set the mess kit up beside it. Next, he placed his collapsible sink on a flat rock and placed their bowls and cutlery on a cloth beside the sink.

Cassie tried to ignore the smell emanating from the latrine by looking at the tall cliff south of her. She loved the way the rocks formed intricate patterns and the sunlight glistened off the different minerals contained within the ancient outcrop. She heard voices drifting across the lake to where she sat. Bob and Carol had arrived.

Brad and Cassie met them at the shore. Their friends were tired and they looked haggard.

"Don't try that portage from Sundew Pond to Little Avery: there isn't one, period. I had to drag that piece of shit across the mud to get it here and I lost a good shoe in the process!" Bob stated before he said hello. He was a tall guy with a receding hairline and scars on his face from a battle with every teenager's enemy — acne.

"It's nice to see you too!" Cassie shot back.

"Sorry Cassie, we just went through hell and I was venting." Bob looked rather sheepish as he apologized for his attitude. The four exchanged hugs and stories as they sat in the warm sunshine. Bob's tension slipped away, evaporated by the sun and the open space.

Steven placed the prospector into the water at the end of the three-hundred-and-sixty-metre portage. The rocky shoreline was a menace to all canoe hulls. Stepping knee-deep into the silt-laden water, he placed his canoe down and climbed into the boat where he floated amongst the logs and debris. He wiped the sweat from his face and neck, tied his wet moccasins to the centre thwart, and placed his life jacket in front of him.

"Susan, you there?" Steven spoke into the radio.

"Steve, what's going on?" Susan's voice drifted into the small bay where he sat.

"Check on site 50 for me. See who's there and if there are any priors, thanks." Steven watched a turkey vulture float in the air currents high above Orley Lake.

"Sites rented to Brad Tomlinson from Toronto, expect a party of four. No priors and they're regulars."

"Thanks, Sue, you're great. I'm going to see if they've had any weird experiences. Something has people's attention out here. I'll keep you posted."

"Steven, do you know if the Jensons moved to the Sherborne access sites?"

"They did. I watched as they headed for the landing, and I could hear her as I sat on site 17."

"What a piece of work that one is. You take care, Steve."

"Ok, Sue. I'll probably stay out in the field tonight. Is 17 booked?"

"Nope, you're clear."

"Thanks, I'll call within the hour." He clipped the radio to his belt and paddled the canoe around the obstacles which seemed determined to keep the boat from entering open water.

Brad and Bob sat near the fire pit which offered a perfect view of Orley Lake. Immersed in small talk, they failed to notice the green prospector as it drifted out from the portage bay. Cassie and Carol were setting up the second tent which was a confounding mess of poles and sleeves when Carol looked up to see a canoe heading in their direction.

"Who's that?"

"I have no idea." Cassie was glad for the distraction from the mess that was supposed to be a tent. "Brad, we have a visitor," Cassie shouted down to the guys. The two looked up and were startled to see a man sitting offshore only a few yards away.

"Can we help you?" Bob called to Steven.

"My name's Steven Stiles; I am with the Sherborne Lake Canoe Trails. Mind if I stop in for a moment?"

"Why don't you make use of your time by fixing the portage to Sundew Pond?" Bob shot out at Steven's bow.

"Wow! That is not why I'm here. This is back country, not some lame-ass resort. Mind your manners, pal," Steven fired back, completely stunned at the cheap shot.

"Shut up, Bob, you freak. Come on in. Sorry, this guy doesn't get out much," Brad said, trying to relieve the stress that filled the air like ink.

Steven paddled to a grassy spot on the shoreline where he pulled the prospector up. The girls had heard the bullshit spewed out by Bob and were completely embarrassed to show their faces. They made their way back to the tent and tried to look busy.

"How long have you been here?" Steven asked Brad.

"I just got here about an hour ago," Bob replied.

"I asked him." Steven pointed at Brad.

"We got to Sherborne two days ago and came here just this morning."

"Mind if we talk for a bit?" Steven asked.

"Sure, do you want Cassie also?"

"That would be great." Steven started heading for a ledge of rock which was protected from the glaring sun by a matriarchal pine. Bob began to follow. "I have no need for you to join us." Steven's stare stopped Bob in his tracks.

Brad and Cassie sat in the shade with Steven. He took the notebook from his pocket and questioned the couple in relation to strange occurrences. Brad tried to cover his obvious fear but Cassie was an open book. She told Steven of the animal on the trail and he could tell from the couple's reaction that the story was real.

"Thanks for the info. I can't tell you what you saw or heard, but you're experienced enough to know that nothing out here will cause you grief — except for him." Steven pointed at Bob who was flailing his arms around trying to figure the tent out. The three laughed and walked toward the tent.

"Sorry about earlier," Bob quietly stated.

"No, you aren't. You're only saying sorry to the badge and that's not cool. That tent is old school; the rods follow the sleeves." Steven laid the tent out and pushed the rods through their respective nylon sleeves. Within minutes the tent was up and the girls were beaming. "Keep your food secured and you will be fine. Call this number if anything happens. I will be on 17 tonight." He ripped the notepaper from his book and handed it to Brad.

"Thanks, sir, we will be fine. I have bear bangers which will scare the shit out of anything breathing." Brad thought he was impressing Steven with his camping skills.

"Doubt you'll need those, but good planning." Steven pushed off and headed back to the portage. As he approached the inlet, four people in two canoes were entering the water. He stayed out in the lake as they paddled past.

"Hey gang, watch that portage from Orley to Little Avery. It's a tough one. Stay on solid ground and don't ever step onto the muskeg," he warned them as they paddled past.

"Thanks, see you later," a girl responded from the second canoe in a condescending tone.

The Park is full of them today, Steven voiced his displeasure to the canoe.

Entering the portage, he noticed a red canoe bag left on the bank. Picking it up, he turned his boat around and chased the group. Steven locked his left arm and drove his otter tail paddle deep into Orley Lake. The canoe responded by shooting forward. The next few strokes brought the boat up to speed and it glided across the lake as if propelled by a motor. The group he was chasing had no idea he was closing on them; only when he passed one of the boats did they notice him.

"Holy shit! Where did you come from?" a shirtless jock in the stern of the first canoe blurted out.

"You forgot your bag back there." Steven pointed behind him. "Normally, I'm not a delivery service, but you guys were close. I figured you would need it." He brought his canoe to a standstill beside the Kipawa they were paddling.

"Thanks, I don't know how we did that," a redheaded teen in the second canoe shouted out.

"Always do a double check when you load the boats. Trust me, if you had put one more portage between you and that bag, you wouldn't have come back for this." Steven tried not to lecture.

"We sure would. Those are my clothes and things; we would have to come back," a blond girl spoke out from the lead canoe.

"Think about that after you finish the next portage. Where are you guys heading?"

"We're camping on Plastic Lake," the jock stated.

"Do you have your confirmation slips with you?"

"Ya." The jock handed Steven a piece of paper with the registration number and the name of John Mathews printed on it.

"All right, please stay clear of the muskeg," Steven said, passing the slip back to John.

"You keep saying that, but we have no idea what you're talking about?" a brunette of about seventeen years old said from the second canoe.

"Gang, listen: I don't know how often you have been wilderness camping, but judging from your gear I would say seldom. There is a section of water coming up which has floating islands on it. These are not solid enough for standing on. If you punched through, the only way out is to swim underwater toward the light. Avoid them. The portage is hard. It is not defined well, but it will keep you on solid ground. Take your time and double carry the canoes if you can, especially the blue one there which looks like a tank." Steven pointed at the second canoe.

"It's my dad's, and you're right; we had a really hard time carrying it up that portage," the brunette said while holding her paddle across the gunwales of the tank, as Steven had called it.

"I don't see a lot of food, guys; do you have any?" He was completely mystified by this group's obvious lack of preparation.

"It's all in that bag there; we're going to fish and stuff," John stated very proudly.

"Ok, have a good time and keep safe."

"Don't worry; we came well-prepared," John Mathews stated while grinning from ear to ear. His redheaded buddy was smiling at the inside joke, which caused the two girls to blush. Steven twisted his paddle, turned the canoe around, and aimed for the portage to Sherborne Lake.

WITNESSES

Small waves pushed up onto the shallow sand beach at Sherborne landing. Five teenagers stood in the ankle-deep water and delighted in the feel of the sand as it worked its magic on their feet. Six canoes, all in various stages of wear and tear, sat on the beach waiting for equipment and supplies to be loaded into their hulls. Small wavelets lapped at the hulls and set off a Morse code-type tapping that signalled all boaters into the water. A yellow school bus, which had just navigated the rough axle breaking Sherborne Lake Road, sat quietly facing away from the lake, as if it were somehow disappointed it could not follow the group on their adventure. People clambered in and out of the interior, each carrying a bag or knapsack, water jug, or crate of foodstuffs. The wilderness sounds surrounding the group suddenly vanished as the diesel engine coughed into life and spewed black smoke from the chimney-like tailpipe.

Mark Evans entered the bus for a final inspection; walking up the aisles, he looked above and below the seats, making sure nothing was left behind. Satisfied that all was well, he thanked the driver and verified the meeting at St. Nora in four days' time. Stepping off the bus, Mark waved to the driver, and the bus lurched forward for the torturous journey out. He watched as the yellow monster climbed up the hill and disappeared around the top bend in the road. Turning to his campers, he called for them to gather around him.

"Ok everyone, we're here!" A loud yell of appreciation erupted from the campers. "I want each group to select a canoe and set it in the water with the bow out. That's the front of the boat; it will have the Algonquin Outfitters label on it." Some people laughed, others were thankful for the added instructions. "Grab your gear and place it beside your boats and I will show you how to load them. Ok, let's go!" Mark issued instructions with the practiced ease of experience.

Gear moved across the beach and was soon strewn around each canoe. Mark showed his wards the best way to stow gear so that it balanced the canoe and would stay in place while they travelled across the lake. Once all the gear was stowed within the boats, Mark gathered the group together.

"Listen up! We have a long paddle ahead of us, and I want no fooling around out there. Stay tight and no splashing with paddles; we want dry gear tonight. We got here late and have about an hour and a half before dark, so grab a paddle and let's launch!" The group turned and ran excitedly to the boats.

"What's that?" a girl said while pointing to the opposite shore which was somewhat shaded. Mark grabbed his binoculars while others took cameras out from their hiding places.

"It looks like a moose," Mark called out. The entire group watched as the moose entered the water and swam to a small rock island. The excitement was electric as all the campers ran to the beach to catch the rare sighting. Harvey Jenson joined the group with his S.L.R. camera and started taking shots.

The large undulate struggled to find footing on the rocky shore. Another large animal emerged from the mainland and dove into the water; the moose found his footing and bounded toward the opposite end of the island chased by something that ran with unbelievable speed.

The campers witnessed the brutality of the kill in which the moose was hit and torn into two. A sound similar to that of a baseball bat hitting a punching bag came a few seconds later. The immense power of the collision threw the moose and his killer into a thicket of low-lying juniper and blueberry bushes. The crowd on the beach was completely silent.

"Holy fuck, what the hell was that?" Nick, a broad-shouldered youth and the unofficial leader of the campers managed to blurt out. The entire beach erupted into conversation, with some people excitedly commenting on the event while others remained mute.

Harvey Jenson ran to his tent and immediately started to take it down. Mary was ahead of him, throwing gear into their BMW. Not one word was exchanged between the two as they frantically packed. The people on the beach milled about, trying in vain to assimilate the vision they had just seen and put it into a perspective their civilized brains could understand.

"Hey!" Mark yelled out as loud as he could to break through the noise. "Listen up, we are staying here tonight. Get your stuff from the canoes and set your tents over there. No arguments! Flip the canoes over on the beach, and get moving!"

The crowd broke into action. People began to move in the direction of the canoes. Three young girls and two boys were inconsolable as they lay on the ground in a huddled mass beneath a ragged maple tree. Almost in unison, they stated that they had to go home. Mark grabbed his cell phone and punched in the number for the Canoe Trails cabin. He relayed the message to Susan and asked for special permission to stay at the landing for the night.

"No problem, Mark; set up there. Get a fire going and hopefully the group will calm down. Steven Stiles is in the area. I will see if I can get him to help you out." Susan felt sick. She looked on the board to see how many campers were in the immediate area.

Steven's radio crackled to life as he was traversing the portage back to Sherborne Lake.

"Steve, we have a serious situation at the landing. A large group of campers, Mark's group, witnessed a moose kill either on 17 or on the island in front of it. They are scared to death and are staying at the landing for the night; their intended sites were 22A and 22B. Everyone at the landing saw it." As Susan's voice filled the void of the upside-down hull of the canoe, Steven increased his pace. Reaching the lake, he flipped the canoe into the water and took the radio off his belt. He pushed the transmit button.

"Susan, I got your message. Did they give you an idea as to what the predator was?"

"No, but I bet it is still there. Where are you?"

"I just put into Sherborne from Orley; I can be at 17 in five."

"Call me back soon; I am sticking around until I hear from you."

"Will do," Steven said as he jumped into the canoe and paddled hard for the island. He placed his camera around his neck and turned the unit on. The canoe shot through the water. He pushed as hard as he could; the shaft of his paddle was bending with the pressure. He closed on site 17 and scanned the island, knowing it was impossible to see it from the landing. Rounding the west side of 17, he aimed directly for a long rocky island situated due south. He paddled hard through the fragile lilies which grew in profusion between the two pieces of land. As he steered the boat through the centre of the channel formed between the mainland and the rocky island, the smell of blood permeated the air. The canoe slid into full view of the dead animal. The moose was literally in two pieces. While his front quarters and head were intact and facing Steven, his large velvety antlers were lying in the water and the eyes were open and glazed. The animal's backside was a mess, torn to pieces, with bits of fur and bone strewn in all directions. Steven searched for the killer. His heart was pounding and his knuckles were white as he took photos of the kill from the relative safety of his canoe. He then placed the camera in video mode and narrated the scene.

Blood is everywhere; the moose, possibly a two-year-old, definitely male, was in full flight when brought down. Appears to have been cleaved into two pieces. Front half relatively intact; back half is a mess; can't tell if it has been eaten; too early to inspect. The predator could still be on site. What animal is capable of cutting a moose in two?

He was reaching into his cargo pants' pocket to grab his note-book when the entire canoe did a turn clockwise. Grabbing the gunwales to steady the boat, he noticed a dark shape shoot under the water toward the mainland. His heart tore into his throat as he saw a large creature with a rippling body structure surface for a second and leap into the forest. Stunned, he sat in his prospector as the boat slowly rotated in the still water. Realizing his vulnerability, he pushed his paddle deep into the lake and pulled for open water. The channel seemed immeasurably long as he made for the eastern edge of the island; his mind felt as if it were imploding. He could hear the breaking of branches within the confines of the forest and knew that he was being hunted. His canoe shot from behind the island and into view of the people at the Sherborne landing. Shouts and cheers rang out over the water and Steven desperately tried to gain his composure. The exertion of paddling helped him dissipate his adrenal reaction, but he could feel the shakes coming on, so he slowed his forward momentum. He was afraid to look behind him.

Get a hold of yourself, man, he chided himself as he closed on the beach.

He was greeted by a group of freaked out people when his canoe slid sideways into the sand; all were looking to him as if he could somehow take the vision from their memories. Harvey Jenson was holding up his camera as Steven Stiles stood in the ankle-deep water and pressed through the crowd to gain dry ground. Lifting his prospector up onto the sand, he turned and told the people to relax and give him some room. When the crowd settled down, he asked them to recount what they had witnessed. As they relived the event, the look of terror on some of the young teens was hard to dismiss. Dusk settled into the camp area during the conversations, and tensions were running high. Steven gathered the people around the fire and recounted the ways of the wilderness and how such a killing was a necessary thing. He explained how such an event fed the entire area from birds to fish, and it was totally natural; it happened every day. He pointed to a fish frying on the fire and asked the crowd if that was any different from what happened on the island. The group understood. Mary Jenson did not.

"I told you there was a bear out here. Why can't you people do the job you're paid to do and get rid of such creatures? We paid our money to have a vacation and all we got for it was bad attitude from you and your office. We can't even leave now that it's dusk; navigating that road in the daylight is bad enough. We're trapped here with a group of loudmouthed brats, this is just great!" she yelled at Steven.

"I have had enough of your crap, lady! I told you before that this is a wilderness park. Consider yourself lucky enough to have witnessed this. And who the hell do you think you are to put these people down!" Steven shot back while melting her with his glare.

"Ya, fuck you, lady!" one of the teens yelled out.

Harvey jumped into the fray, berating Steven for his actions. Steven glared at the impetuous fool in front of him, forcing Harvey to avert his gaze. Steven turned his back to the irate man and asked to see the group's photographic evidence. But nothing that had been captured on the various devices showed the event clearly enough to identify the predator in question.

"Everyone! Gather around for a moment," Steven shouted out to the group. The firelight animated the teenagers' faces.

"I cannot say for certain what killed that moose, but tomorrow I will go and examine the kill."

"Can we help, mister?" the response was voiced simultaneously from a few of the kids in the crowd. Steven smiled.

"No thanks; just go and enjoy your camp. Whatever it was that killed that moose, I can assure you that you are not on its menu or any other animal's menu for that matter, except for the bugs," Steven said, trying to convince the group.

"Get set up for the night, gang; we're going to leave first thing tomorrow morning," Mark instructed the campers while Steven handed the devices back to their respective owners.

Steven walked over to where the green prospector sat on the sand like a beached seal. Grabbing his tent bag and his flashlight, he began the task of pitching his tent. Some of the campers hung around, asking him questions about everything from predators to camping. Steven answered each question with the wisdom he had gleaned during a lifetime of wandering through the forests he loved.

It was around one a.m. when he finally zipped up the mesh door on the tent and climbed into his sleeping bag. He had a clear view of the lake. He took his notebook out and made a few entries.

One: The animal killed - a male moose.

Two: The animal which killed the moose is immensely strong and skilled.

Three: The animal is a capable swimmer below the water.

Four: I am not aware of any predator capable of carrying out this kill.

He put the notebook back into the Ziplock baggie and fell into a fitful sleep while the song of the forest infiltrated the nylon walls of his tent.

THE GAME

The smell of the campfire filled its nostrils as it stalked to visual range and stood motionless behind a clump of cedars. It watched as the group looked at the images on the devices they held. It listened as they spoke of the kill, understanding fully every word of their conversations. Remaining motionless, it waited. Eventually, the humans fell into their tents and silence reclaimed the area. Stalking into the centre of the camp, it lay flat on the ground and closed its eyes. Feeling its pulse mesh with the ground, it pushed the pulsing energy out in a large circle, expanding the diameter until it encompassed the entire camp. It smiled as people stirred within their tents as they felt the pulse move through them. Rising, it then moved to the vehicle which contained the woman and man. With one leap it was on the roof. From here, it jumped up and down and then launched itself into a nearby tree.

"What the hell is going on out there?" Mary shouted from within the vehicle.

"Is that an animal or the kids?" Harvey commented, completely befuddled from sleep. Mary flung the car door open and jumped out with a flashlight in hand; Harvey exited the vehicle from the other side.

"What kind of sick joke are you assholes playing?" she yelled out.

"What's going on?" Mark shouted from his tent while trying to find some pants to put on. Flashlights and lanterns illuminated the camp, casting shadows in every direction. Confusion and anger followed the lights. Mary was fuming and accusations were pouring out of her. Harvey tried to stay out of everyone's way. Steven was up and dressed within moments of Mary's initial outburst.

"Mrs. Jenson, do you mind? Let's take a look at your car and see what happened before throwing around all kinds of accusations!" Steven suggested.

"You're going to defend these people anyway!" Mary was spitting mad.

"Shut the fuck up, you bitch!" one of the campers blurted out.

"You little asshole, you can't talk to me like that; I could have you arrested!"

"Everyone! Calm down, and yes, sorry, the kid can say that. You woke the entire camp up by yelling at them. I don't think Brian's the one that needs arresting!" Mark shouted at the belligerent woman five feet to his left.

"Let's just go and see what the heck is going on. Mark, come with me; everyone else, get the fire going and make some hot tea or something," Steven said to the emotionally charged group. The kids went back to the fire pit with daggers in their eyes pointed squarely at Mary Jenson while Steven, Mark, Mary, and Harvey walked over to the abandoned vehicle.

Steven used his flashlight to check the ground for tracks. He held the unit at hip height, and then he dropped the flashlight to ground level and did a sweep. He found nothing to show that an animal had been in the area. Mark looked at the vehicle and called out to Steven.

"Steven, something was on the roof; look at the indentations."

Steven verified Mark's observation. Something large had been on the roof of the BMW.

"Mr. and Mrs. Jenson, your culprit was an animal. I can't tell what it was, maybe a raccoon. One thing is for sure: it wasn't anyone in the group."

"The SUV shook way too much to be a raccoon; those filthy animals don't weigh enough. I know it was one of those teenagers," Mary shot back.

"First of all, I would hardly call that an SUV. Second of all, a raccoon can weigh up to thirty pounds. You were sleeping; everything would seem larger than it actually was!" Mark interjected.

Harvey Jenson was walking around the vehicle when his toe touched something. Shining his flashlight down, he noticed a running shoe: upside down and laces opened.

"Perhaps my wife is right, people. Who owns this?" The Puma running shoe was highlighted by his flashlight for all to see.

Mark and Steven felt their lips go dry.

"Damn it," Mark said between clenched teeth.

"Let's just go back to the camp and see whose shoe this is, shall we?" Mary said with far too much pleasure in her voice. The four walked into the light of the camp and Mark gathered his group around.

"Gang, we may have a situation here. Take a good look at this and let me know if it is yours." Mark was almost sick to his stomach over the possible ramifications.

"That's mine, Mark; what are you doing with my shoe?" an eighteen-year-old boy said as he came out of the crowd.

"We found this beside the Jensons' car. This is not cool, Phil."

"Fuck that, I put my shoes right by that towel over there because they were wet," the young man blurted out with such truth that it was hard for Mark or Steven to believe he was lying.

"See, I was right; now do something to earn your keep. I read the rules: no harassment of other campers!" Mary shouted out with enough volume in her voice to wake up the entire lake.

"I believe the kid, Mrs. Jenson. Something is strange here, I admit, but Phil is not lying. My shoes are on a log right there. It could have been mine. Let it go." Steven visualized shoving a sock in Mrs. Jenson's mouth.

"None of this would have happened if you'd let us stay at the site we rented. Our treatment has been brutal and I will be informing the township of it. I will have you fired!" Mary Jenson said with pure conviction.

"Mrs. Jenson, I would suggest that from the beginning, it is you who have caused trouble. I am filing a complete report when I return to the base. I have recorded your threats and as such, you will not be allowed to return to this Park for quite some time." Steven turned to Harvey. "Thank you for showing me the pictures; it's a great camera you've got."

"You disappoint me, Mr. Stiles; I would have thought you a stronger person. I will have to agree with my wife on this one. You do recall I am a lawyer." Harvey looked straight into Steven's face while his wife looked on with bloodlust in her eyes.

"Of course you would pull that on me; I would expect nothing different from you." Steven stepped toward the man and stared straight into his eyes. Harvey averted his gaze immediately and then Steven turned and walked away. The Jensons stomped back to their vehicle, talking about legal action. Car doors slammed and the engine fired to life. Headlights lit up the car park area like daylight and the vehicle jostled its way up the steep incline of the road and disappeared at the top of the hill. A huge cheer arose from the campers. Jokes were made and Phil became a hero, even though he was perplexed as to how his shoe had ended up beside the Jensons' car. Steven and Mark walked over to the vacant spot where the vehicle had been parked. They were able to figure out that the only human signs around the vehicle were that of the four adults.

"Wow, that's all it took to get them to leave. We should have thought of that." Mark said as his flashlight panned over the tire marks left in the sand.

Mark and Steven looked at each other and started laughing. Mark made his way back to the group while Steven turned his flashlight off and stared at the dark corridor which was the road. Five feet from where Steven stood, a keen pair of eyes watched his every move.

HUNTING

The smell of breakfast cooking on an open fire drifted on the early morning breeze, bidding all campers to grab their cutlery and plates. They sat in fragmented groups talking in subdued tones and laughing as the conversation dictated. The sun was creeping slowly up the beach by the time the tents were struck and the gear was placed in the canoes. Steven stood on the sand and watched as the wide-eyed campers set off on their delayed journey. He figured it would take them at least an hour or so to reach their destination. They had asked him to stop in sometime in the afternoon and he said he would. Walking back to the tent, his mind went over all the events of the past several hours. Nothing he had experienced in the woods prepared him for the events which transpired a few short hours ago. He stopped and stared at the distant rocky island and just simply could not make sense of what had taken place. His mind spun through several scenarios as he stowed his tent and gear in the canoe. Taking one last look around the camp, he noted that everything was clean and ready for the next group. Walking to the parking area, he looked for any tracks or evidence which would at least help solve one mystery. Failing to see anything worth noting, he made his way back to the beach and pulled his radio from its holster.

"Susan, it's Steve, you there?"

"Hey Steve, how are you?" Sue's voice filled the landing.

"Sue, I am heading over to the kill site. When is the next group due at the landing?" Steven asked while standing ankle-deep in the water and staring at his destination.

"Hold on, Steve." The radio went silent for a few minutes. "There were two eighteen-year-old kids in here asking about the island; it seems that the story's already out. I bet that island is going to get busy fast. The next group is due at the landing by noon. Better take those notes in a hurry."

"Damn technology!"

"Hey, if it weren't for technology, you wouldn't be able to talk to me whenever you needed my expertise." Sue laughed.

"Nice try. I'll call you once I inspect the island. Thanks again."

He put the radio back into its holster. Pushing his canoe into the deeper water, he jumped in and settled into his rhythmic paddling. The canoe closed the distance within ten minutes. Floating off the eastern tip of the island, Steven set his camera on a flexible tripod and pressed the record button. He paddled to the spot where the moose had left the water and he climbed out of the boat, tying the bow rope to a low shrub. He then followed the path of the doomed animal. Upon reaching the spot where he had seen the remains, he stopped in disbelief. *What the hell!* Steven said out loud, completely numb from what he was looking at. It was as if nothing had happened. Broken shrubs and a few random patches of fur were the only traces he found. Steven sat on a rock lip directly within the kill zone and took pictures. He also jotted down notes within his log book. Placing his camera in video mode, he swept it across the area as he spoke.

There are no visible traces of a kill other than some fur, dried blood, and several broken junipers and dogwood. I found some fecal matter from the digestive tract of the moose, but nothing to show that less than fourteen hours ago a massive animal was butchered here.

Steven placed his camera in his pocket and grabbed for the radio. "Hello, Susan."

"Go ahead, Steve."

"Molly Maid must have come through here; there's literally nothing left."

"Steve, I don't understand."

"Sue, the site has been cleaned; I'm telling you there is nothing here to see."

"Steve; given what you described last night, how could it possibly be cleaned up?"

"I don't understand it. I hope we're not dealing with some freaks here." Steven realized how implausible it was.

Susan stood in the doorway of the office which looked out toward the highway. Cars were flying by, their occupants busy with schedules and expectations. "Should we contact the O.P.P.?" she spoke into the radio in a hushed tone as if someone were spying on her.

"Yes, let's do that. If they need to meet with me, it's no problem." His heart sank. He hated dealing with the cops because that just opened up a new level of bullshit.

"Ok Steve, I will call them now. Talk to you soon." Sue did not sound at all happy with the decision.

Steven Stiles sat on the rocky island for another twenty minutes before walking back to his canoe. He paddled up and down the channel, looking for signs of anything which would lend some sense to the puzzle his mind found itself immersed in. Paddling to site 17, he pulled his canoe out of the water, turned it over, and followed the timeworn path to the rounded rock outlook which gave a perfect view of the now mysterious island. Sitting on the rock with his back against the pine tree, he closed his eyes and let the sun pull some of the tension out of his body. Voices intruded on his internal conversation and he opened his eyes to see a couple of young guys scouting the island as if looking for treasure. *Man, news travels fast.*

The pair eventually sat on the rock point and pulled out their cell phones. He could hear some of the words within the conversation and pieced together that the two adventurers were disappointed and ticked off with the apparently wasted time. The two boys stood up and moved to the other side of the small outcrop. They reappeared in a fibreglass canoe and headed toward the southwest channel. He was amazed at how easy it was to observe people; they had no clue they were being watched.

Lying prone, tucked under a camouflaging maze of cedar and pine branches on a rock outcrop forty-five degrees to the human's left side, it scanned the man who was engaged in observing the others on the rocky island. Eventually, the man closed his eyes and his breathing became slow and rhythmic. It moved silently toward the human, stopping three feet from the unsuspecting target. Crouching down, it focused its concentration. The man's mind opened up its doors and it extracted information stored deep within the vaults of the human's memory. Rising with the silence of an ant, it moved back toward the mainland and turned north to Orley Lake.

Bob squatted by the lake while pumping water through his purifier. He watched as minnows searched the shallow water for food and his thoughts wandered. The weather was clear and the temperature was climbing. Carol and Cassie lounged in the water, just around the point of land from where Bob was. Brad busied himself cleaning up the camp area and checking on the tents and sleeping bags. A white-tailed deer emerged from the foliage within the bay which was to Bob's left. He watched as the skittish mammal scanned the area for any threats. The whitetail deer's coat was a reddish brown and Bob thought his head looked too small for his body. He called for the rest of the group, but the deer vanished into the woods before the words were out of his mouth. The smell of the wood fire drifted around the site and everyone was in a good mood.

Brad tried to understand the fear he had felt the other day but was thwarted by an unrepentant memory lapse. Closing his eyes, he could clearly see the portage. He could feel the canoe pushing down on his shoulders and the ankle-breaking stream crossing.

He could see the bow of the canoe rise to an angle-up-pitch as he reached level ground. The memory of seeing the lake was clear, but he had absolutely no memories of that which made him run in terror.

"Guys, I'm going to take a cruise around this pond, want to come?" Brad yelled up to the girls. Bob was not visible.

"No Brad, go ahead. We're just going to hang out here for a while. Ask Bob, he's over by the bay," Cassie called back. Brad gathered his paddle and vest, and he walked over to see if Bob wanted to join him.

"Brad doesn't know the meaning of chill, Carol; he has to constantly move."

"Bob can be like that too, but he has some good points." Carol dried her legs with a small terry cloth towel.

"I don't know about Brad. He's good looking and great in bed, but I don't see anything for the long term." Cassie watched the two men skirt the left shore in the canoe. Their voices were loud and clear even in the distance.

"There are a lot of guys out there, Cassie. I'm sure you will find the right one someday," Carol used the age-old line.

"Maybe. At least he likes canoeing." Cassie smiled.

"You're lucky; I had to beg Bob to leave his computer to come out here." Carol pointed to the boys as they climbed around on an outcrop of rock which pushed up through the surface of the lake, forming the island.

"Why don't we do this on our own, Carol? We could stay down on Sherborne and day trip around the area."

"That's a great idea. Let's do it. Where's your map?"

The two young women walked up to Cassie's tent and opened its flaps and climbed in. Sitting on the ground, they opened up the map and began planning their next outing.

Laying directly behind the green tent, it listened to the females' conversation. Concentrating on the one whom it saw yesterday on the trail, it ensured that she had no memory of the incident other than a recollection of seeing a bear through the mist. It stood and walked into the surrounding forest. Then, after climbing a large pine tree to a high vantage point, it placed its back to the trunk and continued to watch the people below.

COINCIDENCE

"Hey, you know it's like ten. Time to get up, sleeping beauty!" Larry yelled out to Steven.

"Leave him alone, Larry; he gets paid to do this!" Tom added, smirking.

"Holy shit, guys, thanks for the wake-up call. Rough night last night, didn't get much sleep." Steven tried to find his bearings.

"Who is she?" Tom shouted out, laughing, while truly hoping to see a female.

"How's it going, guys?" Steven responded while grinning.

"Great! We heard some kids talking about a dead moose on the island; they passed by this morning and woke us up," Larry said while trying to hold the canoe steady as Bill positioned himself for the tenth time. "Can you just find a comfortable spot, Bill, and stop moving?"

"The whole idea of sitting in a small narrow boat while trying to keep it from tipping is ridiculous," Bill countered. That elicited a response of well-directed paddle shots from the other three men.

"Shit, now I'm soaked! This sucks," Bill glared at the guys.

"That's why we asked you to come along, Bill; it gives us the opportunity to abuse you," Ralph said as he kept the canoe steady. Tom saluted Bill with his middle finger. The echoes of laughter from the five men bounced off the high granite walls surrounding the lake.

"I heard the same story. I saw nothing there. Take a look and let me know if you find anything," Steven said as he stood and stretched his torso.

"See you soon, buddy," Tom shouted out in his usual joking manner.

"See you later, guys." Steven slid down the back side of the rounded rock and walked toward his canoe.

There was a slight breeze which infused the air with the smell of pine and cedar; Steven breathed the soothing aroma deep into his lungs and exhaled his recent worries. Gathering his gear, he placed the canoe in the water, loaded his pack in front of the stern seat, and took his familiar place on the bow seat. Pushing off, he drifted out into the bay and then put his paddle deep into the water. He brought the canoe up to speed as he steered toward site 22A. He wanted to check on Mark and his crew. As he rounded the back side of site 17A, his radio crackled to life.

"Steven, what's your twenty?" the voice of Stan, Steven's boss, filled the canoe and placed a frown on Steven's face.

"What brings you out here, Stan?"

"We have been trying to reach you for about an hour; I sent the boys out toward the Sherborne access point to find you."

"I am on Sherborne; it was one hell of a night. Do Jeff and William have any supplies with them?"

"Yes they do, and they're staying in the area."

"That's different. What's up?"

"There was an accident on Sherborne Road this morning, Steven. A couple totaled their vehicle. Mary Jenson was pronounced dead at the scene and Harvey Jenson is in Lindsay in critical."

Steven's mind went numb. "How the hell did that happen?" he managed to say.

"Cops are still on site trying to piece it together; it appears that they were moving at a good clip when they swerved and rolled," Stan's voice bounced in Steven's brain.

"Holy shit!"

"Exactly! The cops want to talk to you about the events of yesterday. What is the update on that mess?" Stan spoke in his usual commanding bullshit way.

"Stan, there is no update. The moose was likely killed by a cougar; they bury their kill. More than half must have ended up in the water and that would explain the cleanup." Steven was hoping his explanation would preclude further questioning.

"Ok then, please head to the landing and wait for Jeff and William. They should be there shortly. They're dropping off a couple of canoes for Algonquin Outfitters."

"Why are they carrying those?"

"Algonquin's truck got a flat tire on a piece of debris from the Jensons' wreck. Wait for the cops; they want to talk to you."

"Ya, I've got it." Steven was glad to be through with that conversation. He turned the prospector around and headed for the access point. He noticed Ralph and company had pulled into the portage trail leading to Orley Lake. Steve smiled, thinking of how Tom and the boys would react to seeing the women camping up there.

The access point was a hive of activity; people were walking from the cars to the beach carrying all the provisions required for a stay in the bush. Four canoes, all rented from Algonquin Outfitters, were in the water with bows on the sand. The canoes were in various stages of load-out, yet the pile of gear on the beach seemed too large to fit into the remaining hull space.

Never changes. Landing as far as possible from the group, he pulled his canoe up and turned it over. He walked through the grassy area to the right of the path and sat on a small rock which gave him a view of the parking area and the road. He did not have to wait long before Jeff and William descended the tortuous last hill on the road. The windows were down on the old beat-up Ford pickup.

"Hey, ranger dude!" William shouted. Steven shook his head and walked over to them. The trio exchanged handshakes and greetings. Leading the two kids to the back of the truck in order to maintain privacy, Steven asked them to explain what happened.

"We don't really know; the Beamer was upside down in the mud. It bounced off a few trees before flipping," Jeff said. He looked excited yet reserved.

"They must have been flying, Steve; what is with that? That road is wicked, but where they wiped out, it was the flat section just south of site 46," William explained, pulling out the digital camera from his pocket.

"Let me guess, you morbid ass, you probably have lots to show me," Steven took the camera from William. He turned the device on and scanned through forty pictures of the crash scene. The BMW was upright by the time the boys arrived, but its front end was destroyed and the roof was caved in on the passenger side. Clothing and camp gear were strewn all over. "Shit man, that's brutal. No one could walk away from that for sure." Steve was perplexed by what the images showed him.

"You know the lady died and her husband may not make it," Jeff told Steven while untying the canoes on the pickup's rack.

"Yes, I know, guys; the boss informed me about thirty minutes ago. Let's get these canoes to the shore and get the gear out. I'm going to take your truck, and I want you two to stay and guard my stuff." Steven was curious about the circumstances of the accident.

"No problem," Jeff and William replied in unison, looking toward the beach where young women ran in and out of the water. They placed the canoes belly up on the sand and put the barrel of supplies by Steven's canoe. The boys took up positions which afforded them the best view of the beach, while Steven drove the pickup back up the hill.

The road was torturous, as tail pipes, mufflers, oil pans, and transmissions had all succumbed to the access road's relentless need to be dominant. Washouts and large rocks tested even the toughest of vehicles' suspension systems. Steven walked the truck up the hill, and for the rest of the road he worked the brake as much as the accelerator. After what seemed like an eternity of driving, he finally approached the scene. The Jensons' vehicle was loaded on a flatbed truck and the caution tape was being pulled down. Five officers and ten spectators were braving the onslaught of voracious deer flies. Steven smiled when he noticed Lisa.

"Steven, we were coming down to see you," Lisa said while she rolled up caution tape.

"I figured I would save you the trip. What happened?"

She motioned for Steven to follow her and he complied. Out of the earshot of the onlookers, Lisa told Steven the details.

"The Jensons' car was doing at least sixty kilometres per hour when something made them veer off the road. They lost control and flipped at least twice, hitting several trees and ending upside down in the pond. Mary Jenson probably died right away and Harvey Jenson's chances are slim at best. He was airlifted from Highway 35 about two hours ago."

"Ya, I heard the chopper from 17." Steven was visually surveying the site. He spotted his longtime friend Clifford who motioned him to come over. Clifford put his hand on Steven's shoulder and told him to follow.

"We need to keep this quiet, ok?" Cliff said to his friend.

"Sure," Steven answered. The two officers led him into the woods thirty feet from the road and pointed up. Within a slim balsam fir tree was a hunting stand. Lisa turned to Steven.

"We found a third victim here. This guy was not here taking photos. This guy was bow hunting, but nothing is in season. We have informed the Ministry and they are going to do some background on him. The guy's name was Lee Parker from Toronto; he came in by ATV and he was good at staying hidden. We've had the ATV and his belongings taken back to the station. Have you ever seen this guy?" Lisa passed Steven a photo of the dead man.

"No, what the hell was he poaching for?"

"We have two dead deer stashed over there, a female and a fawn. This guy could shoot," Cliff said as he pointed in the direction of a group of white cedars.

"Why would he jump?"

"We figure that the Jensons' vehicle was in a direct line to crash through this area, and Lee Parker panicked and did a header," Lisa explained.

"A tree changed the trajectory of the BMW. This guy jumped for nothing," Cliff said, showing Steven where the poacher hit the ground.

"Amazing, what are the odds. Do you mind if I look around?"

"No, go ahead. By the way, what is with the attack on that moose yesterday?" Clifford asked.

"Possibly a cat. Half of the moose disappeared underwater, and I didn't have time to find the other half," Steven answered carefully.

"That would have stirred campers up," Lisa stated.

"It was a pain." Steven walked toward the carcasses of the deer. The two cops traced their steps back to the road while Steven poked around for any trace of another explanation. He walked to the area where the deer lay and noticed that both had been shot by an expert. He searched around and found a pile of apples within kill range of the stand. *Asshole!* Walking back to the access road, he noticed that the onlookers had left and Lisa was sitting in her cruiser. He walked up to her window and banged on the glass.

"Steven! You ass, you scared me. Find anything?"

"Nope, it's as you said: the guy probably jumped."

"I am out of here. The bugs are wicked, and I'm hot."

"You are all of that," Steven teased.

"Funny guy. Take it easy, I hope it quiets down for you." Lisa touched his hand and put the window up. He watched as she drove away, and then he climbed back into the pickup to catch a break from the deer flies. Leaning back, he closed his eyes. Something about the Jensons' speed made no sense to him. It had been full dark when they left. Mary was in a fighting mood but she was not the one driving, and the road did not allow for that kind of speed. Steven slipped into a fitful dream. He could see the vehicle travelling at a slow speed. The vehicle moved into the S bend and accelerated to an untenable speed. A creature faster than anything Steven was familiar with was right behind the BMW. The vehicle caught a rut and careened into the bush only to be rolled out by the trees and forced to land in the pond.

Steven awoke in a state of disbelief and covered in sweat. *What the fuck!* Climbing out of the truck, he walked back to the S bend. Marked in the sand on the road was the gallop pattern of a large animal. Steven's hands shook as he took photos of the patterns. Nothing in the tracks would lead to an answer as to the identification of the animal, but it fit the unmistakable pattern of a predator hunting prey. He walked back to the crash scene, following, as best he could, the prints and determined that some animal had indeed been chasing the Jensons' vehicle. Steven climbed back into the truck and tried to assimilate the new information.

Placing the truck in gear, he drove slowly back to the landing.

"Steve! We thought they locked you up. What's going on?" Jeff yelled out.

"Sorry guys, filling out reports and stuff. You know how that is."

"Well, we had a great view here so we were just fine," William interjected happily.

"I am glad you enjoyed yourselves. Hey, I'm good to go. There's nothing left to do here, guys, but if you have time, stop by Plastic Lake and check on a group of kids, one of them with red hair. They should be on site 13. I met them the other day, and I have some reservations about them." Steven transferred some supplies from the barrel to his pack.

"How do we get across Plastic?" Jeff asked as if Steven were joking.

"Just use your binoculars, dummy, and let me know." Steven looked at Jeff and smiled.

"Will do, Captain," Jeff responded.

Once again, the old truck rumbled its way up the road, leaving Steven alone on the beach. He readied his supplies and lifted the prospector into the water. The dream he had while sitting in the truck had shaken him up and he needed to put some distance between the accident and himself. Once he was on the water feeling the canoe gently rocking in the small wavelets, his mind calmed. Taking his radio out of its holster, he pushed the call button.

"Good morning, how are you doing?" Susan's voice broke the silence.

"I am confused as hell but a lot better than the Jensons."

"Steven, I just heard that Mr. Jenson didn't make it. He died in transit to Lindsay."

"Holy shit! I just talked to the guy; he wasn't all that bad, just a chicken shit around his wife."

"Who wouldn't be? She was a bitch through and through."

"I know; trust me, I am having a hard time missing her. Do you know if any campers have a very large dog in the area of the accident?"

"There is one couple camping on site 47; they stopped in here to pick up a canoe and paddles. They have a Marmaduke dog."

"Sue; it's a Great Dane," Steven said, laughing.

"Sorry, I am not as gifted as you," Susan replied sarcastically.

"Thanks. I am heading down to site 22A; I want to check on Mark's group and see if they are settled in."

"Ok. Why did you ask about the dog?"

"I noticed some tracks on the road where the accident happened. They could match those of a dog. The couple must have heard the crash and came by to check it out."

"Ok. I have to go; some people just showed up and are staring at me."

"Sure Sue, thanks," he replied. "Jeff, William, do you copy?"

"Hey Steve, go ahead."

"Jeff, can you guys check on site 47? There is a couple there who may have a large dog. Tell them to keep it leashed and ask if they have a cell phone; I want to talk to them about the accident."

"Sure, will do. We're just coming up on the site now," William's voice came through the speaker.

"Thanks, guys. Call me back and let me know."

"No problem; will do."

Steven holstered his radio and paddled toward site 22.

SITE 22

S ite 22 was Mark's favourite campsite for a large group. Hemlock, pine, and cedar served as a canopy facilitating great shade for the tents. Understory vegetation was non-existent, which helped to keep the mosquitoes at bay. The kids roamed all over the site, following each other around and talking. Mark always marvelled at the way a camping atmosphere usually brought people to a place where they could chill out.

"Hey, gang!" Mark called out, "listen, everyone, grab your paddles and vests; I want all of you on the lake to practice your skills." He expected some pushback, but surprisingly, the kids complied without giving him any lip at all. His idea was to get the crew to portage to Silver Doe Lake and then back to Sherborne. This would tire them out sufficiently to guarantee a relatively quiet night. He sat on shore watching them as they paddled around; three of the canoes were in a direct course to the huge rock cliff opposite where Mark sat. He contemplated the age of the rock formation which was created long before any living creature walked the Earth. The cliff was painted in such a way that it would be next to impossible to capture its power with paint or by photography. Water echoed its rhythm from under the cliff at the waterline where over centuries chambers had formed. As the canoes got closer to the monolithic cliff, those echoes were soon drowned out by voices. He watched as the remaining two canoes turned and headed to the same spot as the others. It was then he saw the familiar green prospector heading straight for the camp. Ten minutes later, Steven and Mark sat side by side.

"Where the heck did you get the dog?" Mark asked.

"There's a group of guys camping on 17A. As I passed, Rusty swam out to meet me. I tried to paddle away but the crazy dog would not turn back, so Ralph, the dog's owner, said to just take him for a while. I have to admit: the dog is a natural at this." Steven looked affectionately toward the dog who was completely entranced with checking every piece of equipment within range of his inquisitive gaze.

"The guy just gave you his dog? Don't you think that's weird?"

"Mark, they know who I am. I'll drop him off later this afternoon." Steven turned his attention to the lake. "How's your group after the moose thing?"

"They're great. They haven't spoken a word about it since last night, which I find amazing, but I haven't given it much thought either." Mark frowned, suddenly realizing that it was as if the camp had amnesia.

"I checked the site out this morning and there is literally nothing to see. It was as if someone cleaned the area." Steven became distracted as he tried to figure out where Rusty had gotten too. "Rusty!" Steven called out toward the camp area. Within a few seconds, the excited dog came bounding through the camp with a beach towel clamped in his mouth. Rusty jumped on Steven and licked his face.

"Shit, I would swear that dog is yours."

"I know, it's crazy. I actually wouldn't mind if he was." Steven smothered the dog with back rubs. "I have to take off; take care, and I'll see you soon."

"Ya, sure. I was thinking of taking the kids to Silver Doe later, just for the experience."

"Why bother? Let them hack around for the rest of the day." *Why did I say that?* Steven knew he had crossed a line.

"They have to make the portage to St. Nora in a couple of days and they have no idea how to do it. I figured I would give them a taste today. It'll be good training." Mark clearly disapproved of Steven's suggestion. Steven picked up on it instantly.

"Sorry man, I had no idea you were pulling out at Nora. Ya, give them shit, neither portage is easy." Steven silently berated himself for commenting in the first place. "Speaking of Silver Doe, I think I will head to Silver Buck; I have found unregistered campers there before. Thanks for the idea."

"I didn't give you the idea; you came up with it on your own, buddy." Mark looked at Steven in a perplexed way.

"I swore I heard you say it. Old age, I guess," Steven replied while he stood up. He lifted the canoe into the water; Rusty bounced into the boat faster than the men could blink. Both men laughed while Steven rotated the canoe ninety degrees to the left and paddled toward the portage leading to Silver Doe Lake. As he paddled, he wondered about the latest mind game his brain had played on him.

ALTERCATIONS

Steven lifted the canoe onto his shoulders and started the portage. Rusty ran in front of him searching for anything and everything. The air was muggy and the mosquitoes were out in full force. Holding the canoe balanced with his right arm on the gunwale, he adjusted his shirt collar to help preclude the incessant insects from drawing his blood. The trail rose sharply up from Sherborne and then levelled out, easing Steven's passage, but by the time he put the canoe into Silver Doe Lake, he was covered in sweat. To make matters worse, the horse fly population had tag-teamed with the deer fly clan to make any mammal's life a misery if one should choose to stay near or on the lake. Grabbing his t-shirt out of the pack, he placed it over his head and tied it using its sleeves. This was his way of creating an emergency bug hat. Rusty was also having a rough time of it. He grabbed the flies with his mouth, but for every bug he killed, there were a hundred to replace it. Steven covered the dog with bug repellent; Rusty instantly responded by jumping into the lake to remove the offending liquid. Steven smiled, climbed into his boat, and steered for the second portage which would bring him into Silver Buck Lake. Rusty swam alongside the boat.

Reaching the portage, he pulled the canoe up onto solid ground, shouldered his pack, and walked the one hundred and fifty-metre trail to Silver Buck Lake. Reaching the lake, he climbed onto a point of land which pushed itself into the lake like a finger of stone. He scanned the lake with his binoculars focusing on an island, known as site 77. It was seldom used at this time of year due to the flies and the lack of swimming opportunities. Scanning the island, he could see it was vacant. Swinging his binoculars to the right, he focused on site 76; it too was vacant. Rusty was swimming again, paddling in circles around the base of the outcrop. Suddenly, the Lab's attitude changed. The dog had swung himself around to face site 76. Steven was entranced with the dog's capabilities. Clearly, something had the dog's attention. Raising his binoculars again, he scanned the brush line. It was then that he saw movement. Someone in camouflage gear was moving toward the southern tip of the point. *Shit!* he said aloud. Running off the rocky outcrop and back down the trail, Steven could feel the adrenaline pumping through him. Rusty was excited and ran ahead of him as if clearing the way. He reached his prospector and took the radio off his belt.

"Susan, it's me; are you there?"

"Go ahead."

"Susan, I need you to verify the status of 76."

"Sure, just a minute." Sue's voice drifted through the speaker. He squatted on the ground, waiting for the reply while trying to catch his breath.

"76 is lonely; what's up?"

"I think we have a problem, Sue. I am heading there now to check." He quickly placed his paddles in their sleeves for the portage. Just as he fastened the Velcro ties, he heard the unmistakable sound of a rifle. *Fuck!* Even Rusty looked somewhat nervous.

"Steven, are you ok? You sound winded!" Susan's voice broke through the noise between his heart beating and the echoing of the gunshot.

"Ya! I think there are hunters on 76. I will radio you as soon as I ascertain it."

"Thanks, you've got me worried."

"Sue, relax, how many years have I been at this? I will call soon."
He did not feel relaxed at all.

"By the way, Jeff called in and verified that there is a large dog
owned by campers on site 47A. It chased the boys' truck as they
were driving down Sherborne Lake Road. They would not give the
boys their cell number."

"Thanks, Sue; that explains a lot. I'll talk to you soon." Steven
holstered the radio and lifted the green prospector over his head.

Upon reaching the lake, he was in the canoe within minutes.
Rusty faithfully stood guard in the front of the boat and pointed
his nose directly at their destination. Steven drove his paddle deep
into the lake and pulled the canoe into full speed; the dog rocked
backwards in rhythm to Steven's power strokes. Rounding the tip
of the point, his heart sank. Hanging from a pole trussed between
two pine trees was the carcass of a deer, upside down and draining.
Steven was beyond angry. Without caution he forced the stern of his
canoe onto the rocks and was out of the boat in seconds. He grabbed
the stern line, wrapped a clove hitch around a small cedar, and ran
to the hanging deer. Rusty stayed close to the ranger. Steven scanned
the area and noticed a camouflaged tent set up within the confines of
a tight group of cedars, which had been hacked at to accommodate
the placement of the shelter. A tarp, also camouflaged, had been
set up ten feet from the tent. None of this would be visible from
the lake. Various tools such as saws and axes were cut or punched
into living and non-living trees. Rusty was doing his Lab thing by
checking out the campsite with his keen nose. Steven recorded and
commented on what he was seeing. Rusty started to bark.

"Hey fuckhead, what the hell do you think you're doing?" a disembodied voice boomed from the direction of the shelter. Steven
stood as tall as possible and introduced himself as a Park warden.

"I don't give a fuck. Shut that dog up, or I will!" replied a large,
foulmouthed man who appeared from the underbrush carrying
a crossbow. "I asked you what the fuck are you doing here?" the

large guy stated once again. Rusty was growling, provoking the man's rage.

"Rusty, relax boy, it's ok." Steven desperately tried to control his fear. Rusty, to his credit, stopped growling but had his head lowered and ears laid back. "I'm employed to enforce the laws of the Park; you're clearly in contravention of all of them. Don't ever talk to me like that again!"

"Hey, Mike, did you hear this guy? He thinks he's intimidating," the big guy said to someone Steven could not detect.

"Rick, I'm going to shoot that dog!" the voice replied from somewhere to Steven's left. The report of a gun and the bullet hitting the ground beside Steven sent Rusty flying into the woods.

"What the hell is wrong with you two?" Steven yelled as he fought for control of the situation.

"You're what's wrong with us, asshole!" Rick said as Mike revealed himself.

"I can't let you off, guys — I've already called it in."

"You've got some balls telling us that!" Mike yelled as he ran toward Steven. Steven ducked the fist but the kick dropped him to the ground; Mike jumped on Steven and began beating him. Rick grabbed Steven by the hair, forcing him to stand, and then he dragged him to a dead pine tree which stood beside the fire pit as if it were a sentinel on guard. Steven fought back but only to his detriment. Blood ran into his eye from a cut on his forehead and his leg was numb. Rick's foul breath streamed into his face.

"You're not telling anyone, asshole, and you aren't going home. Do you have any idea of the amount of cash we make from this shit?" Rick pointed to the carcass of a juvenile black bear.

"You fucking guys aren't worth the air you breathe!" Steven's mouth was swollen.

"Who the fuck do you think you are?" Mike slammed Steven in the ribs with his fist.

"Shit!" Steven cried out.

"Let's give this bastard something to think about right now, Rick." Mike had a grin on his face.

"Ya ok; do it."

"My team is on their way, you fucking assholes!" Steven tried to use any leverage he had.

"So what, by the time they get here, we will be gone and you will be wishing you never showed up," Rick spat at Steven as he replied. Mike passed Rick the rifle and walked to the tarp where Steven could see him pick up what looked to be a rubber mallet.

"Fuck guys, back off! You're going to beat me with that?" He began to realize this was the most probable scenario.

"No shit, Sherlock. I hate these fucking forest cops, right Mike?"

"Ya, fucking right."

Steven felt faint; nothing he had experienced to date could match the nightmare he found himself in. Being secured to the pine tree was bad enough, and now he was going to be beaten by two psychos. Steven raised his head and yelled a primal call out to the forest which resonated throughout the area. Mike moved at a fast walk with a mallet in his hands. Steven's legs gave out from under him and he slumped against the tree. The rope, which was binding him, cut deep into the flesh on his arms. Mike approached while Rick turned his back. The mallet rose swiftly into the air. Within one second the man was gone, pieces of him scattered as if a bomb had gone off. Steven stared in disbelief as a creature, unlike anything he could have imagined, moved through the camp. Rick screamed out in terror as the beast closed in on him. Steven tried to comprehend the vision he was seeing. It walked slowly on four legs toward the terrified man.

"Fucking help me!" Rick managed to yell. Steven's heart was pounding as it tried to jump out of his chest. He watched as Rick raised the rifle and in a blur of speed the creature tore the man's arms off at the shoulders. Bright crimson blood spurted from Rick's torso and painted the ground. Rick slumped; his face was a mask of terror. Steven looked on in disbelief as the beast ripped at its prey. Within moments, the thing stood on its hind legs and stared straight at the ranger. The eyes of the predator tore through him; Steven felt his mind let go and he collapsed, bound and totally defenceless.

WAKENING

Bright sunlight woke him from a wicked nightmare but his battered body told him something had gone horribly wrong. He jolted upright. This enticed Rusty to run up and jump all over him, which caused excruciating pain. Steven examined his arms. His memory of the past several hours was vague. He remembered the panic though, raw and powerful as it coursed through his body. *What just happened, Rusty?* He spoke to the dog as if it were able to answer. Rusty responded by licking his hand. Suddenly, into Steven Stiles' mind a powerful thought presented itself as if words were spoken.

"*I am something you cannot fathom.*"

Steven was befuddled. He looked around in all directions in order to see who was talking to him. He saw nothing but the dog. He had heard the words within his mind, but his ears registered only the wind and small wavelets hitting the shore.

"What the hell is going on?" Steven said aloud.

"*I have watched you for a long time. I am allowing you to hear me for reasons I will impart later.*"

The thoughts invaded Steven's mind in a slow melodic rhythm of unspoken words. Steven looked around, desperately clinging to sanity. Rusty ran toward a dense clump of balsams located on the end of the point.

"Rusty!" Steven yelled out to the wayward dog, terrified of what would happen if Rusty ran into the thing which attacked the poachers.

"The canine is ok; he is here with me."

"How the hell is it that I can hear you?" Steven searched the brush for a sign of the speaker.

"Quiet down and listen; there is no need for you to vocalize your thoughts."

The words pushed into Steven's pounding brain which was desperately trying to recall the memories of the last few hours. All he could recall was a feeling of being threatened and helpless.

"I can't remember shit!" Steven yelled to the silence of the surrounding forest.

The response was instantaneous.

"I have the ability to influence others and have been especially diligent at learning the intricate mazes of the human mind." The powerful thought entwined itself in Steven's consciousness.

"How do you know me?"

"As I told you, I've watched you through many seasons and you are in a position of influence over the people who come here. I need you to understand that there is much more at stake here than what you are aware of. If you wish, I can show you and teach you things that no human in recent history has ever known. If it will help you get a grip on this, you can call me Agawaatesin."

"How do I know that I am not going insane?" Steven replied while tears tracked down his bruised face.

Agawaatesin told Steven of the moose kill. He had initiated the hunt for two purposes, the first being that the moose was full of parasites. Second, he wanted to test the ranger. Next, he retold the sequence of events leading to the Jensons' accident. Agawaatesin pushed the ranger harder by forcing him to play witness to the event. Steven's body was trembling and shaking with the exertion of emotion. He could feel the ground under him as he ran at incredible speed behind the Jensons' vehicle. He watched helplessly as the vehicle rolled over and over and came to a stop upside down in the mud. He heard the cries of Harvey Jenson as the man tried in vain to help his wife. Steven could literally see the wrecked vehicle as he circled it; he could feel the mud squish up between his toes as he moved around through the swamp. He walked toward a third victim who lay face down beneath a large balsam tree. His attention was again riveted on the vehicle. Steven saw the horrified eyes of Harvey as he stared at him through the broken windshield. Somehow and impossibly, Steven was at the scene. He watched as a growing number of people gathered at the crash site. He observed as Lisa got out of her vehicle and placed caution tape around trees. Steven watched as the Jensons' vehicle was pulled back onto its wheels by the tow truck which was driven by Josh, his buddy from Big Hawk Lake. It was as if a movie were playing in his head, filmed from a first-person perspective. He observed as he himself drove up to the scene in the white Ford pickup. The perspective was very close. The camera in his head followed as he paced up the road and found the dog's spoor. The mind pictures faded abruptly.

"It was you that ran the Jensons off the road. Why?" Steven asked, weakly.

"I am not bound by your laws or morals. I did exactly what most people who met that woman wanted to do, including you, and I used their vehicle as a means to eradicate two threats. The Jensons would bring far too much attention to your job than I was willing to put up with, and their deaths were not necessarily assured. The poacher's death was not assured either."

The thoughts were so transparent and clear, Steven had no way of refuting them.

"So you choose to attack anyone who is not following your rules?" Steven was shocked that he had the assertiveness to even taunt the nightmare lying concealed near him.

"Humans believe in what they will. I only interfere when much is at stake. Your mind is too sheltered for you to see the truth in what I am telling you, but you will learn."

Steven massaged his neck to release the tension which had a viselike grip on his body.

"I have no idea what you are. This is undoubtedly some trick my mind is playing. Whatever this is, I can't even begin to understand it."

He scanned the area, trying in vain to catch a glimpse of the creature, but he only saw Rusty who was lying down on the ground in front of him. "If you are real, let me see you. Where are you hiding?" Steven was positive he was going insane. *I don't get any of this; I must have a concussion or else I'm drugged.*

"People, like the Jensons and the two I just removed, are plagues, abusing all those that they feel are inferior. They're not satisfied with anything. Give them ten acres of forest, they will clear the whole area and change it so that no life could exist other than that which they choose. Then they will search for more to destroy. Their sheer arrogance and lack of humility have pushed all the wild ones deeper into a shrinking wilderness."

The thought shot through Steven's mind, tearing into his consciousness. Then the radio crackled to life, breaking the conversation and startling Steven.

"Steve, check in please!" Susan's voice filled the camp.

"I'm here, sorry I didn't call you. It was a false alarm at 76."

"Next time call me, you jerk; I was freaking out! You sound really scattered, are you ok?" Susan's tone spoke volumes about her anger.

"Sorry. It won't happen again. Is 17 still available?"

"Yes, it is; I have it booked for you through the weekend."

"Susan, you are a sweetheart."

"Take it easy. And for shit's sake, call me."

"Will do, kiddo, sorry." He placed his radio back into its belt holster. He wandered around the camp and surrounding area for anything which would explain his recent introduction to insanity. He was frozen in some alternate universe where reality and sanity had vacated. Sporadic shivers coursed up and down Steven's body and goose bumps adorned his arms as he tried to compose himself. Succumbing to the dictates of time, he climbed into his canoe followed by Rusty. As he paddled out from shore he turned to see if something or someone was watching, but all he saw was an empty campsite full of questions and lengthening shadows. He looked at Rusty who was curled up in the stern, asleep.

What the hell just happened? he said aloud, which elicited a casual glance from Rusty. Steven knew he had stepped deep into waters he had never before paddled. He could feel an influence and a power within himself which was primal and horrifying.

As he closed in on the rocky point which marked the portage to Silver Doe, Steven slowed his paddle strokes and exhaled deeply to release the huge amount of tension which had amassed within his body. He thought of the voice which had entered his consciousness and wondered how far his mind had slipped. He passed through the portages without paying attention to them as he tried to make sense of the impossible, while his battered body protested the physical exertion. Steven entered Sherborne Lake quietly and stayed close to the shore so as to skirt site 22 where Mark and the kids were sitting around an early evening fire. He managed to pass unseen and paddled steadily toward the site where Ralph and the boys would be awaiting the return of Rusty.

Slowly, stroke by stroke, the prospector moved eastward. The soft, steady sighing sound of the stern as it sliced the water put Steven in a trance. He replayed the events of the afternoon over and over again as the details slipped into the darkening night. He held his course straight, passing campsites where the smell of wood smoke and marshmallows and all things camping drifted to his nose. A sense of normalcy drifted into the ranger's being. He was, for all intents and purposes, invisible to the campers on shore placing him well within his element.

A WARM WELCOME

Steven watched the men as they moved around the site. After drifting his prospector into shore, Rusty jumped out and ran toward the firelight. "Hey, you boneheads, it's Steve."

A chorus of hearty hellos echoed out onto the lake.

Ralph called out to the blackness, "You've finally brought my dog back!"

"Holy shit; we thought you may have eaten him or something," Bill added.

"Mind if I hang out a bit?"

Three men met Steven as he entered the soft glow pulsating out of the Coleman lantern. Larry was once again examining the privy box.

"Sure! Bunk here with us. Bill needs Daddy to hold his hand tonight," Tom replied while laughing. Bill imitated Tom's laugh which set all four men off on a laughing binge. They walked to the fire which drew Steven in as a moth to a flame. The smell of rice and chicken permeating the air instantly provoked his salivation glands into high gear.

"Shit, that smells amazing!"

"Thanks, I have been working on it all day," Larry called out from his perch upon the privy box. The men laughed until their sides hurt.

"Holy fuck! Who did you dick with?" Tom asked, pointing at Steven's face.

"I slipped on the portage and smashed my face against some rocks, hurt like hell." Steven hoped he was convincing.

"See how dangerous this place is? I mean, if a ranger can get hurt, what are my chances?" Bill had unmistakable worry lacing his words.

"Bill, you're a walking moaning machine, man," Ralph stated while rubbing his dog.

"I think I wore him out for you, Ralph. He's one amazing dog. Thanks for letting him come with me." Steven tried to cloak the sadness in his voice.

"Rusty loves you," Ralph replied, with some hesitation. "Larry, get that ass of yours over here; I want to say something."

Larry appeared, walking slowly and carrying a roll of toilet paper.

"I have the shits, man, and it sucks." He opened a camp chair and eased his way into it.

"Make sure to mark that chair, so the rest of us don't ever sit in it," Tom stated while chuckling at Larry's misfortune.

Ralph looked unusually serious as he fixated on the fire. "Guys, I'm getting divorced. Helen threw me out about a month ago. I've been in a basement apartment in the west end since it happened."

"Why the hell didn't you tell us?" Tom looked at Ralph with deep concern.

Steven felt awkward listening to this intimate detail about Ralph's life. Rusty, curled up at his feet, made him feel guilty. Ralph looked at Steven. His voice squeaked with emotion as he tried to formulate his next sentence while holding back tears.

"Steve, I want you to take care of Rusty for me," Ralph broke down.

Bill jumped up and ran to his friend as he slid to the ground. Tom took a long swig of his beer, having no idea what to say. Larry farted. That elicited a round of howls from the guys, including

Ralph, who vacillated between crying and laughing. Steven was completely at a loss.

"I can't keep him in the basement, guys; I love him too much for that. He obviously loves Steve and I have to give him up anyway." Rusty jumped up, ran to Ralph, and licked his face.

It was too much for Tom to take. He stood up, trying to hide his emotions, and walked to the canoes.

"I can't take your dog man," Steven said. "I mean, you've had him his whole life. He is one of the best dogs I have ever seen and that's because of you."

"My ex liked Rusty but constantly bitched about him. I'm not allowed to have a dog where I am, and even if I found a place that let me keep a dog, he would be alone all day. I have to work and it's not fair to Rusty," Ralph said while looking straight at Steven. "I come here at least four times per summer and once in the winter; I can see him then. Rusty has taken to you like nobody else. I have no idea why, but you and your life were made for the goofy mutt."

"Fuck man, what the hell. I love him for sure, but this is nuts!" Steven struggled to keep it together. Ralph stood up, Bill at his side, and walked over to Steven who was now pacing around.

"Steve, I trust you with my dog. Will you take him please?"

Steven looked into the pleading eyes of the man before him.

"I will take care of your dog, Ralph. When you find yourself in a better situation, you can take him back. That's the only deal I'll agree to." The exhaustion of the day gnawed at his endurance. Ralph took Steven's hand and shook it hard.

"Deal! You saved me from dropping him off at some fucking pound or something," Ralph replied as he pulled Steven to him for a big hug.

Bill joined in and even Larry managed to get into the fray. Tom's voice infiltrated the group and suggested they all better drink beer. Laughter and conversation rose from around the campfire and soaked into the forest. Steven would occasionally look around the encampment as if seeing it for the first time. When asked about his constant scanning, he said he was looking for a place for his tent.

"Who said you could stay, you freeloader?" Tom blurted out.

"You did, you goof."

Beer cans lined up around the men like fallen soldiers: some crushed, some open and wounded. Food plates lay on the ground and the men fell into the quietness of camp life.

Steven made his way to the privy box, which was so odorous that sitting on it was a feat of endurance. He mused over Ralph's apparent happiness at their arrangement and realized that if Ralph should want the dog back, his own heart would break. Holding his head in his cupped hands within the darkness, words pushed into his thoughts.

"Good deal."

Startled, he stood and dropped his pants into the dirt.

"Shit!" he inadvertently yelled out.

"Steve, you need a hand or something? I have lots of experience with that box," Larry's voice drifted over from the fire.

"Ya, I can smell it!"

Once again, the camp filled with laughter. Shaken and confused, Steven Stiles rejoined the men at the fire. They talked until the eastern sky became suffused with a pink glow. The fire was extinguished and the exhausted men climbed into their tents and fell into a deep sleep. Steven elected to sleep by the fire pit. The breeze from the lake kept the mosquitoes at bay and he was too exhausted to set up his tent. His last thought before drifting off was that the deal he had made with Ralph may change when they all woke up.

LAYOVER

The morning sun poked through the trees and created dappled light displays on the forest floor. Rising columns of mist floated from the lake as if spirits were released and allowed to dance upon the still water. Bird sounds filled the woods with intoxicating melodies and the smell of wood smoke scented the air with its perfume. Steven sat on a log, nursing a warm cup of oatmeal cereal. Rusty bounced around doing what he did best, investigating everything. Bill was dealing with a bowel issue and the other guys were still snuggled in their sleeping bags. Steven, still exhausted, grappled with the events of the preceding day.

"Steve, I am starting to like it here. I love the mornings; it makes me feel great," Bill said in a low tone as he stumbled toward the fire pit.

"Bill, this kind of thing is more natural for the human body and soul than living in a concrete maze. I'm glad you're starting to enjoy yourself. What's the plan today, are you guys supposed to go home or what?"

"Well, that was the plan, but the guys were debating whether or not we should stay another night." Bill placed a small log on the fire.

"Do you have enough food and stuff?"

"I think Ralph said we did." The sound of a tent zipper drew Steven's attention to where Ralph appeared, standing in his pyjamas and scratching himself.

"Steve, we have tons of food left, but I only booked for three days and this is it," Ralph sounded disappointed.

"Are all the guys in, Ralph?"

"Yep, even Bill wants to stay."

"Let me make a call." Steven looked around for his radio.

"Really? That would be amazing!" Ralph replied while rubbing Rusty.

"Susan, are you there?"

"Good morning, Steve, you ok?" Susan's melodic voice drifted throughout the camp area.

"I am. When are you off, Sue?"

"Saturday and Sunday. I managed to get out for a weekend."

"That's great. Is 17A booked tonight?"

"Nope, there is a group on there until noon today, but it's free until midweek."

"Put me in for it and you can book out 17."

"I'll do it right now."

"Thanks."

"Are you taking care of yourself?" Susan asked.

"Yep, I'm good. Are you going out with that stud of yours this weekend?"

"I am. Are you jealous?" Steven depressed the button to reply when Tom yelled from his tent.

"I am."

"Who was that?" Susan asked.

"Some jerk; I'm about to eject him."

"Damn, that girl gave me a hard-on," Tom called out as he made his way to the nearest tree. Steven and the guys laughed.

"Sue, I will call you soon. What time are you off today?"

"Five tonight, and I'm out of here."

"I am coming to see you today. I want to pick up some fresh clothes and get you to process the digital stuff; is that ok?" Steven pushed a long stick under the coals.

"As long as you're here before I leave."

"I'll give you a big hug when I see you."

"I will too!" Tom yelled out in the background.

"Who is that, Steven?" Susan asked curiously.

"Just some old guy. He can't seem to find his tent."

"Ok, take it easy; I will see you later this afternoon."

"Right on." Steven placed the radio into its holster.

"Man, that girl sounded sexy as hell," Larry said from the confines of his tent.

"Take it easy, you guys; she's all of that, but a hell of a lot younger than we are. You should see her mother, though."

"We're coming with you this afternoon, chief." Tom fumbled for his cigarettes.

"Does that involve the carrying of canoes?" Bill asked.

"Yes it does, Bill. The portage is about five forty in length," Steve replied.

"Five hundred and forty feet!"

"No Bill, it's five hundred and forty metres long."

"I fucking hate metric, Steve; what's that in feet?" Bill looked really worried.

"It's about seventeen hundred feet."

"Shit, I think I'll hang here, then." Bill hung his head down in submission. The camp filled once again with the laughter of middle-aged men who had never really grown up.

"Ralph, the campsite is yours for tonight. If you boys want to stay, you're welcome to it."

The four men ran up to Steven and hugged him; the group fell to the ground where a lot of pushing and pretend fighting ensued. Rusty ran around the group and jumped in where he saw fit.

"Ralph, I have to ask again, man. Are you still considering what we discussed last night, or were you just a drunken shithead?"

"You have one freaky stare, buddy, and yes, I'm serious about Rusty. You'll be doing me a huge favour. I mean, I'll miss the dog — but at least I know he will be in his glory out here," Ralph stated with no sign of remorse in his voice.

"Ok Ralph, I'll look after Rusty for as long as you need me too. Thanks, I've always thought to have a dog would be a pain, but Rusty proved me wrong."

"You're welcome, and thank you."

Silence filled the camp once again as the men moved about, enjoying the first morning of their extended stay.

The sun had climbed high into the July sky, increasing the temperature well into the lower thirties and forcing the forest to cry out for rain. Tom sat on his camp chair with his feet in the water, sucking on a cigarette and feeling completely at home. The camp had grown on him and he was glad to have the extra day. He watched as canoes plied the waters of Sherborne.

Bill busied himself with hanging up his sleeping bag and cleaning out his tent. He had not thought of a newspaper or electronic device for a couple of days and was feeling somewhat liberated, now that he had embraced the whole camping experience. He still dreaded the portage back to the lake where they had parked, but he kept that thought neatly tucked in some far corner of his mind as he soaked in the last day of camp. Larry was finally getting over his bout of beaver fever. His guts were still tender but he was actually able to move around and not have to worry about his proximity to the box. He grabbed his chair and dropped down beside Tom. The two men talked in low tones about the camp and life.

Ralph had walked back into the lot; the excuse was to collect firewood for the night. Rusty bounced around, exuberant as always, and followed him to a rock ledge which looked over the northern section of Sherborne Lake. From here he had a clear view of the landing, and he watched as ant-sized people moved about the beach area. It looked as if a large group had just arrived. Rusty sidled up to Ralph and put his paw on his leg. Tears began to stream down

Ralph's face as he rubbed his dog. Ralph had told the boys that he was in the midst of a divorce. This was true; what he did not disclose, was that he had just recently been diagnosed with prostate cancer. The doctors figured they could get it out in time before it spread, but Ralph was scared. He grabbed the dog and held him close.

"Rusty, I love you, buddy, take care of yourself and that ranger. I'll see you when I can." His throat locked up and tears ran unrestrained down his face. Rusty licked the stricken man and tried to mitigate his turmoil; he pushed Ralph to the ground and jumped all over him. Ralph's tears subsided. Two people in a red canoe shouted their approval as they passed by. The dog jumped off Ralph and barked his reply. Ralph was somewhat embarrassed, but Rusty loved the audience. With his dog in tow, Ralph walked back to the site.

Steven packed and stowed his gear into the canoe; he had to make it to the base before Susan left for home. His travel time would be at least two hours not accounting for wind direction. He told the men he would return by nightfall and hang out with them. Ralph and the boys saluted him as he left the site. He laughed and shot them the finger as he pulled the canoe up to speed. Rusty, tied to a tree, barked his head off. Steven felt awful, but he needed Rusty to stay with Ralph for this last day. Perhaps Ralph would change his mind.

The wind was steady at Steve's back, making the journey relatively simple. He noticed that the wind was coming from the east; this foretold of rain sometime in the near future. The prospector rode up on the small waves and dropped slightly into the trough. This made him think of Rusty and how the dog's weight would be great in the stern to balance out the boat. He thought about the events of the last week and was amazed at the number of incidents he'd had to deal with. Steven was still not convinced his sanity was in check. The events of yesterday were nothing but a blur in his confused mind, but he had retained the memory of a voice which haunted him. He had been knocked unconscious on site 76 and someone had tended to his wounds and then fled the scene.

He could remember nothing, but something was wrong with his version of reality.

A couple of people waved at Steven as he passed by site 20; he noticed that they had set up a stainless-steel camp kitchen. He smiled; it was always a shock to him to see just what people were willing to carry with them to feel secure. He steered his canoe into a small bay hidden by a tree-studded island. His mind was spinning and he needed to quiet the incessant hammering within his skull. With the canoe floating quietly within the protected alcove, he slid his body into the belly of the prospector for a few moments and lay his head on the seat. He could feel his heart beating through the hull of the boat as the pulses meshed with the water and slowed to a steady drumbeat, placing him into a trance. Memories began to creep in from the corners of his mind. He remembered feelings of terror as a threat to his life seemed imminent, he remembered a conversation within his head which seemed to come from somewhere beyond his comprehension, and he vaguely remembered physical violence perpetrated by something which hid well beyond the reach of his beleaguered mind. The canoe drifted, free of his influence, while he searched for the broken fragments of memories which were scattered within his mind as seeds in a wind. As the green prospector drifted, so too did Steven's consciousness. His mouth opened and his breathing slowed as he fell into a deep sleep. Within a few minutes, he jolted up and almost dumped the canoe. He could feel the tremors in his body as he reacted to the vision presented to him in a nightmarish dream of a predator whose very existence was impossible. As he napped, a creature of raw power and unbelievable intelligence hunted him. This predator was capable of mind control and manipulation. Steven's heart strained within the confines of his chest and his breathing was no longer controlled. Deep within, he shuddered at the truth of what could not be real. He turned his attention to the sky and watched as a red-shouldered hawk played in the air currents; he wished he could ask it some questions.

BASE

Susan's week had been hectic with people complaining about everything from weather to outhouses. She had fielded calls from the Ontario Provincial Police and the Ministry of Natural Resources, and she had Stanley breathing down her neck about making sure all the papers were in order following the Jensons' accident. Susan watched the clock as it slowly ticked away the seconds until her release. She walked to the front deck of the building which facilitated a beautiful view of St. Nora Lake. She leaned on the railing, closed her eyes, and inhaled deeply. The warm air and the smell of pine needles helped to release her tension. She watched as a couple of guys boarded behind a modified ski boat, and she smiled as the pair flipped simultaneously off the wake. Susan was impressed; she had never tried the stunt for fear of breaking something. The boat cut in close to the shore and the guys waved at her. She waved back, thinking to herself that her job was the best. As the boat sped out into the lake, she noticed a solitary canoe heading straight for the cabin. The ski boat seemed to be on an imminent collision course with the canoeist. She watched as the boat came to within a few hundred metres and then veered right. The lone person angled the canoe into the oncoming wave and then angled back to a straight course toward the cabin. Susan walked into the office and grabbed the Bushnell binoculars. Then, by training the eyepieces on the canoe, she recognized the unmistakable Mr. Steven Stiles. Even from this distance, Susan thought he looked like shit.

"I see you, Steve," she said into the radio, using her sweetest voice.

Within a few minutes, Steven replied, "Hey, can't you see I'm busy out here with the freaking boarders?"

"Glad to see you too!"

"I'm kidding, Sue! I will see you in about ten minutes. Don't run away."

"Ok, boss." Sue walked back to the desk to place the binoculars back on the hook under the counter.

Heading for the shoreline south of the cabin, his prospector seemed in imminent danger of collision as it closed in, but a small twist of the paddle brought the green canoe sliding in on her port side. Steven jumped into the water and grabbed his pack. He threw it onto the bank unceremoniously while still holding onto the gunwale of the prospector. Lifting his boat up, he carried it several feet from the shore and flipped it over. He examined the exposed hull for any new damage. The entire bottom was a maze of scars which told of many adventures and many unseen obstructions. Steven had memorized almost all of them. He lifted his pack and walked to the cabin.

"You look like shit!" Susan said as she ran out and hugged him. He hugged her back.

"Ya, you should see the other guy."

"Seriously Steve, what the hell happened?"

"I was heading back from Silver Buck when I lost my footing and fell onto the rocks. I actually blacked out; that's all I remember, Sue."

"You realize that if you actually blacked out, I would have to report it to the M.O.L., you stupid jerk?"

"Ok, I didn't pass out. I just fell asleep, right there on the trail."

"You're an ass!"

Entering the building, Steven placed his pack down on the floor and sat in a reclining chair which was tucked into a corner. The two talked about their experiences and brought each other up to date on their prospective worlds which met within the structure they now shared.

"Sue, this particular week has been unusually active with animal sightings and now the Jensons' accident. Can you remember a week like it?" Steven hoped that this was a blip and things would return to the usual chaos of peak season.

"I've been working on a project for Stanley; he wants a list compiled of known incidents within the Park for the past three years. I am almost done; I will print a copy right now before I leave, ok?"

"You amaze me. When did Stan ask you to do this?"

"He asked me about a month ago when we had a problem with that group on Sherborne. You know, those crazies that almost trashed the entire landing."

"I remember them well," he replied while he looked at the papers appearing in the print tray.

"Anyway, Stan is Mister Paper and he wants a record of all reported incidents filed and updated monthly." Susan made a gesture of making herself vomit.

"Really? It is not a bad idea from a management perspective, but they better get us more help here. We're outnumbered." He looked out the window as a black Ford Bronco appeared on the driveway in front of the cabin. Within a few seconds, the vehicle's horn broke the peace.

"Tell that fucking goof to get the hell out of the truck and come get you; he treats you like shit!"

"What the hell?" Susan was visibly upset by Steven's rant.

"Sorry, Susan. I guess I am a bit burned out. Sorry." Steven really meant it.

Susan hugged him and reminded him to lock up when he left. She turned and ran to the waiting Bronco where Kyle grabbed her and pinned her to the door of the vehicle. Steven turned to the papers in his hands. Something about Kyle turned him off and he didn't want to look at the kid. Settling down in the reclining chair, he looked over Susan's recently itemized incident list.

HISTORY

The hot summer sun flattened the ground under its unfalter-
ing weight. Animals and birds moved only to eat or escape
from being eaten. Trees and plants stretched their roots to
reach the buried water which shrank deeper and deeper into the cool
depths of the earth. Steven sat in the cabin, combing over the twen-
ty-page report Susan had printed. She had organized the document
in relation to calendar dates and years. She had also highlighted
people's names who were repeat offenders. Steven recognized many
of them. As he looked through the list, he was shocked by the sheer
volume of ignorant people that visited the area. He noted that the
number of animal disturbance calls had actually increased in the
last five years. Bear sightings were the most common. Twelve people
found it necessary to call in when a noise somehow posed a serious
threat to their well-being. One hundred and eighteen people found
it necessary to report that the sound of the spring peepers was
disturbing their stay. Steven smiled. Raccoons dominated the list,
blamed for everything from torn tents to stolen sunglasses. There
was one report of a raccoon making off with a canoe. The man had
been fishing and in so doing had touched the bow rope on the boat.
The masked bandit, liking the smell, had eaten through the rope
while he was perched on the bow; the canoe had then floated out into
the darkness of Gun Lake. The final five pages contained wildlife

incidents for which no culprit could be identified. Some campers had reported seeing an unidentified animal lurking on shorelines or on portage routes. The details of the animal were vague. The encounters always ended abruptly with the people having no idea how the animal left the scene. Others reported that they were sure someone was spying on them. Steven leaned forward and his brow furrowed as he looked over the pages of the document. People who claimed to have seen the animal and/or felt that they were being watched had made the phone call to the office during the encounter. But when questioned later by Park personnel, not one of the people involved could remember what it was they saw. Steven placed his hand on the document and reached for some water which resided in a heavily stained coffee mug, and he rubbed his forehead as pressure built behind his eyes. He mentally returned to Silver Buck Lake. He could see the camp. As he struggled to remember anything beyond his first impressions, vague images drifted through his head like icebergs on a dark ocean. With his hands to his temples and his elbows on the table, he fought to regain control of his beleaguered memory. Pictures started to form. The memory of a man with an uplifted arm walking toward him materialized from the darkness. That single remembered moment released a flood of memories which turned the half-remembered photos into a full-length video playing within Steven Stiles' brain. Fear crept up his legs and sweat beaded on his forehead. He remembered the deaths of the two men. He saw the speed of the attack and the raw power present within the creature which materialized like a wraith. Words crept into his mind as he formulated sentences which were spoken by the impossible being which had saved his life.

He stood and stretched his weakened legs. Walking to the screen door, he noticed the lock on the aluminum frame. He shook his head at the useless device. Sliding the door open, he walked out onto the covered deck which overlooked St. Nora Lake. He saw people sitting on docks. Some were engaged in conversation, others were looking out at their beloved lake or reading books. Three turkey vultures plied the air with expertise as they scanned the ground with their keen eyes. Seven canoes rounded the point. The white boats were quite a distance away, yet Steven could hear the voices of their occupants. He realized that his world had just been reinvented. He could never look at the forest with any sense of ego. He imagined what would happen to all the cottagers and campers if information of this thing ever reached them. He wrestled with the enormity of it for the better part of an hour as he paced around in the closed office and randomly picked up items ranging from staplers to maps. A Ministry of Natural Environment logo caught his eye.

They can't know about this; they would have catalogued, tagged, and bagged it by now. What the hell is going on? Steven asked the ghosts in the room.

He looked at the notes he had written. Walking to a small wood stove which sat centred within the cabin against the south wall, Steven opened the creosote-covered door and placed the paper in the firebox. Striking a match on the granite hearth, he set the notes ablaze and watched as they curled and darkened, his written words melting into oblivion as the fire ate through the converted wood. Within a few minutes, the paper had turned to fragile black dust, held together by nothing more than a memory of its former self.

Steven grabbed his bag and locked the door. He carried his canoe to the water where waves crashed into the shoreline. Steven glanced back at the cabin which had somehow changed; it had become empty and hollow. He pushed his prospector into the rough water and pulled on his paddle, trying to remember what it was that he had just burned.

LIFE

Slowly emerging from the lake, he shook his fur and stalked into the valley. The musty smell of the hoofed ones floated into his consciousness while he moved quietly toward the unsuspecting prey. The deer stood together, feeding on the green surrounding them. He lay still, flush with the ground, hidden by the tall grasses and plants which grew prolifically in the rich, moist soil. He searched for the one deer which would have a weakness. All were females and one was pregnant. Agawaatesin's attention focused on a deer standing the farthest from him. He noticed that she was constantly sneezing and rubbing her nose on the fur of her legs. Her breathing was strong but had a roughness to it. He watched as she drew in air and exhaled. Upon exhaling, she would shake ever so slightly. The sun slowly crossed the heat-laden sky as the deer continued to feed. Biting flies ravaged the animals' ears, forcing them to shake their heads in response to the incessant attacks. Unsheathing his claws, he blasted out of concealment and leapt toward the terrified animals. The four hoofed ones found their footing and sprinted toward the shelter of the forest. The thick swamp mud hindered them but it also hindered Agawaatesin. Hooves and paws sank into the black sucking mud which seemed determined to claim more organic matter. The power of the deer was inspiring as they moved into a full gallop, broke from the valley, and entered the tree line where they scattered. Agawaatesin focused on the weak one. Feeling the ground solidify beneath him, he burst forward in a blur of speed which his quarry could not possibly match. The female ran with her head down and her ears turned behind her. Her sides heaved with exertion and her nostrils flared, attempting to keep up with the demands placed upon her. Agawaatesin closed the distance. Putting on impossible speed for the final push, he pulled up beside her and dove onto the terrified creature's back. The two animals crashed to the ground where Agawaatesin held the spent deer with his powerful arms and legs. After a moment, he grasped the female's head with his paws. She instantly calmed and he released her. She stood up on legs which shook with exhaustion and stared at him for a short time, her eyes clear and understanding. He would not kill today. The lust of the hunt had dissipated. The doe was not sick enough to die yet. He would take her another day. Agawaatesin lay down in a thicket of balsam firs and ran his fingers through the needles carpeting the ground. He closed his eyes and allowed himself to drift. His consciousness expanded. Locking onto a raven, he steered the intelligent creature to the ranger's location. Within a few short moments, Agawaatesin watched as the man lowered his canoe into the waters of Sherborne Lake. He would find the ranger when the sun fully disappeared from the sky.

ONE FINAL NIGHT

he sun had disappeared from the western sky and the colours of the clouds displayed an impossible mix of reds and pinks, which was reflected onto the lake. Ralph and Tom could hear Bill whistling to himself as he readied the campfire for another round of laughs and gags. Tom threw his cigarette butt into the sand where he ground it in deep. The action bothered Ralph, but he kept it to himself. The two conversed about everything from baseball to cars. Time slowly slipped away as the wilderness was engulfed in darkness. Rusty bolted up from his prone position at Ralph's feet; both Tom and Ralph reacted to the dog's movement. Rusty ran out into the water with his tail wagging; he looked back at the two men as if asking them to join him.

"What's going on, Rusty?" Ralph whispered.

"Hey, boys, I'm back," Steven's voice floated in from the darkness.

"Fuck! It's the ranger; hide the booze!" Tom shouted out into the dark.

Steven's canoe slid into view as Larry and Bill joined the men; Larry shone his flashlight in Steven's face.

"Shit, turn that off; I can't see a damn thing!" Steven called back while blocking the offending light with his hand.

"A little testy, are we?" Larry replied. He motioned to the other three men to turn their flashlights on. Four beams of bright L.E.D.

light blasted Steven's face. Steven put his arms up in the air, accepting defeat.

Rusty was so excited, he tried to jump into the boat. His tail wagged as if it were motorized; it thumped against the prospector's hull, sending booming sounds out into the darkness. The men helped Steven with his gear and welcomed him back. Rusty ran around the campsite, knocking over everything he could. Ralph smiled to himself; he knew his decision was a good one.

The fire created shadows which flickered and danced on the trees within the camp area. The men sat contentedly in a semicircle, facing the warmth of the burning wood. Smoke from the fire filled the air with its ancient comfort and drifted out into the darkness on a soft breeze which moved unseen through the wilderness. Steven sat entranced in the glow of the fire and thought little beyond the very moment in which he found himself. The others were also soaking up the peace and beauty of the camp where the creaking of chairs and the crackling of wood had become the sounds of home.

Bill broke the reverie, "This sucks, guys; it's our last night here and I just began to enjoy the place."

"Yep, you're right, Bill. It sucks that it took you all this time to have a good time," Larry responded while staring at the fire.

"Hey, you've spent the whole time shitting yourself!" Bill fired back.

"I became very acquainted with the shit box. I can tell you exactly how many plants are around it. I've actually named it after you."

The group fell into the type of quiet laughter which keeps on going for no apparent reason. After several minutes, the men settled down again. Ralph complained about his stomach muscles hurting, which began a new round of jokes and banter. The night wrapped the camp in its dark cloak and the lake paid the men no mind as it responded to the subtle breeze which caressed its surface.

Wrapped in her favourite camp blanket, Cassie sat facing the fire. The night air was cool which kept the hordes of mosquitoes from using her as their pin cushion. Her eyes followed the sparks as they broke free of the host log and shot into the darkness of the night. *This is life*, she whispered to the fire as if it were a lover embracing her and keeping her safe.

"Cassie, where did you put my sweatshirt?" Brad's voice boomed out of the darkness from the direction of the tent. The intrusion was awful and she resented it.

"I didn't touch it. You had it on last night, and I have no idea what you did with it." The annoyance in her voice was unmasked.

"Would it be too much to ask for you to help me find it?"

"Find it yourself, Brad; I'm just trying to enjoy the last night here!"

"Fine, just relax, I'll find it myself!" he volleyed back through the darkness.

Cassie was up and off her seat; she walked straight to where Brad was with his flashlight and told him in very precise words to go to hell. The night was ruined. Cassie's mood had turned sour. Brad and Bob had argued earlier in the day, an event which had sent Carol packing. Brad had been an anal-retentive asshole ever since they had left their vehicle at Big Hawk Landing. They had shared a few moments of intimacy during the trip, but the distance between her and Brad was massive. She felt that the night was going to be long, and the return to the city would be even longer.

Wrapping her blanket around her, she retraced her steps back to the fire. The smooth rock outcrops on the site made the journey easy in the inky blackness. Sitting in her camp chair, she reclined and gazed once again into the glowing red and orange coals which seemed imbued with life. Even though the night temperature was well above sixty degrees, the warmth of the fire on her face comforted her soul. Cassie closed her eyes for a few moments and thought of how great it would be to have the courage to do this camp solo. The sound of an owl calling off to the west caused her to open her eyes. Movement next to the water caught her attention.

"Brad, what are you doing?"

"I'm putting new batteries in my flashlight, why?" His voice had come out of the darkness from the direction of the tent. Cassie jumped up and directed the beam of her flashlight toward the water. Two luminescent eyes stared back at her, and then vanished.

Cassie screamed.

"Cassie!" Brad raced down to her side where she stood looking in the direction of the water.

"Something was staring at me, right there!" She directed the beam of her flashlight toward the water.

"What was looking at you?" Brad trained his flashlight in the same direction as hers. The twin beams of light caressed the rocks as they slid over them in an attempt to uncover the identity of the intruder.

"I'm telling you, there was something right at the water's edge and it was looking right at me!" She tried to control her shaking.

"I believe you, but it's gone. I can't see anything down there." He let go of Cassie and started toward the shoreline.

"Don't leave me!" Cassie reached for his arm.

"There's nothing there! Relax!"

Cassie was sick with fear; half-memories of the portage haunted her as she sank to the ground beside the fire. She watched Brad as he walked up and down the shoreline, shining his light out over the black water and back again. Cassie was sitting as close to the fire as the heat allowed; she could hear Brad mumbling and cursing. Something about the eyes glowing from the darkness had burned into her core and left her feeling completely vulnerable. Demons crept into her mind.

"Cassie, whatever it was is long gone, probably a fox or something," Brad's voice joined his body as he came into the light of the fire.

"The thing that stared at me was at least your height; I've never seen anything like it. I felt it as if it were trying to dissect me with its glare," she responded in a hushed, fearful tone which disconcerted Brad.

"Let's get the fire going and just enjoy our last night at camp." Brad placed a handful of wood onto the fire.

Cassie sat back in her chair and let the flames eat away at the dark fear which had possessed her.

Cumulus clouds, rolling in from the east, pulled curtains over the Milky Way. The forest waited in anticipation for the life-giving rains which would fall within the next few days.

HOME

THE ONE PLACE THE HEART YEARNS FOR.

The fire struggled for life in the misty rain as Ralph coaxed it into breathing. He had collected enough dry wood to burn the paper garbage the boys had accumulated over the past few days. Larry busied himself with rolling up his sleeping bag and stuffing it back into its carry bag — a seemingly impossible task. Tom felt anxious to get home now as he had been away from his daughter for a very long time. However, he was torn. Although leaving the camp was decidedly difficult, the wet weather helped him to find an excuse to leave. Bill was busy trying to take down the tent which, in his mind, had kept him safe from predators. He was having difficulty with his emotions. He wanted to stay, but he also wanted to leave.

Steven wandered among the four men, offering help wherever it was needed. He gathered bags and equipment and carried them to the water's edge where he would stop and stare at the clouds in order to judge the extent of the rain. He guessed it would be at least all day before the sun poked out again. He also knew the guys would be soaked by the time they made the trip out.

"Guys, don't pack your rain gear: you're going to need it. It's going to get nasty." Steven grabbed his rain gear from his pack.

"That freaking portage is going to be brutal. It was bad enough when it was dry!" Bill responded as he finally stuffed the tent into its bag.

"Lather up with bug spray, Bill, you're a walking buffet to the mosquitoes and there are going to be billions on that trail," Larry advised while secretly dreading the next few hours. The men were in sombre moods, and so Larry's comment fell on relatively deaf ears.

All of the canoes were loaded and positioned for the final push off. The rain had increased to the point where the trees on the other side of the channel were not easily discernible. The men stood beside the remains of their morning fire. Ralph, with his hands in his pockets, admitted he felt like bawling. The others used his admission as a way to hide their own sadness and Tom told Ralph to grow a set.

"I had a great time; thanks for putting up with me," Bill said with a sappy voice.

"Fuck Bill, without you, camp wouldn't be the same," Tom replied while blowing a kiss to his victim. "Hey Ranger, you better have the Park dudes clean out that crap box; Larry filled it." He threw the remainder of his cigarette into the fire pit.

"We might have to close the site for the rest of the season!" Steven responded.

"My ass is raw; I swear you brought sandpaper instead of toilet paper," Larry retorted, trying to gain pity from his friends.

"One hundred grit!" Ralph smiled at his own comment. "Well guys, let's head out, we have at least two hours before we make it to the landing. Check over the campsite and make sure you have everything."

"Yes, Papa. Can you put some butt cream on Larry before we leave?" Tom replied while kneeling down and acting like a child. The five men chuckled and broke off to search for anything left behind. Climbing into the canoes, they turned their eyes away from their campsite and began the journey home. Rusty stood in Steven's green prospector with his front legs up on the seat, seemingly oblivious to the rain. The three canoes drifted out into the mist and slowly became shadows.

The campsite lay empty. The sand where the canoes had been beached was marked with three distinct indentations from the bows of the boats. It also contained the distinct impression of a paw which contained five digits, claws showing.

Steven slid his canoe into a landing beside the rocky shoreline of the portage route through to St. Nora Lake. Rusty jumped out and ran around, searching and exploring every nook and cranny he could stick his nose into. Steven lifted the prospector from the water and turned it over on the smooth outcrop of the Canadian Shield. He placed his pack and paddle under the boat. Camp gear was strewn on the shoreline in a haphazard fashion and everyone was soaked.

"Hey, take a look out on the lake," Larry said as he was slinging a pack onto his back.

"Holy shit, the whole lake's leaving!" Tom pointed at the phantom canoes materializing out of the mist.

"Let's get out of here, guys!" Ralph interjected while dragging the canoe up on the rocks. Steven winced as the Kevlar hull grated across the rock.

"I recognize that crew. This portage is about to get crowded; I agree with Ralph." Steven put his pack on his back and adjusted the straps.

Bill picked up the food barrel, which he had thrown on the rock close to the water. As he hefted its weight onto his shoulders, his right foot slipped and forced him into a pirouette spin. He cried out in despair as he realized his destination. Bill fell into the lake and became submerged in slow motion. Reappearing, the waterlogged man struggled to climb back up onto the shore while swearing that camping sucked. The four other men collapsed in hysterics. Rusty joined the fray by licking Bill's contorted face.

"Damn Bill, only you can make us laugh like that!" Tom spat out between bouts of uncontrollable laughter.

"This fucking camping is killing me! Fucking lake!" Bill dragged the shoes off his feet and drained the water from them.

"That's a YouTube moment," Larry said while wiping the tears from his eyes.

"Shit man, that was too much." Steven wiped the tears from his eyes.

"I'm fucking soaked!" Bill replied, completely ticked off and trying to be menacing. The look on Bill's face sent the guys into another fit of laughter.

"We should move," Steven suggested while trying to catch his breath. The men grabbed their gear and hoisted the canoes. They left the landing in a ragged line. Steven hung back and looked out at the lake to judge the distance of the oncoming canoes.

"*A storm is coming.*" The thought pushed into Steven's head and made his eyes flutter. His knees weakened beneath him and he struggled to regain his balance.

"What are you?" Steven managed to say through the fog of pain which filled his head.

"*I'm real.*"

His mind contorted, trying to put some semblance of reality on the situation. The rain was intensifying and the oncoming canoes were closing on the landing. He gained control of himself, hoisted his canoe onto his shoulders, turned, and jogged down the portage road. Rusty barked at the oncoming canoes, and then he ran after Steven.

The portage was designated as a novice trail; however, when Bill set the barrel down on the sand at St. Nora, he was exhausted and spent.

"Holy shit, I have steam coming off me!" Bill said as he slumped on the wet ground.

"Ya, that's fascinating. You look like a waterlogged seal," Tom replied as his lungs strained for oxygen. He leaned over a branch which held his torso up as if he were a slab of meat.

"Funny, you look like a wrinkled old monkey." Bill rubbed his calves in order to get the blood flowing again. The rain had increased in intensity and there were flashes of lightning to the southeast.

"We have to get on the water, guys, or wait it out here!" Ralph said, genuinely concerned about the oncoming storm.

"We should make a run for the landing; we are all soaked and I'm freezing. Let's go!" Larry added.

"Are we all in?" Ralph asked. Bill nodded his head in agreement and Tom put his thumb up as he hoisted himself off of his branch.

"I'll follow you guys; this storm is going to get wild and we need to get you home," Steven interjected as he joined the crew.

"Does that mean you actually like us?" Tom hugged himself and stared at Steven.

"I'm not worried about you; I have to get to that nice cozy cabin over there to get away from you goofs."

"I love you too, buddy." Tom punched the ranger in the arm.

Steven threw mud at his assailant. Bill threw mud at Larry. That, in turn, caused an all-out mud fight. Rusty got involved by barking and jumping on anyone he could.

The three canoes were loaded and the men took up their positions with Rusty jumping in with Ralph. Steven purposely arranged the setup so that Ralph could be with his dog again. The rain was coming down in earnest with lightning streaks parading through the cloud cover; the five men pushed out onto St. Nora Lake and paddled hard for the landing.

Agawaatesin came out of concealment and stood in the mud and sand where the five men had just been. The heavy rain beaded on his long guard fur and dripped to the ground, and vapour rose into the air from his exhaled breath. The lake was calm and shrouded in mist as the cold rain mixed with the warm summer air. He watched as the three canoes drew slowly away into the distance. Turning — he ran back up the trail.

THE PORTAGE

Mark was apprehensive. The storm was closing in faster than he wished and he worried about the paddle across St. Nora. The kids were novices and nobody was safe on the water if lightning were present. He watched as the crew saddled their loads and sorted out the canoes. Mark thought of his options. He decided to push the kids hard toward the Canoe Trails cabin and hopefully beat the main thrust of the storm.

"We have to move, everyone; the weather is closing in and we have to beat it before we're stuck here. Are you guys ready for a challenge?"

The entire group yelled out in unison that they were pumped and ready to go.

"Good, let's move!" Mark shouted.

Nick picked up one of the largest packs and two paddles. After jogging across the wooden planks which crossed a bog, he entered the portage followed by three of his camp mates and quickly became winded.

"Hold up, guys; I have to tie one of my shoes," he said while trying to maintain his composure. The boys following him happily accepted the momentary break. Nick bent over to pretend to tie his shoe when one of the other boys shouted out the one word which incites panic in campers.

"Bear!"

The three other boys snapped out of their weariness and looked to where their friend was pointing. Less than twenty yards away, something large was moving and paralleling the trail. Despite being fully loaded, all four ran as fast as they could toward St. Nora Lake. Not one of them bothered worrying about the people who were behind them.

A couple of girls had heard the call and froze in place, south of the wood-planked trail. This created a people-jam, and by the time Mark showed up to sort through the mess, the entire crew was panicked.

"Those jerks are kidding you. Come on, I'll lead, just watch I don't hit you with the canoe, ok?"

Mark walked with a measured and sure step as he negotiated the terrain with the canoe over his head; the rest of the campers followed behind, shouldering loads which seemed too large for the bodies carrying them.

By the time the group made it to the St. Nora end of the portage, everyone was soaked and spent. Mark walked the four boys several metres away from the main group and spoke sternly to them.

"What the hell is wrong with you guys? You scared the other campers and we still have a storm to contend with!"

"We saw something that was following us; we swear it was a bear, sir!" Nick said, looking like he had seen a ghost.

Mark's anger sloughed off him and mixed with the mud on the trail. "I'm sorry, guys; I believe you saw something. You're experienced enough to know nothing is going to hurt you, so just relax. Now, let's get the other canoes. Martin will stay here and organize the group. Let's get moving." Mark started the return journey.

The rain had slowed to a light mist which allowed Mark to pick up his pace; experience had taught him that the storm was just catching its breath. He jogged up the trail with the three boys following close behind. They chattered and glanced into the surrounding woods with apprehensive looks. Mark tried to calm them by telling them that the bear would have long since vanished from the area.

By the time they reached the planked area, they had slowed to a walk. The boys were panting and Mark was reaching his limits. The party traversed the planks in a tight group. The fear from the boys was palpable and Mark was confused as to why. The boys had seen bears before. He reasoned that the kill on the island had somehow made them insecure and he hoped that it would not taint their love of camping. Reaching the Sherborne end of the portage, they barely took the time to catch their breath before loading the rest of the gear onto their backs. Mark took up the rear position; he had a seventeen-foot canoe to shoulder and he wanted to maintain an eye on the boys. The rain was still holding off but the mist was thickening. As they walked, there was very little talk; Mark could hear the sound of the buckles on the packs and the grunting of the boys as they climbed up the first rise of land. His canoe bumped its stern on a rock as he climbed up the small rise. He silently gave himself a lecture on the proper way to carry a canoe.

The stress of the hike pulled hard on the boys' reserves; their legs started to burn and fatigue was adding weight to their burden. Kurt was directly in front of Mark; though slight, he was lean and tough. Kurt's shoulders began to ache which forced him to place the pack down at the halfway point on the portage.

"Sir, just go around me; I have to rest my arms for a second," he said as he placed the pack on the ground just to the right of the trail.

"I'll hang here, Kurt; we're almost there."

"Ok, my hands were numb. That's all," Kurt replied as he picked the bulky pack up.

When he turned, his face told Mark a story which no words could. He had gone white and his eyes were as wide as saucers. Kurt tried to speak but only a strangled noise escaped from his mouth. Mark watched as the boy turned and ran with the pack in hand at top speed toward St. Nora. Mark's nape hairs had made themselves known. Kurt had obviously seen something which triggered a flight response and Mark did not want to hang around to see what that was. Fighting the instinct to run, he picked up his pace and tried to fight the demons his mind was conjuring up. His legs responded well to the adrenalin coursing through his arteries and he could feel the pumping of his heart as sweat poured from his face. Rounding a portion of the trail which marked the final fifty metres of the portage, he increased his pace as he desperately tried to control the fear which threatened to overcome him. Without warning, his canoe was violently shoved from behind. The force made it swing to the left and crash into a tree. Mark lost his footing and fell with the boat. Swearing at the world, he jumped up, ready to assail the prankster. The trail was empty, and he saw nothing but rocks, forest, and mist.

"Fucking assholes!" Mark yelled out. Picking up the canoe and balancing it on his sore shoulders, he made his way to the St. Nora side of the portage.

Mark was shocked to see that all the canoes were loaded and everyone was floating several metres offshore. "What the hell is going on, guys?" he shouted out to the group.

"Sir, there was a huge bear or wolf or something on the trail right behind us; I saw it following you!" Kurt blurted out as he slouched low in the bow of a canoe. The entire group was convinced that something was indeed following them and they were on the verge of panic.

"We heard you swear; what happened?" a thin, blond girl asked.

"I thought one of you pushed my canoe; I was blaming them," Mark said, pointing at the three boys who were clearly distraught. He continued, "It's pretty clear someone else is out there. Have you seen anyone enter the trail while I was gone?" Mark looked over each of his campers. The fear painted on their faces was real. A couple of voices assured Mark that no one had entered the trail while he was traversing it.

"Head to the landing; I'll load the rest of the gear in my boat and be on the water in a few minutes. The rain is going to catch up with us and it'll suck to be on the water." Mark slid his canoe into the water, stern first, and then he began to load the remaining barrels and bags. He watched as the crew paddled into the mist which encapsulated the lake. Within a few minutes, he was, for all intents and purposes, alone.

Mark looked back on the portage trail which he knew intimately, but this time it had changed. The trail was obscured with the heavy mist which floated like smoke around the dark shapes which were once trees. The silence was complete: nothing moved and the trail itself seemed to taunt him. His heart was thumping and he could feel the tremors in his hands; never before had he been frightened to enter a trail. Forcing himself, Mark picked up his paddle and re-entered the portage to Sherborne Lake. His muscles were tense and his eyes darted back and forth as he tried to regain the courage which had so recently been his. The mist moved around the trees as if it were caressing them. Water dripped from the branches and the trail had small rivulets of water running along it. The fear building up within him was almost unbearable. He desperately tried to reason his way out of the feeling, but every cell in his body told him to run. He stopped for a moment to readjust the Velcro strap on his right sandal; kneeling down on his left knee, he glanced downwards. When he looked up he saw a dark shape on the trail ahead of him, shrouded in mist, masking details. His skin crawled and his scalp tingled. Panic caused his logical mind to fight for his attention as he stared in disbelief at something which stood on two legs and was slowly moving toward him. He turned and ran as fast as he could move. He could hear the animal running behind him; daring to look back, he saw the mist-cloaked creature following him on two legs, matching his speed. Mark's heart was breaking under the strain and his mind fought for control. Reaching the sand, he pushed the loaded canoe into the water and dove into it without hesitation. Within a minute he was a few dozen yards out on the lake and paddling as fast as he had ever paddled. He looked behind him, and nothing but the mist-covered shoreline could be seen. Slumping over the centre thwart, he broke down and shook violently. His stomach heaved and he felt as if his muscles had turned to jelly. The rain had returned and its cool touch helped Mark to overcome his paralysis. Putting his paddle into the water, he pulled on the blade and drove his canoe toward the landing.

The campers were exhausted and soaked. Gear was strewn all over the cement launching ramp and the canoes had been dragged up without care for the gel-coat finishes. All of the campers shouted out when Mark appeared from the gloom of the lake. An eerie silence pervaded the area as the assembled crew moved their gear toward the dirt parking lot behind the cabin. With all the equipment finally piled up and the rental canoes placed on the racks, the group anxiously awaited the bus which would take them to a place where warm food and dry beds existed. Mark was asked a dozen times by as many campers what it was that Kurt had seen on the trail. He simply shrugged his head and admitted to being wet and tired. He said that all of them would feel better after a good long shower and some hot food. The sound of vehicles racing past on the highway was loud but very reassuring.

CHANGE

INEVITABLE.

The Canoe Trails barracks building was a paradise to the five men who now enjoyed its warm showers. Rusty lay on a heap of towels in the corner of the men's change room. Five showers produced enough steam to plunge the room into a near sauna-like atmosphere. Humour had returned and everyone was in great spirits.

"Thanks, Steve. That was awesome. All we need now is a beer," Tom said as he paced around looking for a place to sit and dry his feet.

"You're welcome, guys."

"Glad these stalls have curtains; imagine being in the same stall as Bill," Larry interjected.

"You love me, Larry, I know it."

"You're right, Bill. After this camp, I feel strangely attracted to you," Larry's reply elicited a gusty round of laughter which filled the steamy room with echoes. Rusty added his own version of laughter by barking which in turn made the men laugh harder.

Dressed in dry clothes, the men grabbed their gear and walked out into the rain which was teeming down. Lightning was streaking throughout the area.

"Fuck me, we didn't miss that by much!" Ralph said while trying to hide his head in his shirt collar.

"I'm glad we're out of here," Bill added.

"It's good you pushed hard across Nora. We could be stuck in this shit right now!" Steven said. He watched as Rusty attempted to stay dry under Ralph's poncho. Ralph held the dog's leash in his right hand. The group crossed the highway to the parking area and threw their gear into Ralph's truck.

"Thank god we loaded the canoes earlier; that was a great call, Ralph," Larry said while climbing into the front passenger seat of the large vehicle. Bill had taken refuge in the back while Tom considered trying to light a smoke. A loud bang of thunder changed his mind and he dove into the back seat next to Bill. Ralph turned to Steven.

"Steve, take care of my pup. I'll be back next month. Do you have my number?"

"Ya buddy, I do. I'll take care of Rusty for now, ok."

"I've got to go." Ralph knelt on one knee and hugged Rusty hard. Tears were streaming down the man's face, forcing Steven to look away. A loud clap of thunder broke the two apart. Ralph jumped up and mopped at his soaked face with his left hand. Hugging Steven goodbye, he climbed into the driver's seat and closed the door. The vehicle coughed to life and then the truck edged out onto the highway and disappeared. Steven lowered his hand and rubbed Rusty's head as he grappled with his emotions. A loud crack of thunder shook the ground, pulling Steven out of his internal dilemma, and Steven and Rusty ran toward the cabin.

Steven placed his hand under the deck of the paddle shop; his fingers encountered the familiar feel of the keys. He slipped them off of their hook and ran to the door just as another loud clap of thunder echoed across the sky. When the door opened to the persuasion of the key, Rusty ran in and jumped on the Ikea chair. Steven stripped his clothes off and obtained a dry set from his day pack which he had placed in the cabin earlier. He walked to the kitchenette and plugged in the kettle. The kettle gurgled and popped as the element coaxed the molecules in the water into a boil. The windows of the kitchenette looked out toward the south of the building where canoes rested upside down on wooden racks. He noted that two of the rental canoes were on the ground and upright, collecting the rain which was pounding the earth.

"Who the hell did that?" Steven said aloud, knowing he was not going out to correct the situation while the thunder gods played hardball outside. The kettle hissed loudly and then clicked as the internal thermostat shut the element off. He poured the boiling water into a mug which was stained from years of use and instantly the aroma of the tea worked deep into Steven's nasal passages. He closed his eyes, breathed in deeply, and then exhaled. Looking up from the counter, he noticed a piece of paper which had been placed in a Ziplock bag and then stuck into the window frame of the main office area. Steven opened the front door and retrieved the note. Sitting in his favourite spot by the wood stove, he opened the Ziplock bag and extracted the letter. The letter was addressed to him and it was written by Mark.

Steven, I hope you find this note. It's raining like hell so who knows if it will stay dry. I need to talk to you. The kids and I saw some strange animal on the portage trail from Sherborne to Nora. The thing chased me and scared the hell out of the crew. Call me on my cell. I didn't get a good look at it but I did see enough of it to know I've never seen anything like it.

Steven's mind was doing somersaults. The relaxed attitude of a few moments earlier had vanished. His heart beat like a drum within his chest as he thought of the possible scenarios of destruction such an animal could cause. Steven's elbows rested on the armrests and his hands supported his head. Rusty's bark brought his head up from its prone position to see the dog run past him toward the windows overlooking the lake.

"What's up, Rusty?" Steven stood and walked over to the window where Rusty was standing on his back legs, looking through the glass, and wagging his tail. The storm was fierce, lashing the trees violently; a bright flash of lightning lit the area with such intensity that Steven noticed something crouching beside a large pine tree. Steven walked to the desk and grabbed the binoculars which hung from a hook under the counter. He aimed the eyepiece and adjusted the focus. His breath caught up short when the binoculars revealed the identity of the animal crouching in the lashing storm. Staring back at him was the thing Mark's letter described. The creature did resemble a large wolf from a distance, but under the scrutiny of the binoculars, this animal was, without a doubt, unclassified. Steven watched as it rose from a crouch and stood on two legs. Its eyes bore into Steven's mind. This caused him to drop the binoculars; he watched the creature as he closed the distance between the tree and the cabin at a slow, methodical pace.

"Open the door." The command was forceful and received by Steven's mind as if the words had been spoken.

"Fuck that!" Steven's verbal reply was instant.

"Let the canine out; I will not harm him."

Steven resisted, but then he opened the door as if he had no choice. Rusty burst through the opening and ran straight at the nightmare which closed on Steven's position.

"You are wondering why I terrified the man you know as Mark. I had to get them to move fast. This storm was closing in; the group would be in extreme danger if they had not been pushed. Do not misunderstand me; I have little love for people. This world would be far better off if they did not roam around on her back. Go and sit in that chair you enjoy so much and relax. You and I are going on a journey."

Steven saw the words within his mind and felt the power of the creature's control. He knew he was trapped and he struggled at keeping his mind his own.

"Tell me to leave and I will. If you wish me to disappear from your life, I will erase all memory of our encounters. You are at a junction point which will dictate the rest of your existence here. The choice is yours to make."

Steven walked to the recliner by the fireplace and dumped his tired body into its embrace. He grabbed his mug and guzzled the remaining tea.

"I have no idea if I'm insane or not, so any decision I make will be troublesome. Let's go on that journey you spoke of." Steven's hands tightened on the padded armrests of the chair.

"Relax, you have nothing to fear." The words sank into Steven's head as he stood and walked to the front of the cabin. He locked the door and then turned off the light which had illuminated the area over the kitchenette. Steven then walked to the rear porch door and called out to Rusty. The Lab ran up the steps and blasted past him with great enthusiasm, soaking both the man and the room in the process. He noticed the storm intensifying and shuddered at the calls which would invariably inundate the office by sunup the next day. He looked for the creature which haunted him but could see no trace of him.

"I am still here. Close your eyes and relax; I'll do the rest."

The words once again formed somewhere deep within his mind. Steven walked to the recliner and pushed the seat back. He could feel his pulse in his feet.

"I'm thankful that you have chosen not to fight me on this."

There was a long pause.

"The question as to whether or not you have a choice can be simply answered as yes."

"What the hell are you?" Steven's hands clenched as he asked the question.

"There is much I need to say, and the storm is a perfect backdrop."

"Tell me about it."

"I exist only as long as the Earth dictates. A very long time ago, humans would understand this statement, but their arrogance and ego pushed the possibility of understanding deep into the dark caves within their minds. You are the first person I have found in a very long time who may have the ability to learn."

"I think I'm going insane; how the hell is this possible?" Steven was dropping into despair.

"Humans have developed many of the belief systems which you have experienced. The common thread of these is fear. They are all designed to keep your population ignorant. The wilderness, with all of its power to enlighten, was and is vilified for the sole purpose of keeping people from finding their own power. In order for you to understand how I exist, it must be impressed upon you that there was a time when humans were part of the world and not lords of it. Knowledge was shared, but now it is hidden within the shadows of the remaining wild places. I carry that knowledge." Agawaatesin paused, allowing Steven to process the information while he himself struggled with his own misgivings about sharing this intimate knowledge.

"How the hell can you expect me to believe this?"

"I'm right outside that door; do you need another look?"

"I know you're there. I can't help but question my sanity, though. You are telling me that you carry knowledge of some sort and that you think humanity is a plague. Why the hell doesn't the Earth just get rid of us and be done with it if all you have told me is true?" Steven was bordering on anger.

"I can erase all that has transpired within one beat of your heart. Do not use anger when addressing the issue!" Agawaatesin pushed hard into Steven's mind. *"We do kill when it is absolutely necessary. You have witnessed that. I have no concern for your politics or for the power-hungry people who trick the rest of you into believing in them. I care only about the survival of the species which I share this time with. The energy I tap into is elemental. Your phone is going to ring in a moment. Answer it; you're needed."* Agawaatesin fell silent when the phone resting beside Steven filled the cabin with uninvited noise. Steven picked up the receiver.

"Steven, it's Sue. I need your help!"

"What's up?" he replied. He tried to understand Susan's words as she sobbed through the phone. He could hear Kyle yelling in the background. Susan whispered to Steven that she was scared and was hiding in a washroom. "Can you get through the window, Sue?" he asked.

"I think so, but where do I go?"

Agawaatesin pushed a picture of a white shed into Steven's mind.

"There is a shed to the right of the building you're in. The door's unlocked and there's a boat which you can hide in until I come for you," he said, shocked by the clarity of what he saw.

"Ok," Sue replied.

"Do not hang up; talk to me when you reach that shed." Steven heard the sounds of a window opening and the crash of something falling. Several moments passed and then Susan spoke again.

"I'm in the boat. How did you know about this?"

"Doesn't matter; did you close the door?"

"Yes."

"I am calling the cops! I can't get there fast enough. How psycho is the prick?"

"Steven, don't get them involved, please."

"Susan, this jerk has done this before. Enough is enough, man! Ok, I won't call, but what's the address?" Susan hesitated, and then she told Steven the address. "Keep your head down. I'm leaving now," Steven sprinted to the counter and grabbed the keys for the Chevy pickup.

"I have to get to her!" Steven yelled out.

Steven opened the front door and ran for the Chevy with Rusty right beside him. He jumped into the truck and Rusty bounded over him, taking the passenger seat. Steven started the motor and gunned the pickup out onto the dark highway heading south. Rusty panted excitedly while the headlights pushed the darkness to the side of the road. Steven glanced at the mirror on the driver's door and noticed a large animal running beside him, just off his left front bumper. He looked at the speedometer which showed a speed of eighty kilometres per hour. *How fast can you move?* he wondered aloud as the rain slashed at the windshield and pushed the wipers to their limits.

R. G. Wright

The Chevy vibrated as it sped down Highway 35. The needle indicated one hundred and ten kilometres per hour as his foot pushed the accelerator down as far as he dared while still maintaining control. Headlights of oncoming vehicles appeared and vanished within mere moments, causing momentary blindness for him. The storm was battering the Highlands with vicious winds and powerful flashes of lightning which were followed by unbelievably deep heart-pounding crashes of thunder. The pickup held the road but he knew he was pushing his luck; all he could think about was Susan hiding in a shed while her drunken asshole boyfriend wandered around looking for her.

The storm had grown to a maelstrom; trees highlighted by flashes of lightning were bending at impossible angles. Debris covered the highway and forced Steven to slow the speed of the vehicle to an agonizing sixty kilometres per hour. His hands were gripping the steering wheel tightly, cutting off the circulation to his fingers, and he had a tension headache which threatened to explode his cranium. When he took a hard left and turned off the highway, the tires of the truck slipped on the wet pavement. This momentarily put the truck into a fishtail; Steven corrected and pushed the accelerator. The Chevy sped through a four-way stop and jumped off the hill which preceded the driveway where Susan was holed up. Locking the brakes, the pickup ground to a shuddering stop. Steven pulled the keys from the ignition and ran to the white shed which was exactly the image he had seen back at the cabin. Pulling the door open, he called to Susan. The wind stole his voice and threw it into the air. He tried again. "Susan!" A brown canvas tarp used to cover a boat lifted and Susan popped her head out of concealment.

"Steven!" she cried out as she jumped from her hiding place and ran to his arms. He hugged the distraught woman and began to retrace his steps to the pickup.

"Where are you going, bitch?" Kyle's voice boomed from the darkness to the left side of the pair.

Steven stopped in his tracks and held Susan tighter. "Back off; you're scaring her," he hollered at Kyle who was approaching him with what seemed to be a piece of lumber.

"Fuck off, old man; she's mine!"

"Not tonight, asshole; I'm getting her out of here!" Steven shouted back. "Sue, here are the keys. Now get into the truck and lock the door." He held Kyle with his eyes. Susan ran for the truck, which Rusty was desperately trying to vacate. Kyle increased his gait and changed course to cut her off. Steven intercepted him. The two men fell heavily to the ground and momentarily disengaged from one another. Kyle swung the two-by-four at Steven's legs. Steven jumped back and then lunged at his attacker. Once again, the two men fell. Kyle had the advantage of alcohol and youth, while Steven felt his body protest against the punishment he was receiving. He lay on his back in the mud with Kyle straddling him. Kyle's fist slammed into his cheek and rocked his head violently to the right. Rusty was incensed and barked as if demented. Kyle's rage was powerful; he rained punches down on his victim until Steven released his own rage. The power surged from his core as he pushed the young man off of him and onto the rain-soaked earth. Steven used the heel of his hand to beat Kyle's face. Steven raised his fist in order to deliver a killing punch when he was brutally thrown off Kyle. The harsh landing jarred him from the dark place he had occupied seconds earlier, and he looked toward Kyle to see Agawaatesin posed over the semi-conscious man. The power of the creature was unmistakable; his stance and demeanour forced the acid taste of fear to rise in Steven's mouth. In slow motion, his eyes filmed the stage which shook with the violence of the storm. Kyle had his arms outstretched in the air, trying to defend himself against the hellish thing straddling him. Susan's eyes were wide with horror as she stared in disbelief through the passenger window of the truck. Rusty was running in circles around the combatants. Steven felt as if he were made of sponge. He watched in horror as Agawaatesin placed his opened paw on Kyle's face.

"No!" Steven cried out.

"You were about to do the same, Ranger." A flash of lightning wove its web across the sky and blinded Steven for a mere second. When he looked back toward Kyle, the creature had vanished.

"Leave him where he lies; he will not remember this," Agawaatesin's voice entered Steven's mind as he stood and walked to Kyle. The man's chest rose and fell as if he were in a deep sleep. Kyle's face was bloodied and bruised. Steven limped to the pickup, climbed onto the driver's seat, and put his head on the wheel.

"You beat the shit out of him!" Susan punched Steven in the arm as she berated him for his action.

Blood dripped from a gash in Steven's forehead onto the steering column.

"Susan, that prick could have killed you!"

"We have to move him; we can't leave him there."

"Trust me, he'll be fine. Let's get out of here before he stands up." Steven turned the key and started the truck's engine. He turned the truck around and started to pull away.

"Stop!" Susan yelled out while pulling on the release for the door. She jumped out of the vehicle and ran to Kyle, who was sitting up and wiping his face with the front of his t-shirt.

"Susan!" Steven yelled out as he stopped the vehicle and climbed out into the rain. Kyle was standing by the time Susan reached him. He placed his arm around her shoulder and she guided him back toward the house.

Steven could not believe what he was seeing.

"Susan, what the hell are you doing?"

"Shut up, Steve; I can't leave him out here!" Her voice was full of reprisal.

"Fuck!" Steven yelled out into the blackness which surrounded him. He retraced his steps back to the truck and climbed in. Rusty took up residence on the passenger seat. The heater was cranked on and the heat slowly worked its way into his bruised and cold body. He tried to find some semblance of logic in the decision Susan had made. Running through the events over and over again, he drove back toward the highway by pure instinct. The storm was a perfect background for Steven's emotional state.

The Chevy's headlights highlighted the cabin as he drove into the parking lot. Steven walked around the vehicle and released Rusty who jumped down and took up shelter under the eaves of the building. Steven splashed though the water and muck, mumbling to himself. The door protested slightly to the disturbance as Steven swung it open. Rusty bolted in and took up residence on the Ikea chair which rocked slightly under the dog's weight. As Steven turned to close the door, a large lethal paw was placed just above his hand. He jerked his hand away and fell backward onto the wood floor. Agawaatesin stood framed in the doorway, his silhouette resembling nothing living on the planet. The creature entered the cabin, grabbed Steven by the leg, and pressed his claws into his flesh. Steven cried out in pain and panic.

"Ranger, you did not fail tonight. The female has no idea of the danger she faces. In time she will learn." Steven felt the words as they formed within his straining head. The paw released its grip.

"She called me for help, I raced like a lunatic to get to her while risking my own life, and this is the thanks I get!" Steven felt used.

"She has seen both sides of men tonight. That lesson will never be forgotten. She will, one day, thank you for what happened."

Steven closed his eyes and lay his head on the floor of the cabin. When he lifted his head to speak again, the creature was gone. Lightning flashed, highlighting the trees beyond the cabin door. Steven kicked the door closed and walked in the darkness to the bunk bed where he had placed his sleeping bag. He stripped down to his shorts and slumped down onto the mattress. Rusty joined him and tucked himself into the crook behind the ranger's knees. Steven pulled the sleeping bag over his body. The last noise Steven's ears registered was the sound of a horn on Highway 35.

PLANS

Light rain tickled the windows of the cabin as Steven lifted his head from the pillow. Sitting up, he stretched his back, scratched his head, and wandered into the bathroom to look at his face. It was bruised and he had a swollen lip and a laceration on his forehead, but otherwise he thought he had gotten off pretty easy. He looked at the calendar which was hung over the desk. July had turned into August during the night. He lifted the page and looked at the photograph of a black wolf. He noted how the animal's eyes showed intelligence far beyond its reputation. The phone broke him from his reverie and he reached for the handset. "Trails office, how can I help you?" He looked for a cup to put some water in.

"Steven, is that you?" Lisa's voice sliced through his cluttered brain.

"Lisa — how are you?" he managed to reply.

"I'm great, but I hear you had a rough night. Sue told me everything. Don't worry, Kyle is fine."

Steven let out a sigh. "How's your daughter? That creep really scared her last night."

"She's ok. Sue's hardheaded, but I think she realizes she can do a hell of a lot better than Kyle. I'm going to watch him and nail his ass if he so much as does five kilometres over the limit," Lisa said with humour in her voice. Steven did not doubt her sincerity though.

"That's good to hear. There's no shortage of studs lining up to date your daughter. I am sure she won't be single long." He remembered Lisa in high school.

"There's another matter I have to ask you about. Do you have a few minutes?"

"Ya sure, fire away." Steven watched as the rain painted lines on the lake.

"A couple of guys from Toronto were camping in your area, and according to their families, they have not returned home yet. The names are Rick Glaff and Mike Slessor. Do you have any bookings under those names?"

Steven heard the words as they drifted out of Lisa's mouth into his battered head. His knees suddenly felt weak and his pulse intensified. The names drifted through his mind in half-formed memories, coalescing and then dissipating like wraiths.

"Neither had a reservation. I caught up with the pair on Silver Buck and asked them to leave. As far as I know, they did." Steven wiped his face with a paper towel he had hastily pulled off a roll attached to the sink cabinet. Something was missing. He could not place the day or time. Grabbing his notebook from his pack, he leafed through the past several days and could not find one entry for Rick Glaff or Mike Slessor. "Lisa, how long have they been missing?"

"They were supposed to be home several days ago." Lisa paused, and then offered, "Hey, I am up for a bit of paddling. What do you say, would you like to accompany me to Silver Buck Lake?" Lisa threaded her fingers through her hair.

"Consider me in; just tell me when and where we're meeting."

"Tomorrow looks good as far as weather is concerned. I can be at the cabin by seven; is that ok with you?" She looked at the Weather Network on her tablet.

"Sure. It'll take about an hour and a half to reach Silver Buck if we paddle from here. How about launching at Sherborne Dam? That will shave off forty or so minutes."

"That sounds great. I will be there by seven," Lisa said with the authority that cops learn while performing their duties.

Steven felt a twinge of rebellion but he let it go. "Ok boss, I will be here and ready to go." He looked in the mirror and touched his bruised face.

"Thanks." Lisa paused before asking, "Are you at the cabin tonight?"

"I'm not sure. I have no plans to head out into this stuff, so I may just take the day to run some errands and restock. I guess I'll crash here for the night," he answered while wondering why she would ask.

"I will give you a call later, take care." Lisa hung up.

He looked at the phone and shook his head. *What was that about?*

Steven looked out through the window to the sullen day which seemed determined to sap happiness from all those who were caught in it. He thought of the Park's visitors who would be huddled under tarpaulins and in tents, waiting out the weather and cursing their luck for picking this time for a vacation. Tents would be dripping with moisture both outside and inside, and unprepared campers would face the prospect of sleeping through the night in wet clothes and sleeping bags. Mosquitoes would be clinging to the tents like hungry hordes of winged vampires waiting to feast on the soft-fleshed humans. Yet with all the misery soaking into their lives, very few groups would leave their campsites to enjoy the comfort of a climate-controlled environment. Steven had learned long ago, that the instinct to den-up in inclement weather was as strong in humans as it was in the wild ones.

Lisa filled her time by catching up on the arduous task of filling out the paperwork which had been neglected. She had spoken with her daughter regarding the incident of the previous night and Sue had assured her she would be leaving Kyle. Sue's adventures with young men reminded Lisa of her own youth, and she mused over the similarities they shared. She remembered her prom year. Graduating from grade twelve was a huge deal at the time, yet the passing of twenty-four years had mellowed that milestone down to almost nonexistent. Lisa opened the bottom left drawer in her desk and took out her grade twelve high school yearbook. She leafed through the time capsule while memories flooded back into her from a long-lost file stored away within her mind. She read one of the comments written on the second back page signed by Brian Fendrik:

"Hey gorgeous, don't forget the time on the bleachers in grade ten."

Her mind instantly gravitated to the night that the football team had won their match against some other high school which she had long forgotten the name of. The night was unusually warm and a whole gang of students had filled the now darkened field. Brian had wooed her and she gave into him on the bleachers, well out of sight from the crowd below. Lisa shook her head to rid herself of the memory and continued to leaf through her book. Turning the pages to the graduating class photos, she glanced at each face staring at her from the past and recalled details of each person. *What the hell did I see in that guy?* Lisa asked herself out loud in the unoccupied office as she stared at a long-haired Brian Fendrik whose eyes seemed hollow and stoned. As she continued to scan the pictures, she came across Steven Stiles. His hair hung down to his shoulders and his mouth showed a slight, forced smile. Lisa could hardly remember even seeing him at school. He was in a lot of her classes yet he remained invisible to her memory. She closed the book and put it back into the drawer.

She reached for the freshly inked file of Rick Glaff and Michael Slessor. Opening it, she read the descriptions of each of the men. Although the information was light, it did hold some valuable insights. Both were avid outdoor enthusiasts with a love of fishing and hunting. Both were reputed to have excellent bush-craft skills and they apparently knew the area of Sherborne Lake very well. Lisa picked up the phone and dialed the only number listed in the file.

"Hello?"

"Hi, it is Constable Lisa Denton calling from the O.P.P. detachment in Minden. Can I speak with Mrs. Glaff?" Lisa waited as she heard the phone get placed on some hard object.

"Have you found them yet?" a gruff female voice entered Lisa's ear.

"With whom am I speaking?" Lisa replied as politely as she could.

"Millie Glaff, have you found my husband?"

"We have not found him. I need to know what colour of canoe or water craft the men used, Mrs. Glaff; do you recall?" Lisa held her pen over her notebook.

"They took a sixteen-foot aluminum canoe with a motor."

"How did they get to the Park, Mrs. Glaff?"

"I drove them to the landing at Hawk Lake five days ago. They were supposed to call me when they were done but I haven't heard from them yet."

"What were they doing, Mrs. Glaff?" Lisa asked, puzzled by the way Millie Glaff replied to her question.

"They were just fishing; what does that have to do with anything?" Millie Glaff said defensively.

Lisa paused.

"Can you provide me with their phone numbers and provider? I'll see if I can get the location of the phones."

She wrote the numbers down as Millie relayed them and then reassured the woman that she would do everything possible to track the men down. Lisa looked at her calendar as she twirled the pen in her fingers. She turned the calendar to the new month and looked at the photo of a black wolf staring back at her. Picking up the phone, she dialed the Trails' office once again.

Steven was dealing with a woman who was complaining about the rain and wanted a refund when line two lit up.

"Please, it is a wilderness park. We cannot control the weather. If you want that, go to Great Wolf Lodge or something." Steven hung up and picked up line two.

"Hey, it's Lisa. I have to change our plans. Can you be ready to roll in about two hours?" Lisa's voice resonated in his ear and he felt the usual increase in his heart rate.

"For sure, come and get me out of here!"

"I should be there around ten thirty. What do you need me to bring?"

"Just your clothes. I have the food covered as long as you don't mind eating dehydrated stuff."

"That's great; I want to close this file as soon as I can. Sorry for pushing it."

"I'll be waiting with great anticipation, Princess," he replied, purposely knowing that it would piss her off.

"You goof. I'll see you in a bit. Bye." Lisa smiled as she hung up. She hated being called a princess, but Steven never let her forget the grade twelve commencements where she and Mike Denton were crowned King and Queen of the ball. Lisa pursed her lips as she remembered that night. Her memory played the movie as she drove home from the office. She and her King got high in the back of a modified Ford Econoline van. Red shag carpet and black lights adorned the interior and hormones played their games. A few years later she and Mike were engaged with a child on the way. Mike was controlling but tolerable for the first little while. He joined the police force in Huntsville where he quickly rose through the chain of command and eventually was voted onto the local council. He helped her get onto the force where he could keep his eye on her, but tensions escalated and eventually Lisa left Mike and transferred to the Minden detachment. Mike still controlled her though; his reach was long and he had many people who would do his spying for him. She gripped the steering wheel harder as she realized the control his highness still exerted over her. The trip to her house was just a blur of trees and rock as she revisited the memories which refused to stay hidden.

A deer ran across the highway and Lisa swerved deftly around the wide-eyed undulate. "*Holy shit!*" she yelled as it disappeared into the foliage on the opposite side of the road. With her reverie broken, Lisa prepared a mental list of what she would pack for the run up to Silver Buck Lake.

Back home, the hot water felt great as it rolled off her body. She pumped the soap from the dispenser and rubbed the solution all over her skin. Her breasts felt a little hard and she wondered how long it would be until her next period. She did not need it when wandering around Sherborne. Lisa dried off with a terry cloth towel and looked into the mirror over the sink. She never liked what she saw reflected back, as she could see the strain and stress of forty-two years written on her skin. Taking her makeup out of the drawer, she applied cover up to the areas on her face she thought needed improving. She then took a pencil and darkened the edges of her eyelids. Mascara followed; with deft hands, she applied it quickly and lightly. She pulled on a sports bra and quick dry panties; looking into the full-length mirror on the back of the door, she scanned her body for signs of aging. Her breasts were still relatively firm and her waist had only increased marginally. Her face gave her age away and she thanked her makeup kit for the wonders it achieved. She changed into cargo pants and a long-sleeved shirt. Then she packed her bag and was out the door within the same hour she had entered her home.

The light rain required only low wiper attention in order to facilitate Lisa's ability to see the road. The highway was relatively deserted and the lakes she passed were completely devoid of boats. She wondered if she had been a bit hasty with her desire to head to Silver Buck Lake, but her penchant for getting the file closed was stronger than her desire for comfort. The cabin slid into view and she eased her car into the parking lot. She smiled when she noticed the white Chevy pickup loaded with Steven's canoe strapped to the racks. She turned her head, looked at the building, and saw Steven leaning on the door frame. He was wearing a shirt which was open to his breastbone and beige coloured pants. Moccasins completed the look and she found herself catching her breath as she took in the sight of the man who she once thought was a geek.

"Hello, Lisa; are you a cop today or just one of us ordinary citizens?" he called out through the misty rain. Rusty bolted from the cabin and ran up to Lisa and proceeded to make her as dirty as he was.

"Nice try. I'm undercover, special assignment detail. Whose dog is this?" Lisa reached for her bag and desperately tried to see her image in the water-soaked window while fending off the earnest canine.

"His name's Rusty and he's my new buddy. Come in, I'll show you what I've packed and then we can take off." Steven turned and entered the cabin.

Lisa scolded herself for her weakness, but something powerful and primitive had stirred within her. She walked into the cabin followed by the muddy dog and was instantly calmed by the smell of wood smoke and the energy contained within the walls of the building. A warm mug of tea waited for her on the table while Steven busied himself with organizing snacks and food items for the trip.

"Thanks for the tea, and thanks for being so accommodating." Lisa took the warm liquid and sipped it, hoping it would calm her down.

"Anything for you; you know that."

Somehow his voice flowed through her and she felt herself go weak. Speech became difficult as she fought desperately for composure. Lisa looked at the gear as he explained it to her, but she heard nothing at all. She was too busy giving herself a thorough scolding for loss of control. Hoping to break the spell she was under, she asked him if she could see the bookings for the last two weeks. He pointed to the desk and the pile of paper which he had just printed off. Lisa walked over to the desk and leafed through the papers.

"Can I read over your report about the incident on Silver Buck?" Lisa asked while sorting through the names on the papers she held. He walked over to the computer which took up a corner of the desk and typed in his password. The monitor lit up and a beautiful picture of a sunrise on a mist-shrouded lake filled the screen.

"Wow, that's gorgeous. What lake is that?"

"It's Sherborne; I took it last September. There was nobody on the lake and the mist seemed surreal. I remember being close to shore. When I looked through the mist toward the shore, I saw something watching me. It gave me the chills." He wondered why he had opened his mouth.

"That's freaky; why didn't you take a picture of it?"

"I thought I did; in fact, I swear I did. Anyway, I downloaded the photo and that's the one you're staring at." He opened the file aptly named Mike Slessor and Rick Glaff. "It's all yours." Steven walked back to the table to pack the equipment.

Lisa sat in the padded chair and scanned the report. She took her notebook out and jotted down a few particulars. The report was dated a few days' prior and it was very sparse in detail. She wrote down the body of the report.

- *Arrived on Silver Buck Lake at nine thirty a.m.*
- *Noticed campsite number 76 was occupied*
- *Sixteen-foot aluminum canoe with a motor tied on shore*
- *Encountered two men camping without a permit*
- *Both men left the campsite as requested, but with some hesitation*

"Steven, are there any trails in the area?"

"Sure, it's a bit rough, but the place is lined with logging trails."

"Could they have gotten lost on those trails?" Lisa pulled up Google maps on the computer.

"Lisa, there are so many trails in there; they could have gone in circles. My guess is they show up in a day or so, tired and completely pissed off. If you don't have a GPS or a good compass and map, you will get twisted around." He sat on the edge of the table and watched

Lisa as she leaned into the computer monitor. Memories of Silver Buck Lake taunted him from hidden recesses within his mind.

"The bag is packed and I'm ready to go, the taxi is waiting and he's blowing his horn."

"Funny guy, I'm ready too." She switched the computer off and pushed the chair into the office desk. The pair left the cabin and climbed into the pickup that would take them to the Sherborne Lake Dam.

CATCHING UP

S teven kept his speed to a smooth ninety kilometres per hour. He was well aware of the woman sitting beside him and he had difficulty focusing on the task of driving. Rusty sat between the two which helped defuse the tension they both felt. The Lab was busy panting and staring intently at the road as if he was going to be the one who would be driving home. Lisa and Steven caught up on the events and situations in each other's lives. By the time they reached Sherborne Lake Road, the two were engrossed in a deep conversation centred primarily on control freaks. She broke down a few times, showing Steven her vulnerable side. This flattered him. He felt as close to her as if he had been with her his entire life. Memories floated in and out of his consciousness ranging from grade school to present. He remembered his feelings of ineptness around her and was surprised that at the present time they were and always had been the best of friends.

Sherborne Road started out smooth for the first few kilometres of their journey, and then it turned into a ball-joint-breaking road from hell. Steven navigated the road as best he could while Lisa pointed out the tire-eating potholes. The rain had abated to a fine mist when they arrived at the dam. Lisa took the packs to the shoreline while Rusty dove in and swam in circles. Steven released his canoe from the Chevy and carried it to a grassy area just north of the landing. He slid it into the water and tied its bow to a small tree root.

"Where are we getting in, Captain?"

"Right here, Princess. I've seen people slide off that rock and I would hate to see you get soaked." He had a grin on his face.

Lisa picked up her bag and threw it at him. The aim was perfect and he was shocked by the power behind it.

"Not bad!" He placed the pack in the centre of the canoe. Lisa carried the larger pack over and placed it behind the bow seat. Steven went back to the truck and grabbed three paddles and two life jackets. He called Rusty who bounded out of the water and dove into the canoe. The trio headed off into the mist-shrouded waters of Sherborne Lake.

The Precambrian outcrop provided him with perfect cover. He watched as the couple approached and listened to the mind chatter each had. The ranger was trying hard not to expose his feelings for the female who, in turn, was doing the same. As the canoe slid past, the canine stood up in the boat and looked up. This prompted Steven to follow the dog's action. Neither dog nor human saw Agawaatesin as he lay prone on the ancient rock. He smiled as the trio moved from view. Standing, he stretched and unsheathed his claws. Placing all four paws on the ground, Agawaatesin burst from the rock in a blur and vanished into the surrounding forest.

The granite walls and dark green forest slid slowly past as Steven and Lisa paddled toward the portage trail which would take them from Sherborne to Silver Doe Lake. The rain had commenced and both of them wondered why they had ever bothered to undertake the journey. He found himself looking at Lisa's back more often then he should and he scolded himself for letting her get to him. She, in turn, was well aware of the eyes on her and she was thankful for the raincoat which masked her form. They passed campers who sat sullenly around sputtering campfires holding cups of warm liquid; some waved and shouted out expletives about the weather. Rusty would shake every now and then, which threatened the stability of the canoe. Steven usually saw it coming and would place his paddle on the gunwales to balance the boat, but Lisa had no idea it was coming and would scold the excited canine, convinced that the canoe would overturn. Steven smiled every time it happened.

"Relax, the canoe's a prospector — hard to tip even with a shaking dog," he told her as he manoeuvred the canoe around the point of land into the bay in which the portage to Silver Doe Lake resided. He noted the sign and pointed it out to Lisa.

"How long is this portage?"

"It's only about six hundred metres, straight uphill at first but it slopes down from there. It will be crazy with mosquitoes though, so I suggest we button our sleeves and spray on the bug juice." He reached for his pack.

Lisa pulled the drawstrings on her hood and readied herself for the inevitable onslaught of bloodsuckers. Steven brought the canoe in broadside and steadied it as Rusty bounced out in a cloud of water spray. She grabbed the sides of the boat, still frightened that the craft would spill them into the water.

"Does that dog do anything gently?"

"He's a Lab: they're either asleep or running; they have no other speed." He braced the canoe. "Well, here we are, Princess. Do you want to carry the canoe or the pack?"

"I'm a princess, remember? You said it yourself." She picked up the large pack and started the trail. Steven smiled, put the small pack on his back, and lifted the sixty-pound canoe onto his shoulders.

The rain, which intensified as the pair traversed the trail to Silver Doe Lake, made the portage miserable; shoe-sucking mud and ankle-breaking rocks had to be avoided and the bugs were wicked. Lisa trudged along, trying to keep her spirits up, but the rain seemed determined to drive her insane. Steven kept relatively dry due to the canoe over his head, but he found it tricky trying to negotiate his footing while fending off hundreds of bloodsucking insects. They finally reached Silver Doe Lake where Steven propped the canoe up on a tree branch to create a shelter.

"This sucks. I had forgotten the bad parts of canoeing. Is this shit ever going to let up?" Lisa pointed up to the sky as the mosquitoes clouded around the pair.

"Let's get out of here; we're already soaked and these vampires are getting worse." Steven tipped the canoe over and unceremoniously flopped it into the waters of Silver Doe Lake. The paddle to the portage trail leading to Silver Buck was short and relatively bug-free. The pair repeated the load out of the first portage and pushed on through to Silver Buck Lake. Rusty ran ahead and seemed oblivious to the humans' plight. He splashed through every puddle he could and was completely immersed in exploring. Steven watched the dog and wished he could be just as exuberant in such lousy weather.

Once on Silver Buck, Steven and Lisa jumped into the canoe while Rusty was content to run along the shoreline. The rain had increased and thunder rolled heavily in the west as they met Rusty on site 76. Steven pulled the canoe up and turned it upside down. After tying the bow-line to a small tree, he grabbed the pack and carried it the short distance to the tent site. He opened the pack and reached for the shelter which had remained dry.

"Lisa, can you help me out with this rain fly? That storm is rolling in fast and we need to get out of it." He was seriously concerned that another strong storm was on its way. Lisa ran over to him and they had the tent set up in a few minutes. Steven threw the gear into the tent.

"Get in there and change out of your wet clothes. I'll bring the canoe closer for the dog to stay under; he's not coming in the tent to soak everything again." Steven walked to the lake to grab the canoe. He laughed at the dog paddling around in the lake, oblivious to the storm.

Lisa crawled into the tent and stripped off her jacket which she placed on the ground in the vestibule area. This was followed by her shoes which were saturated. Steven placed the canoe upside down by the tent and secured it so that it would not move in the strong winds which he suspected were rolling in. Steven walked toward the tent. Lisa had left the door flap open but had closed the bug screen. This allowed him to see Lisa within the tent. She had her top off and was undoing her pants. He turned his head, feeling guilty, but within moments he looked back toward the tent. Lisa was now only in her bra and panties which were both soaked and showed her smooth skin beneath the fabric. She rummaged through her pack and pulled out a dry shirt and some pants. He walked toward the lake. His heart was pounding and he found himself struggling to breathe.

Shit. Now what? he said out loud. This made Rusty bounce toward him. The dog shook right beside him which broke the sexual tension he had been grappling with.

"Steven; it's your turn!" Lisa yelled out as the wind grabbed her voice and sent it in shards through the air.

Crouching down into the vestibule, he kicked his shoes off and draped his soaked jacket over a guy wire. He unzipped the screen mesh and entered the confines of the shelter where he took up position opposite Lisa who sat on a sleeping bag she had unrolled from the pack.

"You had better change. I won't look."

"I looked at you, by accident though. You left the door open."

"What! What did you see?" She acted shocked.

"Not much, no I mean it was awesome, shit, you left the door open," he grasped for words which made sense.

"I hope you turned away!" Lisa hid her embarrassment beneath feigned indignity.

"I swear, honestly. Now turn around and let me change; I'm getting cold." He unbuttoned his shirt in front of her. Lisa watched for a moment as his chest hair was exposed. As the shape of his chest became visible, she turned and faced the wall of the tent. She listened as he took his shirt off and placed it on the floor. He stood up and faced the other wall of the tent to take off his wet pants. Lisa waited for the sound of the pants to hit the floor; she turned to face him as he was tossing the garments out of the door. When he turned around, she was looking at him.

"Now we're even, Ranger." She tried not to visually feast on the man.

"Shit! I should have worked out; there is not much to see here. By the way, when did you start calling me Ranger?"

"I don't know; it just popped into my head."

Steven could hear Rusty barking his happy bark not far from the tent. He thought of Agawaatesin and became concerned.

"What's wrong?" Lisa had noticed the hint of a frown on his face.

"Nothing, I just wanted to leave a better impression."

"No worries there," Lisa mumbled as she turned to face the wall once more. Steven looked at her while he covered his underwear with his hands. She sat leaning on her right arm. Her long sleeved shirt hung loosely from her torso while her yoga pants hugged her butt perfectly. A loud crack of thunder broke his trance and he quickly changed into his dry clothing. The rain intensified and beat on the tent with deafening relentlessness.

Steven opened the zippered vestibule on the tent and called to Rusty who seemed completely oblivious to the torrents of water cascading from the sky. The dog tried to jump into the tent but Steven managed to grab him. He dried the dog as best he could and allowed the exuberant canine into the confines of the relatively dry shelter. Lisa and Steven lay in their respective sleeping bags and talked for hours. She relived her marriage to Mike Denton and her messy separation. She told Steven of the pressure her ex-husband placed on her by continuously following her and calling her at home and work. The storm drummed a rhythm on the nylon walls, adding a fitting background noise to the storm playing out in Lisa's life. Steven listened in silence, loving the melodic sound of her voice and worrying he may put his foot in his mouth if he said anything. He did mention a few failed relationships.

"You just haven't met the right girl," Lisa suggested.

"You know what, I actually have met her. She doesn't know how I feel, but I've known her for a long time." He listened to Lisa's breathing less than three feet from him.

"Is it anyone I know?" She felt a tug in her stomach.

"Not sure if you do, Princess; and no, I won't tell you her name."

"I'll get it out of you. By the time we leave tomorrow I will know her name." Lisa's emotions vacillated between jealousy and disappointment.

"Ok, the bet's on."

The day drifted away as the pair talked of life and living. Eventually, they fell into the mystery of sleep as the wilderness performed its symphony outside of the small green shelter.

A CALCULATED RISK

Lisa woke up to the haunting calls of a loon and the serenading of frogs. The interior of the tent was dark but the ambient light from the star-filled sky allowed her to see the outline of the poles holding the shelter up. She pulled herself out of her sleeping bag, put on her jacket, and exited the tent as quietly as she could, followed by Rusty. The stars were gorgeous, filling the sky with a million twinkling diamonds. She stretched and breathed in a lungful of fresh air. Lisa busied herself with lighting a fire and boiling water. Rusty was a dark shadow running from one adventure to another; she watched the dog for a while and found herself being jealous of his freedom. The fire was small but it radiated light and warmth to all the right places. She sat with her back to the forest and watched the fire lick its way over the resinous wood. She mulled over the conversation with Steven and found herself actually upset at the idea of a mystery woman in his life. Entranced in thought, Lisa failed to notice the shadow which drifted along the shoreline.

Agawaatesin moved to within twenty feet of the female. He looked deep into her mind to find out why she was there and who she was. He crouched lower onto the ground and closed his eyes.

Lisa felt uneasy and tried to pin the emotion on some logical explanation. She thought of her ex. If he ever found out that she was camping with Steven Stiles, shit would hit the fan in a very ugly way. She dusted off old memories and remembered the young Mike Denton. He was the most revered guy in school and he made sure his status never changed. She fell hard for him and his chiselled looks; she gave in to him and spent the next twenty years of her life trying to make him actually see her. Mike had the Hollywood flair and used it to get his way with almost everyone he had contact with. Their life together was tumultuous and she felt helpless around him. Lisa had tried in vain to tell her side of the story to her friends and people she knew, but Mike's influence was strong and he had most people fooled. She suffered in silence for years until she found out that Mike had fathered two children by two other women. She left with the help of her family and had been hunted by him ever since.

Lisa's mind drifted to the present and she looked toward the tent where Steven slept. She relived the moment when he had taken his shirt off and she felt the sexual tension rise within her. Scolding herself, she busied her hands with the fire and soon had a blaze burning which seemed to match her desire. Lisa walked to the shoreline to fill the pot with water and then she scanned the lake which was slowly coming into view in the predawn light. A small island in the middle of the lake with stunted pines looked as if it were a sunken galleon which had somehow found its way from the ocean to this tiny body of water within the Highlands. Sitting on an outcrop of rock, she let her mind wander. Wrapped in thought, she failed to notice the creature laying ten feet from her left leg.

With his eyes barely open, Agawaatesin watched and listened to the woman who had entered his world.

Steven awoke as the predawn light lit the tent up with its soft and subdued touch. Rusty ran to the door and begged to be let in to properly greet him, but he let the Lab drool outside while he got his pants and shirt on. He had the door of the tent partially unzipped when the dog bounded inside and knocked any sense of organization within the shelter to oblivion. He laughed and wrestled with the overzealous canine.

"Hey Steve, I've made coffee," Lisa's voice floated to Steven's ears.

"I'm on my way." He went to a nearby tree to relieve his bladder. Following the trail to the fire pit, Steven planted his eyes squarely on Lisa's butt. *Damn!* he said aloud as Lisa turned to ask what he meant.

"I have a stone in my moccasin; sorry for the outburst."

"No worries." Lisa handed him a steaming cup of coffee. He took the cup and held it between his hands.

"How long have you been up?" He tried to find conversation which was relatively neutral.

"I think it was four or so; I couldn't sleep. I forgot how beautiful it is out here." Lisa looked straight into his eyes.

"Don't stare at me like that; I may bite you." He struggled to hide his rising lust.

"Sorry, I couldn't help it. Your eyes are weird, you have a freaky stare. I've never noticed that before." She was fighting off her own desires.

"The morning light around here reflects off things and makes everything weird. Thanks for the coffee, but I don't drink the stuff. It's keeping my hands warm though," Steven replied, trying in earnest to break the spell she was casting on him.

"Shit, you could have told me when I handed it to you."

"I was too busy trying not to stare at you. There, I said it, now I can relax." He took up a position next to the fire on a log which was losing the battle to decay. She was taken aback for a moment and not sure how to reply.

"I'm not going to lie; you've had my attention since grade school. Now here you are in my world, life-sized and gorgeous. I couldn't help but stare at you. Sorry if I'm blunt, but shit: looking at you sure beats the hell out of staring at the goofy Lab," Steven blurted out without really considering if he should.

Lisa felt dizzy as the rush of endorphins engulfed her brain. No one had ever been that forward with her before. Steven had said it without the sales job she had heard from others. He said it from his heart and she knew he expected nothing in return for the compliment. For the first time in her life, she saw Steven Stiles and she felt the raw unadulterated wilderness exuding from his core. Lisa shivered as if she were cold.

"Are you comparing me to Rusty?" She tried to break the spell woven in the morning silence.

"Well, you smell a hell of a lot better, that's for sure." Steven smiled his unique grin.

Rusty broke the tension by running past the fire pit and knocking the pot of coffee off of the metal grate it was resting on. Sparks flew out of the pit and Steven danced around, trying to beat the dangerous embers to death so they would not spread to the forest.

The sun flooded site 76 and tendrils of water vapour rose from the lake as the heat tricked the water to leave its resting place. Steven and Lisa combed the lot for clues of the missing men. The rain of the preceding days had obliterated any track which would have been left by the men. Lisa worked in ever-widening half-circles, eventually ending on a rough trail which had been hacked through the woods by would-be adventurers. She followed the trail for five hundred metres in each direction, but the trail was devoid of any relevant information. She retraced her steps back to the camp where Steven was busy packing the gear back into his canoe.

"I can't find a trace of them. Where could they be?"

"That trail runs south where it splits: one branch leads southeast to the marina at Hawk Lake, and the other branch leads to Partridge Lake Road. They could have gone in either direction; most people using aluminum canoes and motors have carts. Maybe they moved to a different site by trail?" Steven put his pack into the prospector. He watched as Lisa pulled her cell phone from her pack. She punched a number in and he listened intently to her conversation with the disembodied person on the receiving end.

"The guys can be on the trail in an hour or so, Steve. The ATVs are already loaded. Can we hang here for a while until they arrive?"

"Sure, we can paddle around the lake for a bit and see what we can find."

She completed her conversation with the dispatch in Minden and closed the phone.

"They're on the way. Any excuse to ride those four wheelers is a good excuse for those guys. Thanks for putting up with this, but we might as well cover all the bases while we're here."

"I totally agree. Let me call the cabin and let them know that I will be out of commission for a bit." He picked up his two-way radio and called the office.

"Hey, what's happening?" Sue's voice filled the site.

"I am holding your mother hostage on 76; just thought I would let you in on it."

"Shut up, Steven. Really, what's going on?" Susan had an edge of concern in her voice.

"I really am here with your mom, but relax: it's a search and find expedition. Your mom wants to follow up on the two guys I had a run-in with up here but we've come up with a negative on all counts. I have to hang here and wait for the ATV patrol to show up, so I will be out of the loop for a bit."

"No problem. Jeff and Will are out on patrol; I'm sure they'll call you if they have issues." Sue was trying to control her voice. She was still upset with Steven for the way he abused Kyle.

"Thank you, Susan."

Sue waited for a lengthier response, something more in keeping with Steven's style.

"Ok, remember Mom's a cop," she voiced into the microphone only a few inches from her mouth.

"That I am well aware of," Steven's voice filled her right ear and then silence.

I'm so pissed with him! Susan said aloud to the counter and the windows as if they were somehow listening. Her mind gravitated to the storm where mayhem ensued and fear stalked. She recalled the fight where Steven pummelled Kyle into the mud and she vaguely remembered a vision which tore at her soul and ripped the voice from her mouth. It was like a half-remembered nightmare where reason was dissected and found completely inept. Shaking her head, Susan reached for a mug which was highlighted on the counter by the brilliant sunlight streaming through the window.

The sound of approaching machines broke the stillness of Silver Buck Lake. Steven swung the prospector's bow toward the campsite as Lisa placed her notebook and binoculars into her pack. The canoe slid into the muddy landing with a sigh as the reeds caressed its hull. The sound of the machines abruptly stopped and Steven could hear the cops as they made their way to the site. He watched from shore as the two officers approached Lisa and he instantly recognized Billy Hamilton who carried himself as if he had a pole rammed up his ass.

"Hello, Stiles," Billy called out as he grabbed Lisa and hugged her hard. Lisa pulled away from the burly cop. Steven acted as if he had not seen Billy's blatant disregard for personal space. As he tried to reason with his confusion and disappointment, his face felt flushed and his pulse elevated to the point where he could feel it in his legs. Steven cursed his insecurity and set about loading the canoe with his gear.

"Billy and Raymond found nothing on the trail. It is as if Slessor and Glaff vanished," Lisa said as she walked toward the lake where Steven stood looking out over the water.

"Sorry if this was a waste of time. I'll keep an eye out for them when I'm patrolling." Steven was desperately hiding his emotions, fearing she would see right through him.

"I was the one who asked you. I thought I may find something, but we didn't. The guys asked if I wanted a ride back. Would you mind if I take them up on it? I can get back and make some calls to the families of the two missing men." Lisa watched his body language.

"No problem. I should check out Sherborne and see if everyone survived the storm in one piece." He felt rejected and used.

"Thanks, I'll call you tonight. And thanks for reminding me how awesome getting out here really is." Lisa approached Steven and hugged him close; he put his arms gently around her shoulders and lightly hugged her back.

"Are you ok?" Lisa felt the awkwardness of the situation.

"Ya, we're being watched. Best get going, kiddo." He pointed to Billy who was staring in their direction.

Lisa picked up her pack and waved goodbye to Steven as she and the two other officers followed the trail back to the ATVs.

Steven made his way to the fire pit where the smell of coffee still lingered and Rusty was digging through the warm ashes. He rubbed his companion's neck and sat down on the ground. A million thoughts collided in his head as he tried to reason his way out of the hole he found himself in. The sound of engines starting and the deep growl of motive power filled the site as the vehicles pulled away. He thought of Lisa hanging onto Billy as he guided the ATV along the trail.

No doubt the egotistical stuck-up bastard has a grin from ear to ear on his face. He poked a branch into the fire pit as if it were a skewer.

Rusty bolted from his excavation in the fire pit and ran into the surrounding forest. Steven jumped up and called to the crazy Lab as he disappeared.

"What the hell, man! Now even my dog has left!" Steven shouted out to no one. He felt the pressure behind his eyes before he heard the voice.

"I want you to tell her what happened here." The push was strong and not negotiable.

"Shit!" Steven recoiled from the pressure. *"I can't tell her; she's a cop and will hunt you down. There is no way I could make her understand,"* Steven pushed back to the creature which lay concealed.

"What are you hiding from me, Steven?" the soft stern voice of Lisa filled Steven's ears and forced him to jump up and spin around to the direction from which she spoke.

"What the hell is going on; I thought you left!" he managed to blurt out while grappling with the situation.

"I was testing you; do you really think I would leave you after dragging you here?" Lisa smiled at the stricken man's confused countenance.

"I thought you had to get back and make some calls. I'm no good at this crap!" Steven floundered for words.

"I know you're holding something back. I need to know. I have no idea what it is, but I need to know."

"What makes you think I am holding something back?" he blurted out, feeling like he had no direction in which to flee.

"I have no idea how I know, but it's intense and impossible to ignore."

"What's with Billy grabbing at you like that?" Steven felt stupid for saying it.

Lisa laughed and looked at him. "Are you jealous, Ranger?"

"No, that's dumb. I mean, what the hell," he sheepishly replied. Lisa walked up to Steven and kissed him on the cheek.

"Billy is a stuck-up asshole who is in the pocket of my ex. Mike controls him. Billy did it to see if you would react. If you had, he would suspect you and I had something going on and he would tell Mike. Get it?" Lisa looked straight into Steven's blue-green eyes.

He grabbed her and hugged her close. Lisa snuggled into Steven's chest and listened to his pounding heart. She looked up at him and kissed him on his lips. Rusty dove into the couple and bounced around like a furry black rubber ball. Lisa and Steven laughed hard at the goofy dog but held onto each other tightly.

The sun slowly slipped down the western arc of the sky as Lisa and Steven wove the stories of their lives into the memory of each other. The stories would merge and separate again as the pair relived moments shared and moments spent far apart. Eventually, the stories coalesced around Steven's incident with Kyle and Steven relayed most of his recollection to Lisa. As she lay against his chest with the fire radiating heat and light into the darkening forest, he told

Lisa of Agawaatesin's involvement. He could feel her tense up as she lay against him; she turned to him and told him to cut the crap. He looked straight into her eyes and told her he was not kidding.

"Lisa, I need you to hold on to me tight, and listen, just listen," he pleaded with her. He could not afford for this to go wrong.

"What are you saying?" Fear and confusion showed in her eyes.

Steven's eyes began to well up; tears formed and followed the contours of his face to drip off his chin.

"What's wrong?" Lisa looked at him with grave concern; she was also tearing up. He held onto her tightly and buried his head in her hair.

"I am the creature of which the ranger speaks." The voice, harsh and assertive, broke into the woman's mind; she grabbed onto Steven and looked into his face to see if he had said the words. Steven pointed his hand to a spot just beyond an old dead tree by the fire pit. Lisa looked over and was struck mute with terror at the sight which confronted her. Standing twenty feet away was Agawaatesin. Its eyes reflected the firelight and its power was beyond imagining. She cried out in terror for a moment, and then she fell silent. A wave of comfort suddenly washed over her and she relaxed into the arms of the man who held her. She stared in wonder at the creature which stayed just within the shadows the firelight created. Steven spoke to her in whispered softness.

"He came to me. I have no idea how or why, but he chose me, and now you. Let him tell you his story." Steven kissed her hair and hugged her tight.

Lisa watched as Rusty ran up to the creature and lay down beside it while chewing on a stick he had hunted and killed. She tried in vain to put some semblance of reason on the events transpiring in front of her. Time stood very still as Agawaatesin relayed his story to her without ever opening his mouth. Steven sat quietly behind her, embracing her with warmth she had never truly experienced. The forest had grown very dark by the time Agawaatesin's story went silent. The fire had retreated to small embers and Lisa's body ached from the sustained position she was in.

"I guess we're staying an extra night." Steven's voice seemed loud. It was as if she was hearing speech for the first time. "You'll get used to it, Princess. The whole listening inside your head thing." Lisa turned to him and hugged him close; he, in turn, wrapped his arms around her and enveloped her.

"This is unreal. What if we are being held hostage by that thing; what if it controls our minds to the point that we have no more free will?"

Agawaatesin's voice entered Lisa's head gently and firmly: "*You are free to do whatever it is you wish. I can control your mind, Lisa, but I'm not. If you choose to not accept this reality, I will vanish as quickly as I appeared. You will not remember a single word or vision you witnessed here.*"

"*Can I touch you?*" Lisa's mind sent the thought to the creature before she realized it.

"*Yes.*"

She looked to Steven to follow her as she crossed the distance separating them from Agawaatesin. Rusty jumped up and ran to her side where he licked her hand.

The wildness of the creature was tangible; its body was unlike any other wild animal Lisa had ever seen. With her hand outstretched and her heart beating rapidly, she made contact with the creature's ear. Agawaatesin kept his head prone on the ground as the woman's hand reached toward him. Buried memories of a woman's touch rose in his mind and he flashed back to a distant time when that touch was magic, calming his world down, making everything right. Lisa's trepidation slid from her and she moved her hand to the top of Agawaatesin's head. She ran her fingers through his soft fur.

"*Hey, I'm getting jealous again,*" Steven pushed to her. Shocked that she could hear him, Lisa released her hand from Agawaatesin and turned to Steven.

"How did you do that?" she said aloud.

"I had no idea I could."

"Just think it and send it, not unlike the electronic messaging you humans are addicted to," Agawaatesin pushed.

Lisa looked into the ranger's eyes, and said, "This is a dream, right?"

Steven whispered into her right ear, "No." Then he kissed Lisa gently. She smiled, opened her eyes, and then turned to look at Agawaatesin. It had vanished. Rusty had another stick he was intent on subduing. They walked over to the fire pit and within a few moments, flickering fire light bathed the campsite in dancing yellow and orange colours.

Dawn broke free of the confines of the night and bathed the area in a warm cloak of yellow light. Birdsong filled the air with each musical note conveying a message to those that understood the melodies. Steven and Lisa busied themselves with packing up the camp while Rusty sprang from adventure to adventure. The heat was starting to build and Steven wanted to get through the portages from Silver Buck to Sherborne by midday. He was conflicted; leaving this spot would also mean facing the world. He loaded the prospector with Lisa's pack and then squatted by the water's edge to ponder how people would handle the news of this development. When Lisa's hands draped over his shoulders, his body relaxed and he closed his eyes.

"We'll figure it out," her soft voice pushed into his mind as he soaked in her touch.

"I know."

The sun made itself known as it poked its brilliance over the tops of the trees adorning the eastern side of the lake. The faint sound of a motorized boat reached the confines of Silver Buck Lake and bounced its echo from shore to shore. The green canoe slid through the water, leaving a liquid wake of silver behind it. Rusty rested in the centre of the canoe, his head leaning on the thwart, his ears ever vigilant. Steven gently propelled the canoe toward the portage trail as Lisa dragged her left hand through the water.

BROTHERS

IRREPLACEABLE.

Agawaatesin lay on the edge of a precipice, eighty feet above the water. The decision to invite the woman into his world was a calculated risk; he was prepared to remove her if the need arose. He closed his eyes and searched for her. From the eyes of a crow, he watched as the couple approached the dam where they had parked their vehicle. Her influence over the man was strong.

Agawaatesin pushed the crow to circle the area. The two humans embraced. She reached behind the ranger's head and pulled his lips to hers. The exchange was long and passionate. Agawaatesin disconnected from the bird and opened his eyes. He turned on his back and spread his arms out on the soft moss which grew lush and thick as it absorbed the minerals from the ancient rock. Letting out a sigh, he pushed his mind into the forest which surrounded him.

Leaping from creature to creature, he travelled north. From the eyes of a fisher he followed one of his kind. It was stalking a group of four people who traversed a portage trail. Agawaatesin felt the darkness surrounding the being; anger had entombed its soul. It would not hesitate to kill.

The fisher ran at the humans; they in turn yelled and ran as fast as they could. The group reached the end of the portage, tossed the boats in the water, and paddled quickly out into the lake. A long howl broke the air from within the confines of the trail. The group on the lake stared at each other in disbelief.

Agawaatesin disconnected from the fisher and connected with a grey jay. He flew down the trail and found the creature. It was ripping apart an old tree stump in frustration. Agawaatesin released the bird and opened his eyes. The darkness that had taken up residence in that being to the north would soon become a serious threat.

He looked over the edge of the cliff to the water below; a group of people were sitting in their canoes admiring the ancient outcrop of rock. He prodded them gently and they looked up to his position. He stood, making himself visible; they saw a raven.

Sitting down, he pondered how easy it was to influence human minds. The creature that was ripping apart a stump, north of his position, would have an easy time stalking vulnerable prey. He eased his body into the soft cushion of moss, closed his eyes, and let the wilderness run over him.

The wolves ran hard toward the sleeping animal. The ground slid beneath their paws which made just a whisper of sound as they contacted the earth. Their lungs drew the oxygen-rich air of the forest deep into their chests through their open mouths as their keen eyes scanned the woods through which they passed.

Breaking to the left of the pack, the leader pulled up short of the dormant being. The pack formed a semicircle around it as their leader approached the sleeping animal. He growled. Agawaatesin opened his eyes and stared into the yellow eyes of the wolf. Assured his brothers would stay close, Agawaatesin allowed his mind to shut down as he drifted off.

EXPLANATIONS

Merging onto the highway was surreal for Lisa; the ribbon of concrete and asphalt seamed invasive and wrong. Holding Steven's hand helped, but a feeling of helplessness tugged at her soul in a way which she had never previously felt.

"That's why I do this job, Lisa: the walls are closing in, and developers are lobbying to destroy this area. The only thing protecting it is provincial law. It's reliant on a user pay system, but the people who use it don't understand its fragility. Every time I run into one of the ignorant jerks, I want to beat them as they beat the land. I try to educate them without sounding preachy, but it never works. I am limited by the very rules I am employed to enforce."

"How did you know my feelings?" Lisa looked at Steven's profile as he drove.

"I have no idea." He took his eyes off the road for a second to look at her.

"Hey, I could hit you up for distracted driving; keep your eyes on the road, mister."

"Can't seem to help it. Why in the hell do you have to be so damn cute?"

Lisa squeezed his hand a little tighter.

"Why did it pick you? Why now? Why has it taken this chance? Not just with you, but with me?" Lisa's thoughts trailed from her mouth in a quiet, slow monotone.

"Something unprecedented is happening. I think it needs us to help. I'm guessing it has something to do with being its eyes and ears. I can't imagine what it is that we could do for it, but if it didn't need us, we wouldn't be aware of its presence."

Steven turned the truck into the parking lot at the cabin where he parked it and turned the engine off. The sound of the waves hitting the cement ramp helped to fill the silence which had entered the space between the two occupants of the vehicle.

Sue stared at the window above the main desk and watched as a large, grey horsefly roamed over the smooth surface in a vain attempt to extricate itself from the prison it had flown into. Rolling up a piece of paper, she raised her arm in preparation to strike at the winged vampire. As she took aim, a pickup truck pulled into the front yard. She instantly recognized the canoe strapped to its rack.

"*Shit!*" She abandoned the death blow to the horsefly and walked into the washroom to formalize her complaint before confronting the man who had beat up her boyfriend.

Susan waited until the screen door protested the intrusion of Steven before leaving the bathroom to vent her disapproval. Entering the main room, she stopped short when her mother greeted her.

"Hi Sue, how's everything going?" Lisa felt completely exposed.

"Mom, where's Steven?"

"I was with him over on 76 trying to tie up the Glaff case. And yes, we stayed a couple of nights."

"I know, Mom; your car's parked right over there."

Lisa smiled at the expression in her daughter's eyes. Rusty blasted through the door and took up ownership of the Ikea chair. Sue turned and scolded Rusty for getting her chair wet. Rusty replied by rolling on his back and wagging his tail.

"This dog is just like Steven; he's impossible to deal with!" Susan was totally exasperated.

Steven walked in and stopped short as he took in the scene which was playing out in the office. Sue's attack was instantaneous. She yelled at him for pouncing on her drunken boyfriend who was now so traumatized he did not want to leave the house.

"Holy shit; hello to you too, Sue!" Steven managed to say before Susan unleashed more accusations against him. Lisa jumped in and tried to calm her daughter down, but to no avail. Susan stormed out of the cabin and paced over to the empty canoe racks south of the building.

She stared at the water for a few moments and watched the waves as the sunlight danced across them. Sue felt the rising bitter taste of jealousy and she fought hard to put it into proper context.

Lisa had instantly recognized the symptoms Susan was feeling and needed the matter to be settled before it grew into something large and formidable. She walked over to where her daughter sat and leaned against the canoe rack.

"Can we talk?"

"Mom, I'm ok, just a bit pissed."

"I get it, and I need to explain some things to you."

Susan stared at the water while she and her mother talked in lowered tones for the better part of an hour. Lisa explained the events leading up to the past few days and she explained her fear of Sue's father. Lisa and Sue had the conversation which all mothers should have with their daughters about partners and life in general.

Steven paced the floor as if he were an expectant father. He had no idea what had happened, and even worse, what was going to happen. If a member of the public walked in at that moment, he was not sure if he could formulate a sentence which would make any sense at all. He tried to peek out of the bathroom window which gave the best view of the south side of the cabin, but the canoe racks blocked most of what he needed to see. Walking back out to the office area, he noticed the horsefly on the window. Steven took a glass from the small cupboard and a piece of paper from the desk; he placed the open end of the glass on the fly and slid the paper underneath it. Walking to the screen door, he opened the protesting hinges and walked a few steps from the porch area. Just as he released the fly to its rightful place, Susan yelled out to him.

"I almost killed that thing!"

"Not really giving it a fair chance; they won't bite when they're inside." Steven tried to avoid eye contact.

"I'm sorry if I lost it. Mom explained everything."

"You still pissed about the Kyle thing?"

"I am, but I know you were protecting me. Sorry, Steven. I don't understand why Kyle's a wreck and seems to be scared of his own shadow. You traumatized the hell out of him."

"He had the upper hand; I was getting my ass kicked! The booze won out and let me drop him. I'm surprised he hasn't tracked me down and kicked the shit out of me." Steven meant every word of it.

"He couldn't find you if he wanted to; we didn't know you were kidnapping and seducing my mother."

Steven smiled. Susan hugged him lightly while Lisa looked on from the edge of the water.

A cacophony of squeals broke out from the marshy area left of Lisa's position. She turned quickly and witnessed the struggle of a muskrat as it fought in vain to retain its life. A mink had it locked in its grasp and chewed relentlessly on its head. The struggle lasted a mere few moments and resulted in the mink dragging the muskrat's lifeless corpse to a secluded spot. Lisa stared at the now vacant area and shuddered at the fierceness of the attack.

"Mom, come on up." Susan's voice broke through the wall Lisa's mind had just built. Glancing back to the area once more, Lisa scanned for a sign of the mink. It was as if nothing had happened. A red-winged blackbird alighted on a cattail head and sang its song as if the world was a peaceful place. Lisa released the tension in her shoulders and walked toward the cabin. As she approached the porch, a large horsefly buzzed around her head trying to find a way to get to her skin. Lisa bolted for the front door. She flung the screen door open and ran into the building, complaining about pesky horseflies. Steven and Susan looked at each other and laughed until their sides hurt.

RAMIFICATIONS

The Ontario Provincial Police building was busy with conversation as Lisa walked through the corridors. Fellow officers looked at her and smiled or frowned as their personal perspectives dictated.

"Hey Lisa, how did the mall cop treat you?" Billy's voice rebounded off the walls as she stepped into the room which served as a kitchen.

"Billy, back off! I really don't need the badgering, ok!" Lisa felt her face becoming flush with embarrassment.

"Just asking. You two seemed really friendly, that's all." Billy smiled as if he had just bagged another trophy for his wall.

"I'll send Mike the photos myself. No need to worry, Billy."

"Hell, I'm just looking out for you. I can't figure out how a guy like Steven Stiles could even get a second glance from a woman like you."

"Are you jealous?"

"Come on, Lisa. You're Mike's wife. Translation: off limits."

"I am not anyone's, and if you could get your head out of Mike's ass, maybe you could look in the mirror and see why it is that no one shares your bed!" Lisa's response was spontaneous and delivered with the intensity only a ticked off woman can deliver.

Billy showed her his middle finger and walked quickly away in the direction of the men's change room. Several witnesses gave Lisa the thumbs up signal which lightened the mood within the area significantly.

The summer rush was on and neighbourly dispute complaints were the staples of the day. Lisa received her dispatch orders and walked out of the station.

The morning sun was already intense as she moved through the parking lot to the allotted vehicle; she noted the numerous cars and trucks that paraded by on the highway and hoped August would move quickly so that some sense of peace would replace the frenzied craziness which was gripping the region. Doing her circle check, she noted the tin cans which had been tied to the rear of the vehicle. Lisa smiled, pulled the cans off of their tethers, and began her day.

Dorset was buzzing with activity. Steven checked the time on the Chevy's radio. *Man, it's only eight and this place is nuts,* he voiced to Rusty, who was panting and looking out the side window trying to capture every movement he could. Wagging his tail, he looked over at Steven as if to say he agreed. Steven smiled, climbed out of the truck, and walked around to the passenger side to release the exuberant Lab. Rusty almost broke away, but Steven grabbed the leash and restrained the dog before he could gallivant his way into an adventure which would inevitably be deemed unfavourable by the vast majority of the people who were within range of the dog's investigative abilities. He crossed the street and walked through the parking lot which serviced the L.C.B.O. and Robinson's hardware store.

Three women, dressed in outfits designed for turning heads, walked by Steven and commented on Rusty. This elicited a smile and subdued response from Steven. Siding up to a post which held up the second floor of the store, he watched as the women flirted their way through the parking lot with any man who looked in their direction. Rusty had found a Mars bar wrapper and kept himself busy by trying to clean any remaining residue from its plastic prison. Steven smiled as the intelligent canine used his left paw to hold the wrapper from escaping while his large tongue searched its creases and folds. People became a background blur as Steven pictured the panic which would surely follow if Agawaatesin entered the scene.

Tethering Rusty to the post, he entered Robinson's General store and quickly picked up the items on his list. The store was busy; however, the lineup for the cash was small. Steven picked the lane where Wendy worked.

"Hey Steve, how are you?" Wendy was serving the customer in front of him.

"Great, Wendy. It's busy; how are you holding up?" Steven glanced at the guy in front of him knowing that he was getting upset by the conversation.

"I'm good, punching out at two today. Patrick and I are heading out your way for some R and R; I think we're on site 17."

"Damn, that's my site, lady. Who gave you permission to stay there?" Steven smiled and winked.

"Do you mind focusing on me?" The customer played his hand and proved Steven's suspicion as to where he called home.

"Sorry if we offended you, sir. Is that cash or debit?" Wendy gave Steven her thoughts through eye contact.

"I have a busy day and just want to get a move on it, if you don't mind," the man responded while handing Wendy a credit card and eyeballing Steven.

"Chill out, dude; that is, after all, why you come here, right?" Steven locked his gaze onto the impatient fool in front of him. Something in Steven's glare made the man hastily drop his stare. He left the store, muttering something about small towns and their inhabitants. This made Wendy and Steven laugh.

"It's getting worse. I would say three out of five people are like that guy. I barely converse with people now; it's not worth it. Do you see the same?" Wendy asked as she scanned in the bug repellent.

"I just had a run-in with the same make and model a few days ago. It makes for a shitty day if you let it get to you," he replied, staring at the growing line up of customers coming to Wendy's station.

"Drop by; Patrick would love to see you."

"How long are you there?"

"Three full nights and I can't wait."

"Ok, I will see you there. Thanks, and keep on smiling."

"See you, Steve." Wendy reached for the next customer's items.

Steven left the store and was greeted by Rusty who had somehow managed to escape from the post. His heart skipped momentarily as his mind rummaged through all the things that could have happened. He grabbed the Lab and hugged him. Leashing the dog, he walked through the parking lot and across the road. Looking toward the truck, he noticed the dreaded shape of a yellow ticket on its windshield.

Damn! What the hell?

Taking the offending yellow paper off the windshield, he noted it was not a ticket but a warning about parking outside of the yellow lines. Steven smiled; where he had parked was a dirt parking lot which had no delineated lines. The ticket stub was a clear indication that Lisa was right and the pull of her ex-husband was strong.

Taking his eyes off the yellow paper which was clutched in his left hand, Steven looked up and noticed that the parking lot was filling with vehicles. Excited visitors meandered all over the place at random. He put the key into the ignition and cranked the engine over, bringing the old girl to life. Rusty's tongue hung out of his mouth as he watched the commotion. With the crowds becoming dense, Steven placed the truck into drive and pulled onto Main Street.

The day was turning out to be a scorcher and he wanted to get back to the cabin where he could catch up on the sleep he desperately needed. Steven's mind wandered through a maze of thoughts centred on Mike Denton and how far his power reached. He tried to deduce the extent of the trouble coming his way. The rock cuts and guard rails of Highway 35 flew past with hardly a mention in Steven's mind.

INFLUENCE

"Hi, Mike!" Janice called out as she passed Mike Denton when he entered the front doors of the Huntsville Civic Centre.

"How are you, Janice? Your tan looks gorgeous." Mike poured on the charm which was second nature to him. She smiled and was glad the tan would hide her blushing. She found Mike Denton to be the sexiest man in Huntsville, as did most of the women she knew. He had a flair about him which women were drawn to like moths are to a flame, and he knew exactly what needed to be said in order to set the proverbial hook.

"I take all the sun I can while we have it; winter's not far off." Janice felt like a young girl trying in vain to compose herself in front of a major crush.

"It's great you have that balcony. You have to watch for those new drones, though; I may have to invest in one." Mike made her feel that she should be flattered.

"I will keep an eye out, Mike; the balcony is still open if you would like to stop by."

"Thanks. Glad to see I am still on the invite list."

"Always," she replied in a soft voice while touching Mike's arm in a manner which was an invitation for further exploration. Mike responded by hugging her closely and whispering the time of his arrival. She walked away feeling lightheaded and moved through the front doors into the sunlight which pushed down onto the pavement. She climbed into her Mercedes and pushed the start button which brought the car to life. *Turn the AC to full,* she spoke aloud in the interior of the vehicle. Pulling the visor down and opening up the vanity mirror, she checked her face for any discernible flaws. After smiling at her reflection, she placed the visor back to its original position.

Mike Denton's office was lavishly appointed and had multiple photographs of him in various public settings adorning the walls. Pulling his chair up to the sprawling desk, he punched in his access code and password into the computer which brought him into the world of instant information. A couple of keystrokes later, Mike Denton was looking through the lens of one of the new webcams located on the small log cabin nestled beside St. Nora Lake. Mike smiled as he brought up the images provided by the five cameras. Four of the cameras showed various external views of the area around the cabin while the fifth camera showed a view of the interior. He could see clearly a couple of campers who were standing at the counter looking at a map. Mike reached for his desk phone and punched in the requisite ten digits.

"Stan, it's Mike. Just checked on the cameras and they're perfect. Your employees and the public should feel safe knowing that you have security now. Give me a call when you get the chance." Mike depressed the actuator on the phone base and dialed another ten digits.

"Hey Mike, how are you doing?" Billy Hamilton's voice spoke directly into Mike's right ear.

"I'm great, Billy; did you drop the note off to our good friend?"

"I did it this morning. I watched him pick it off his windshield. I think he got the message."

"Stan has just recently installed some security cameras at the Canoe Trails office. The clarity is amazing; I'm staring at them right now. Be careful how you conduct business around there. Stanley and

I have full access to all five cameras; the public only has access to the boat launch camera." Mike highlighted the parking lot camera on his screen.

"Shit, this stuff makes me nervous because you can forget they're there," Billy responded while turning his Jeep Cherokee onto the highway southbound from Dorset.

"You're a cop; relax. I've got to go; keep me updated." Mike placed the phone back into its base before Billy had a chance to respond.

Fuck me! Billy swore at the handset. Being under the thumb of Mike Denton had been a lifelong job and he had no idea how to get out from under the oppressive weight. As he passed the Canoe Trails cabin, Billy noted the beat-up Chevy pickup parked in front of the barracks building.

Sucker! Billy said out loud within the confines of his Jeep. He reached for the radio, tuned the dial to his favourite station, and adjusted the volume so he could listen to Alice Cooper complaining about being eighteen.

TIME OFF

The sun had long since passed over the building and was highlighting the west wall when Steven crawled out from under his bed sheets. Moving to the window, he noted that the temperature gauge which was attached to the wooden window frame read twenty-eight degrees. Steven led Rusty down the hall and let the dog out. The heat blasted him as he stood with his left shoulder leaning on the door frame. Rusty ran straight to the lake where he dove in and swam in circles chomping at the water, almost choking himself in the process. Steven called to the Lab who sprang out of the water and made a beeline for the open door where he shook his coat.

Damn, you could have done that somewhere else! Steven wiped the water from his face as he berated the dog.

Rusty scampered down the hallway with absolutely no remorse whatsoever. Fifteen minutes later, Steven and Rusty crossed the open space and walked up the ramp to the cabin. "Steve!" Jeff stood at the counter and reached across the surface to punch Steven in the arm. Rusty barked with more exuberance than what was required, and both Steven and Jeff cringed at the volume.

"Check out our new additions," Jeff pointed above the desk.

"When the hell did that happen, and how many did they put in?" Steven felt suddenly trapped in a place which he had long called home.

"This morning. The guys from some security company in Dwight installed them."

"How many are there?"

"Five. One apparently is a live webcam which is viewable to the public." Jeff looked completely despondent.

"One, my ass! They're all live, Jeff. I have seen this set-up before and it's bullshit! Who the hell ordered these? Can you access them so I can see the images?"

"I already have them on the screen." Jeff turned the monitor so that Steven could see the images projected on it. The image was that of the canoe rack area and everything within the northwest corner of the cabin.

"Man, that's clear! This sucks; did Stanley order these?"

"Apparently he did." Jeff stared in fascination at the images displayed on the screen. "The cameras update every ten seconds; and as far as I can tell, the lag time is less than a second."

"Where's the hard drive for this stuff?" Steven looked around the room.

"They put it in the closet next to the bathroom. It stores up to six months of data; I've already made a sign to remind me, see?" Jeff held up a paper which simply had the word camera on it.

"Nice sign." Steven shook his head. "I'm not supposed to be back on the trails until tomorrow, but now I'm thinking of leaving. Are you stuck in here today?"

"Ya. Susan called in sick, and Stan put me behind the desk. William's out in the truck checking up on a disturbance on Plastic Lake."

"What kind of disturbance?"

"Some kids got plastered and caused some mayhem; a couple from Kingston called it in." Jeff grabbed the complaint sheet from the clipboard which was appropriately named complaints.

"Can William handle it?"

"We called the cops; they sent Cliff out with Will. They should be on location now."

Steven took the radio off of the charging station and depressed the button. William's voice filled the room. William relayed the information that the kids had threatened him, and that's when the police got involved.

"William, stay on the site and watch them as they pack. Make sure they have all their garbage and equipment. Take some photos and call me when the site is clear. Can Cliff stay with you?"

"Ya, no problem. He said it beats dealing with the crowds in Minden," William replied to Steven as he watched the campers pack their gear.

"What is the name of the person who booked the site?"

"The guy's name is John Mathews," William responded.

"Shit, how many are on the site?"

"I've counted ten."

"Where are they heading to get out?" Steven was fighting rising anger.

"Two vehicles are parked at the landing here on Plastic."

"I'm on my way; don't let them leave until I arrive. I should be there within the hour."

"Ok, Steve, will do." William ended the conversation.

Steven placed the radio back in its charging station and grabbed his own device.

"Jeff, call up Mathews' name and tell me his group size and sites he has booked."

"I already have it; he was booked for three nights on Little Avery Lake, site 100; and three nights on Plastic Lake, site 13. His group size is four."

"I guess he's going to have to figure out how to pay for the fines he is about to receive, the dumb shit. Thanks tons, Jeff. I am going to send a message to Stanley; don't get offended. You're not the target."

As Steven left the building, he glanced at one of the external cameras and shot it the middle finger. Steven smiled when he heard Jeff's laughter issuing out of the open window.

The group was milling about at the parking spot on Plastic Lake when Steven and Rusty arrived in the Chevy with the green prospector loaded on the rack. Steven got out and opened the door for Rusty who immediately ran around to everyone as if he was the one who was going to interrogate them. One girl ran to the nearest vehicle, screaming about the vicious dog. Steven picked out John Mathews right away and walked over to him. John's buddies looked on while they swatted at the horde of horseflies buzzing around them.

"John, you started off well, but you ran into it now," Steven said while trying to keep his words as professional as possible.

"Some buddies called me and I told them where I was; they showed up and crashed with us." John fought against the hammering in his head which was fueled by recent encounters with booze.

"I get it, John; it sucks. The inability to say no just cost you big-time. I'm writing fines for the following: noise violation, too many tents and people on a site, and staying in the Park without a valid permit. The fine totals five hundred bills, so you might want to work out the financial details with your friends. If that's beyond your comprehension, there are ten in your group; I figure you can spread out the love and cough up fifty bucks each. Your parents have been notified as a precaution and yes, since you're not nineteen, I'm obliged to make that call. I had a feeling something was up when I met you on Orley Lake. I've been doing this for a long time, and trust me: if you kept everything above board, we would not be meeting here." Steven handed John the notices.

"This fucking sucks; how am I going to pay this shit!"

"I told you to spread out the pain."

John looked at Steven with disdain.

"Get over it; I don't give a crap how much you despise me. By the way, I sure hope that you packed all your garbage out. I'm going over there to check. If I find anything that's not supposed to be there, another two hundred will be added to your total bill. Want to come with me to make sure I don't plant something?" Steven stared at the young man.

"Ya, I think I will."

"William, stay here. I am taking young John back to the site. He seems to have trust issues."

"Sure Steve, will do."

"I know there must be at least one vehicle at the Sherborne access site. Two kids can go and get that vehicle and by the time John is back, you will be ready to go," Steven said as he placed his canoe in the water.

Steven pushed off from shore and drove his paddle deep into the waters of Plastic Lake. On the way, he remained silent and let the canoe do all the communicating to the young man in front of him.

Searching the site, Steven found one tall boy can. Steve flattened it and returned to the boat where John had stayed seated, refusing to participate in the investigation.

"All's well. Next time, just play by the rules. Can you imagine what would happen if everyone treated this place as your group did?"

Steven launched the boat and propelled it back to the road. John sat stoically in the bow and did not utter one word. By the time the canoe reached the access point, all the cars were present and accounted for. Three cars and one minivan were loaded in record time and John and his friends were driving toward home. As they left the parking area, John shot a middle finger at Steven who smiled, knowing exactly how good it felt to do that.

"Thanks, guys; I knew I had to deal with this one. I am sure those kids have done this before. Hopefully, this will end all of that crap," Steven said to Cliff and William.

"No worries, Steve. I have had my time with kids like that all summer long; can't wait until the silly season's over," Cliff responded while shaking the ranger's hand. Cliff walked back to his cruiser and climbed into the driver's seat. He started the engine and dropped the passenger side window where he motioned for Steven to come over. Steven approached the vehicle and hunched down.

"Steven, you sure made a hell of an impression on Billy Hamilton; I know he put a ticket on your windshield. Just watch your ass around him. He's so far up Mike Denton's ass, you can't see his boots." Cliff had real concern in his voice.

"Mike Denton is a stuck-up jerk. I know how much pull he has and it ticks me off that everyone seems to buckle under his gaze. I'm serious: if that dude pulls his shit on me, we'll have complications."

"Steve, I am a cop, and that sounds like a threat. I love it, though. Keep your eyes open for Billy; maybe we can get him for harassment or something."

"Precisely. I'm for sure going to nail both of them with harassment and I think a restraining order should also be included in the package." Steven smiled from ear to ear, meaning every word of it.

"You're the man to pull it off. If you need any encouragement or help, you know where I hang out." Cliff placed the vehicle's transmission in reverse.

The two friends said goodbye and Steven watched as the cruiser sped down Sherborne Lake Road chased by a thousand horse flies. Steven said a farewell to William as the young man drove away with the nose of the vehicle pointed at the Sherborne Landing. The silence filled in quickly. He took his bandanna off his neck and wiped the sweat from his face. Walking to the lake, he submerged the cloth into the water and placed it back around his neck. He locked his vehicle and pushed the canoe back into the water. Rusty took up his usual position in the stern, still dripping wet from his water excursions. The water sighed as the hull of the boat interrupted its slumber. As his paddle dipped and pulled through the water, Steven looked back to watch the eddies created by the blade. In doing so he noted writing on the inside hull of his prospector. The capital letters were written with a Sharpie pen. On the inside stern of his beloved canoe, the message said:

Fuck you, old man.

Goddamn, that frigging shithead, Steven voiced loud enough for Rusty to lift his dripping head. Steven made a straight run to shore where he quickly sprayed the offending letters with a liberal dose of the bug repellent. Mixing some sand into the liquid for some major abrasive power, Steven managed to dilute the ink to the point where it was not readable. Steven racked his canoe and drove straight back to base.

The afternoon was wearing thin as he pulled into the parking lot. Rusty jumped out of the truck and dove into the water as Steven released the straps holding his canoe to the rack of the truck. Carrying the boat to a grassy area abutting the parking lot, he placed the canoe belly down. He immediately went to get the liquid cleaner he would require to remove what was left of the ink on his prospector. Within a few moments, he had returned and removed any trace of John Mathews from his canoe. Sitting beside the boat and using it as a backrest, Steven pulled his phone from his left front breast pocket and punched in Lisa's number.

"I thought you had forgotten about me." Lisa's voice had a narcotic effect on him.

"As if I could forget about someone I have thought about since high school. Has your day been ok?"

"Fine, but I seem to be having a hard time getting back into the swing of things. I heard your little cabin had some upgrades, funded by a certain politician in Huntsville. I also heard that you received a non-ticket, ticket." Steven could see her smile through the phone.

"I think intimidation is the operative word," Steven replied while he tried to fend off a very exuberant wet dog from drying itself.

"I have a plan that may get him off our backs. How about you and I set up a table in front of one of those cameras, and indulge in a candlelit meal?"

"Wow, I think that's called entrapment or something. You're the cop; is it legal?"

"I have no idea what you are referring to. I just want to thank the man who took the time to take me to site 76. I figure hot food and some root beer should do the trick."

"That's brilliant. We'll need a bug tarp, which I just happen to have. When do you want to eat?"

"I think I can be there by nine, or is that a bit too soon?"

"You're on; what's the menu?"

"Godfather's pizza. What would you like on it?"

"You pick, not vegetarian though."

"I miss you and will see you by nine. I have to wrap a few things up here at work so I better get back at it. See you soon."

With that final statement, Lisa's voice was replaced by a dial tone and Steven flipped his phone back into its closed position. Rusty made a big deal out of Steven's excitement and the two rolled around for a few minutes, wrestling like puppies on the sunburnt grass which abutted Lake St. Nora.

The sun crossed the western tree line of Highway 35. As it did, the pines around the cabin extended their shadows far out from their trunks toward the east, reminding the sun where to show up in the morning. Steven moved a picnic table to a spot in front of the camera which pointed to the canoe racks on the south side of the cabin. Entering the building, he opened the closet where some promotional material for Sherborne Lake Canoe Trails was kept. He found the screen tent residing quietly in a corner. Within a few moments, the screen was set up and the table was ready for two companions to enjoy some pizza and conversation.

LIGHTS OUT

C rickets filled the hollows of silence with their strident strumming as the stars slowly circled Polaris. Mike drove up his driveway carrying with him the memories of Janice's passion. Exiting his vehicle, he stood and steadied himself by placing his hand on the roof of his car. The wine was working him over and his legs took a few moments to register what it was his confused brain was trying to tell them to do. Taking a few steps from the car, he noticed the unmistakable lump of a raccoon which sat immobile on his front porch. The animal was accentuated by the incandescent light illuminating the entrance. He flung his arms around in an attempt to scare the omnivore off, but the creature made no move to show it was in any way concerned. Mike was now feeling somewhat perplexed as to the raccoon's refusal to leave. Picking up a small stone from his driveway, he tossed it at the defiant animal. The stone bounced off the brick entrance and landed one foot from the raccoon. The animal slowly rose on its four legs and walked toward the confused human, who responded by backing up to his vehicle while fumbling for his keys. Opening the door, he jumped into the car. He pulled the door closed while maintaining eye contact with the animal which was still slowly walking in his direction. As the raccoon passed the car, it stopped and stared directly at Mike who was now actually terrified by the animal's behaviour. The animal stared at him for only a few moments before quickly running from the area in the tank-like manner all raccoons employ. Mike sat in his car and wondered if the wine had intoxicated him enough to misconstrue the incident. Pushing the actuator for the window to open, he stuck his head out the opening to learn if indeed the assailant had actually left. Finding the path clear, he quickly exited the car, briskly stumbled up the remaining length of his driveway, and entered his home.

He walked straight to his office and opened his laptop. He punched in the necessary keystrokes and brought the device to life. As the machine was booting up, he went to his wine rack and picked out a bottle which had recently been opened. Once the red liquid was sitting in his glass, he returned to the computer and sat down. With a few more keystrokes, Mike Denton was looking through the lens of a camera at the Canoe Trails' office. He could clearly see the boat ramp and the driveway leading to it. Another couple of keystrokes and the interior of the office jumped onto his screen. The office light had been left on but the office itself was unoccupied. He then scrolled to another camera and found himself looking directly at his wife and Steven Stiles as they sat, arm in arm, facing the building with an open pizza box and a bottle of Hires root beer.

Fuck that! Mike yelled loud enough to stop the cricket music from playing outside his walls. Standing, he grabbed his cell phone.

"Billy, get your ass to the Canoe Trails' office. I am watching Lisa right now on the fucking camera as she cuddles up to that fucking Stiles!"

"What do you want me to do about it, Mike? They're not breaking any laws that I know of!" Hamilton struggled to find an excuse not to have to leave his television.

"Just make something up and break up that party!" Mike reached for his keys and wallet.

"Okay, I'll check it out. I mean fuck, Mike! Shit!"

Within a few moments, two vehicles were approaching the cabin — one travelling south and the other travelling north. Steven and

Lisa were sitting and talking about everything and anything. The water lapping gently at the shore kept enticing Steven to launch his canoe and drift upon the flat calm surface, but he managed to place the siren call of the water into a spot reserved for future deliberation.

"Do you think they will come?" Lisa looked into Steven's eyes as she voiced her question.

"They are both on their way," Steven replied, kissing Lisa's forehead. He noticed her shaking slightly. "It's ok, it'll be ok."

The moon had poked its head over the eastern shoreline when a vehicle pulled into the parking area abutting the building Steven called the bunker. The lights of the vehicle were off. Lisa watched as the brake lights illuminated the ground behind the vehicle and then silence and darkness filled the area.

"That's Billy, now one more," Steven said calmly.

"Are you sure Mike is on his way?"

"Here he comes." Steven pointed to the two beams of light which broke the darkness on Highway 35. The vehicle turned into the parking lot. Its lights were extinguished and only the amber running lights were visible. The vehicle's engine went silent and they heard the opening and closing vehicle doors.

"Here we go," Steven said. Lisa cuddled into his chest. The sound of heavy footsteps brought their heads up.

"Hey dick-head, you think you're a big man now?" Mike yelled as he approached the pair.

Steven jumped up and exited the screened enclosure. Mike did not hesitate to throw a punch at Steven; the fist hit him square in the jaw and rocked his head back abruptly. Steven fell backwards onto the gravel and was then kicked by Billy Hamilton who yelled something about Steven being a mall cop. The pair continued to physically assault the downed man. Lisa ran to Steven's defence and was also hit by Mike who was incoherent with rage and booze. The fist caught her nose and she screamed in pain as she too fell to the ground. Steven's hands clenched as the boots worked him over. The area flooded with light. Denton and Hamilton winced as their eyes attempted to cope with the sudden illumination.

"Mike Denton and Bill Hamilton, place your hands on your head!" Clifford's voice entered the scene, emanating from high beams to the south of the area.

"What the fuck, you set me up, you bitch!" Denton yelled out.

"This, Mr. Denton, is what we like to call a criminal act, caught not only on camera but also witnessed by two uniformed officers and one off-duty officer whom you just assaulted. Now, both of you, please blow into this machine for me; it will analyze and retain your blood alcohol level." Clifford held the machine up to Billy's face. He complied with the order and the machine remained silent. He then held the machine to Mike Denton's face, but Mike abruptly pushed it aside.

"Once more, Mr. Denton, and it will be an automatic D.U.I.!" Cliff held the machine to Denton's mouth. Denton blew into the device and it instantly registered an alarm.

"Mike Denton, you are under arrest for assault and battery, driving a motor vehicle while intoxicated, and conspiracy to commit a crime." Cliff pushed Denton against the nearest cruiser and placed handcuffs on him. The other officer, Craig, read Mike Denton his rights.

"Billy Hamilton, you are under arrest for assault and battery of a civilian and conspiracy to commit a crime," Lisa said as she placed handcuffs around Billy's wrists.

"Do you have any idea who you're dealing with?" Mike yelled out as he was placed in the back of the cruiser.

"Ya, we do. I think we're dealing with an asshole!" Steven yelled out while holding his side. Steven walked over to Lisa and hugged her close. He kissed her without hiding it. This elicited a hearty response from the two other cops.

"Well done, Cliff; thanks, buddy. I'm glad you could join us for dinner. I owe you huge." Steven grabbed Clifford's shoulder.

"You owe me nothing; you just did this township a huge favour. For years we have been trying to nail Denton, and now he's done. Thanks for the pizza."

"Anytime, Cliff. I have to get Lisa to the hospital, buddy."

"Jump in with Craig; he will take you with lights flashing." Cliff hugged Steven.

Lisa and Steven walked to the cruiser where the young officer stood waiting and they climbed into the back seat together. With the strobe lights flashing, Craig pulled the cruiser onto the highway and turned south for Minden.

"That was unbelievable; I love this job!" Craig said as he looked in the rearview mirror.

"Thanks, Craig; you did well," Lisa managed to say while holding her nose with both hands.

"Holy shit! What the fuck was that!" Craig yelled out.

"What are you talking about?" Steven shot back.

"Some huge animal was running directly beside the car, and I'm doing ninety!"

"Now that's impossible!" Steven replied while Lisa looked at him and smiled.

DECISIONS

The sun was a huge orange ball as it rose above the eastern tree line of St. Nora Lake, foretelling of a windy, sunny day to come. Steven sat on the dock watching Rusty as he waded through the water in search of anything he could chase. Steven's mind coalesced around many thoughts seemingly at the same time, but he primarily focused on the *get-out-of-jail-free* card Mike Denton had received. It irked him that Denton was freely roaming the streets once again, albeit with a couple of restraining orders in hand. A loon floated into the peripheral of Steven's vision, making him turn his head and focus on the red-eyed water missile. Its body moved about on the water as if it were propelled by a motor, and every thirty seconds or less it would poke its entire head beneath the surface to check for a meal. The body of the loon always reminded Steven of a canoe. He stood and stretched, receiving a doggy shower from Rusty in the process. He made his way over to the scene of the standoff at the cabin. Leaning his back against the paddle shack wall, he saw the entire scene play out once again and found it to be absolutely fascinating that the plan had succeeded at all. After taking the screen tent down, Steven entered the cabin and placed the tent back in the closet where it would sit until the following spring. He noted that the hard drive for the security system was missing. In its place was a police sticker showing that it had been removed as part of an ongoing investigation. He smiled at the unexpected bonus of last night's endeavours.

Rusty's barking brought Steven to the front door of the cabin. When he opened the screen door, he was greeted by the scowling countenance of Stanley.

"What the hell was that all about last night, Stiles?"

"I was having dinner with a couple of friends and I'm sure you know the rest."

"Bullshit. You had your hands dirty with this from the outset. Do you realize that Mike Denton is a huge contributor to this place? What do you think the council will do when they find out? Look!" Stan thrust several local papers in Steven's face.

"Shit, they're fast." Steven tried to not smile.

"You think this is funny? It could cost you your job, and in fact, I could suspend you until the end of the season for inappropriate use of public resources. And I want that dog out of here!" Stan walked over to the main desk and sat at the computer.

"Stanley, you are aware that my contract clearly states that while I am here at this or any other site within the jurisdiction of the township, I'm on duty twenty-four seven. Denton's got his hand so far up your ass he's making your lips move, so back the hell off!" Steven was helpless to control his anger.

"Who in the hell do you think you are? You're terminated!"

"Try it. Let's see how far you get. The only reason you can strut your stuffed shirt around is Denton. Now he's on the rocks, man, and your boat is about to hit them too!" Steven raised his voice so loud that Rusty began to bark incessantly.

Stanley rose off his seat to confront Steven who was standing framed in the front door. Once standing, his countenance changed and he quickly sat again. He supported his head in his hands and stared at the table.

"Are you ok?" Steven was both concerned and confused at the same time.

"I feel weird, like dizzy or something."

Steven rushed around the desk and helped the embattled man to the recliner chair. Steven grabbed the phone and called for an ambulance.

"I don't need an ambulance," Stanley stated weakly as he tried to raise himself from the chair. Steven took a blanket and placed it over him. By the time the ambulance arrived, Stanley was pale, clammy, and non-responsive.

The ambulance sped away southbound. Steven stood with the volunteer fire personnel from Algonquin Highlands in front of the office cabin.

"This place is sure getting a lot of attention lately," Josh stated as he put his equipment away.

"Tell me about it. My ribs are cracked, a cop has a broken nose, and now the boss has had some kind of stroke!" Steven looked at the highway, wondering what the hell had just happened.

"Did you read the papers yet?"

"No, Stanley kind of pushed them in my face just before he had his breakdown."

"Read them; it's amazing how much shit Denton has pulled off. The Huntsville reporters are taking it easy on him but the rest aren't; it sure beats the hell out of the usual news."

"I will, Josh. But right now, I just want to get back out into the field."

"Drop by the hall someday, you fucking recluse."

"Ya, I will."

"Sure you will, I've heard that before." Josh pushed Steven's shoulder as a gesture of goodbye. Steven shook the hands of all the guys and watched as they drove off to whatever their day had to offer them. Rusty kept himself busy chewing on a ball cap which he had found. Steven smiled at the canine's crazy ability to find fascination with anything and everything.

Steven Stiles walked into the Minden hospital, which was almost deserted, and approached the main desk. "Sally, how are you?"

"Steven, thank god you're here. Stanley just passed away!"

"What!"

"Stanley just passed away. They believe it was a stroke, but the docs aren't sure what happened?" Tears formed in the corners of her eyes.

"We were arguing and suddenly he collapsed; he was agitated as all hell over the Denton thing." Steven's brain tried to grasp for any semblance of normalcy it could.

"This place is going to be full of white shirts soon, so put on your poker face if you actually have one," Sally suggested.

"I actually don't know how to play poker, but if you insist, I'll do my best."

Sally smiled weakly as a tear rolled down her cheek. He hugged Sally then walked to the waiting room where magazines and papers were stacked neatly on end tables. By the time the reporters and the councillors entered the hospital, Steven had read the articles from three current newspapers regarding the events of the previous night.

Steven had to deal with the myriad of questions pertaining to the last twenty-four hours. He was worn out by the time he had answered all that was asked of him. He needed to see Lisa and then get home to his little room where he could collapse and recuperate. He drove his truck into the Canadian Tire gas bar where he pumped in fifty dollars of fuel and cleaned the kamikaze bugs off of the windshield. The drive to Lisa's house was uneventful as he purposely kept the radio off and tried to focus on nothing. Upon arriving, he commented on her newly minted face. Lisa and Steven talked about the recent events. A grandfather clock beat a steady rhythm on Lisa's wall and chimed out the indicated time of six p.m. precisely when Lisa's phone rang. She answered; Steven could hear Susan's voice emanating from the headset.

"It's for you." Lisa handed the phone to Steven.

"Hello." Steven placed the headset into speaker mode.

Sue's voice entered the room. "Are you coming back soon? Rusty is driving me nuts; he has all but destroyed the place. By the way, how is Mom?"

"She's fine. I will be there soon; leave Rusty in the cabin and take off. Don't wait for me, Sue."

"I will. He thinks everything in here is his. Anyway, he plastered me with mud and there's a hole in the parking lot deep enough to bury a small car." Susan was exasperated at the dog's capacity for trouble.

"Sorry; I'll deal with it. Close up and head home. Thanks for watching him for me. You heard about Stan, right?"

"Holy shit, I can't believe it?"

"I'll fill you in when I see you tomorrow, ok?" Steven stroked Lisa's hair with his right hand.

"Ok. Let me talk to Mom again."

He handed the receiver to Lisa who stood up and wandered to the kitchen. Steven walked to the door, put his shoes on, and waited for Lisa to return. When she did, the two embraced, kissed, and then Steven walked out of the front door. As he approached his vehicle, he noticed a blue Ford Focus parked several houses away on the same side of the street. Someone was sitting in the driver's seat with the sunshade pulled down and the car was idling. As he backed out of Lisa's driveway and pulled away, the Focus pulled away from the curb and followed him. Steven merged onto the highway and drove through Minden; the Focus stayed back but was moving at the same speed. Approaching the town of Carnarvon, Steven accelerated to one hundred and ten kilometres per hour, pushing the vehicle fifty kilometres per hour over the posted limit. He flew through the yellow light at the intersection of Highway 35 and Highway 118. Steven pulled into the lumber store parking lot and backed the truck in tight beside some docks and rafts. Within a few moments, the Ford Focus sped past. Steven put his truck in drive and pulled out onto the highway. Catching up to the Focus, Steven kept a sizable distance away from his target, but the Focus accelerated and was soon lost to Steven's sight. Steven drove a steady ninety kilometres per hour all the way to base, where he pulled into the lot and parked his truck. Just as he shut the engine off, the blue Ford sped past, northbound. Steven shook his head, climbed out of his vehicle, and walked to the cabin from which issued the exuberant barking of a dog. Rusty clearly knew his partner was home. The door was barely open when Rusty sprang at Steven and knocked him over. The dog jumped all over the hapless ranger who tucked himself into a fetal position in order to protect his ribs from further injury.

When Rusty was finished greeting his partner, Steven entered the cabin expecting a disaster. Besides a few mud stains and remnants of various chewed articles, the place was perfect. He sat in the recliner. Rusty curled up beside him on the throw carpet.

"Ranger, I'm here."

Steven's eyes opened as Agawaatesin's voice pushed through his clouded thoughts.

"Where?"

"You are wondering why all this is happening. Come outside," Agawaatesin pushed gently. Steven reluctantly got out of the chair. Rusty bounded up and clawed at the door. Steven crossed through the open area and moved toward the canoe racks; he was thankful the nighttime temperature was cool enough to limit the activities of the vampire bugs which called the area home. The sight of Agawaatesin's outline as it stood silhouetted against the lake made Steven's hair rise. He was reminded of how lethal the creature was and wondered how he had gotten mixed up with it. Steven climbed into a canoe which had been left with its hull down on the grass. He lay in it with his head resting on the stern seat. The feel of the canoe allowed him to stay relaxed and open to what Agawaatesin had to say. The energy of the creature was almost overpowering and Steven's head began to throb as it approached the boat in which he lay.

"What happened to Stan?" Steven closed his eyes and pushed the thought to Agawaatesin.

"He's dead; what is it you are really asking?"

"Did you kill him?"

"Why would that be of concern?"

"Did you kill him?"

"I don't live under the burden of human rules." Agawaatesin moved closer to Steven.

"Did you kill Stan?" Steven said once again, feeling the anger move through his veins. Suddenly, Steven felt his body go limp. His brain felt as if it were floating free within the confines of his head, yet there was no pain; it was as if he were paralyzed. As quickly as it started, the symptoms vanished and Steven jumped out of the canoe, hurting his ribs in the process.

"Holy shit! Is that what happened?" he said out loud.

"Yes."

"Why?"

"Time is short and you're part of a larger story. Stanley chose his path and I changed it. Don't question me again on this. I do not enjoy doing what needs to be done, but that is precisely why I am allowed to exist." Agawaatesin's energy could be felt deep within Steven's heart.

"What larger picture?" he pushed quietly back to Agawaatesin.

"There is," Agawaatesin paused, *"there is something similar to me roaming in Algonquin Park. It has stepped outside its duties and has taken it upon itself to incite fear into as many humans as possible. I have watched it for several seasons and his influence is growing. In choosing to stray from its purpose here, it has also chosen to lose much of its power. It does retain the power to influence humans and that is a process it has mastered. This creature, as you call us, is capable of confusing human minds to the extent that they will do its bidding when directed. When a human mind is under its influence, they have no choice."*

"That is what all this is about!" Steven was angry.

"Everything that has happened to this point was engineered by me. I needed you to see what this energy is capable of and I needed you to understand that there are forces at play here which are very much outside of what humans would consider normal, or for that matter, provable."

"What the hell can I do?"

"You will help me find it."

"You're fucking nuts! I'm a middle-aged guy with zero experience in anything like this. How the hell can you expect me to help?"

"You'll be the bait."

"No way you're going to use me as bait! Do you think I am insane?"

"That depends on your definition of sanity. One day you will realize why you have been chosen for this. You can choose to help or you can choose not to help."

Steven recoiled at the thought of having a choice at all. The nighttime sounds of the area filled the space between the two beings while Steven's mind juggled with the balancing act it was just presented with.

"Leave Lisa out of this and I'll help you." Steven felt the helplessness of his predicament.

"It'll be her choice, yet I'll assure you that she will not be part of the actual hunt."

"What the hell did I just sign up for?"

"You were signed up for this before you were born." Agawaatesin lowered his stance to lie on the ground with Rusty who was curled up and sleeping.

"What do you call that thing?" Steven asked.

"I don't. It is powerful and incredibly dangerous; however, it has lost its ability to use the minds of any other animal so it is cut off from seeing as I do. Name it whatever you would like." Agawaatesin pushed a picture into Steven's mind which made him recoil at the voracity and unbelievable physical power of the creature depicted.

"I think I'll just call it scary." Steven looked to Agawaatesin for guidance.

"Call your mother; she needs to speak to you. Call her and then get some sleep. We'll talk again soon."

The ranger felt faint from the information overload. *"I suppose I don't need to ask how you know this, right?"* Steven commented while getting out of the canoe. When he looked around, he could find no trace of the entity which had altered his life. Agawaatesin was gone and Rusty was doing his best to fill the vacancy.

PLANS

Steven armed the alarm system in the cabin and then locked the front door. His head was so full of half-formed thoughts that he failed to notice the beautiful August night which had descended upon the Highlands. It took Steven only a few minutes to settle into his room and heat up a pre-cooked meal in the microwave. After feeding Rusty, he sat on his couch, picked up the phone, and called his mother. His mother had indeed been trying to reach him. She was concerned about the news reports. His mom told him exactly how she felt about him messing around with a separated woman and especially the wife of a politician. Steven relayed as much information as he dared in order to alleviate his mom's fears. Eventually, his mother relaxed.

"Steven, I was rummaging around in the basement and found an old trunk that belonged to your father. I can't get the darn thing open, but I would like you to get it out of here and help me clean the rest of the place up. I am going to have to move one day and I don't want to contend with all the junk. Will you be able to come over and give me a hand?"

"Sure, Mom. How about tomorrow? I have some time off." Steven pushed gently on his lower right rib cage to remind himself to take it easy.

"That would be wonderful! I will be here until noon. Then I'm going over to Mae's for a tea. When can you come?"

"I should be there by eight or so if that's ok. I have to bring Rusty; he's worn out his usual dog sitter."

"Who's Rusty?"

"I'm taking care of a friend's dog, Mom."

"Ok, Steven, as long as it doesn't mess up my house. I will see you at eight."

Steven's mother talked for twenty more minutes about the state of the world and the loss of morals before Steven was able to tell her he had to go. He ate his dinner as he watched the Weather Network. The forecast for the coming days was unsettled as a low-pressure system moved into the area, bringing with it rain and thunderstorms. Steven shook his head, thinking that his life had just become a mirror image of that report. He dialed Lisa's number.

"Hi trouble, I was just starting to miss you." Her nasally voice made Steven smile.

"Hey, can I talk to Lisa please?"

"Shut up, you jerk; quit making jokes about this."

"Sorry, how are you feeling?" Steven paced back and forth in the room.

"I'm sore but ok. The meds are kicking in so I won't be able to drive for a bit."

"I'm going to my mother's tomorrow to help her clean some stuff up. If I have time, I'll drop by after I'm done; that is, if you want me to."

"That's a date. When do you think you will be done?" Lisa touched the edges of the tape which was securely fastened on her nose.

"I don't know; I have no idea what I'm getting into."

"Watch those ribs; I need you to heal."

"Thanks, Princess; it sounds as if you have plans for me."

"I just want you to get better." Lisa realized her concern was real and she had fallen deeply for Steven Stiles.

"Lisa, I have a small favour to ask."

"Sure, what's up?"

"Can you dig up any information regarding unusual events in Algonquin Park?" Steven's pacing increased.

"What do you mean?"

"See if there have been any incidents that the cops had to deal with. I'm going to check from this end, but you have access to a larger database."

"Why are you asking this?"

"I've been asked to help out a friend up there who is dealing with some issues relating to campers and stuff." Steven fumbled his sentences.

"You're full of shit, Steven; what's going on?" Lisa's voice echoed her concern.

"Ok, our pushy friend needs us to track down the information without raising suspicion. Agawaatesin claims something is causing trouble and needs our help." Steven felt as if a weight was lifted from his shoulders.

"Why did you make up the other bullshit story, and are you telling me there is more than one?"

"I'm sorry about the bullshit; and yes, there's more than one."

"Now I get why it befriended us; we're its ears."

"You're right."

"I guess it'll give me something to do while my face is healing." Her mind was jumping at the thought of another creature and she wanted desperately to delve into the matter. "I'm going to start searching tonight; I can't sleep with this broken nose so I might as well dig into this now."

"You don't have to do it tonight. Why not start in the morning when I'm at my mom's?" Steven felt guilty he had asked her to search in the first place.

They discussed the information search for a few more minutes and then moved onto other topics which put their conversation well into overtime. Eventually, the conversation ended and Steven climbed into his bed, pulled the sheets up over his face, and drifted off into what would be a fitful sleep.

Agawaatesin lay close to Steven's window and listened to the couple's conversation. He wondered at the complexity of human life. He waited until the ranger was fast asleep, and then he began teaching him the lessons he would need to know to stay alive when he encountered the darkness to the north which would show him no mercy.

FORGOTTEN

Steven opened the door that led down into the cool musty confines of his mother's basement. Childhood memories of paralyzing fear jumped to the front of his consciousness. He could see himself, standing in front of the closed door and staring at it, imagining all kinds of horrors waiting for him should he turn the knob. The door was made of rough pine boards which had been painted white. Time had faded the pigment and it bore the handprints of people who dared to descend into the depths of the dimly lit underbelly of the old house. It had taken young Steven years to even venture close to the door and several more to actually open it and walk down the timeworn steps. Rusty ran past Steven and clattered down the stairs to disappear into the darkness of the basement.

"*Well, if he can do it, so can I.*" Steven smiled as he listened to his buddy rummaging around in the dark.

He reached for the light switch which was loosely secured to the wall and pushed it upward. The cellar jumped from darkness to light and revealed the hand-piled rock walls which formed the foundation of the house; they stood as they were originally placed. Mica, granite, quartzite, and a myriad of minerals reflected the tungsten glow of the dual light which hung from a hemlock joist covered by the silk-woven trails of generations of spiders that had combed the basement, hunting down insects who claimed the basement as home. Steven walked slowly down the steps which groaned their disapproval every time his foot hit a tread, bringing to the mind every horror movie he had ever seen.

It took him twenty minutes of sorting out junk and carrying boxes up the stairs before his trepidation was replaced with frustration at the sheer volume of work. After several hours, he was able to put order into what was a chaotic mess.

The mouldy, foul-smelling boxes went into his pickup truck. Random articles were placed alongside his mother's house for her to rummage through and make the final decision as to where the junk would go. Then he focused on the trunk that Rusty had been chewing on all morning.

It was bound in leather and had once been a piece of brilliant workmanship. It now bore the scars of dampness and neglect, relegated to sit in the corner of his mother's cellar like a prisoner left to languish in a medieval dungeon. Steven tried to lift it, but the leather handles tore off thanks to Rusty's efforts. Placing a piece of cardboard under it, he dragged it across the uneven floor and walked it, corner by corner, up the stairs. He managed to eventually get the trunk into the back of the truck which was now overloaded. Steven's mother had spent most of the morning talking on the phone to her friend who she was to have tea with, which made Steven wonder what they would have left to say when they actually did meet. He hugged his mom, called Lisa to let her know this was taking longer than he had expected, and drove directly to the dump where he tossed his mother's treasures into the pile of other discarded treasures. By the time he pulled into the Canoe Trails parking lot, it was six p.m.

Rusty ran directly to the water and swam in circles. Steven climbed into the bed of the pickup to examine the last remaining article, the leather trunk. The brilliant sunshine highlighted the extent of the damage to the old piece of history. The leather was cracked and discoloured and the leather bindings were well past their useful life. He looked closely at the brass catches which fastened the lid to the body of the trunk; pushing and prying at them proved to be a futile endeavour as the catches failed to release their grip.

Steven resorted to using a flat blade screwdriver which he inserted under each catch. Forcing them to open damaged both in the process. His progress was interrupted by the arrival of a busload of adventurers who piled out onto the grass area next to where his truck was parked. This caused him to alter his plans. He used a dolly and wheeled the trunk into his room where he could open it in private.

Rusty lay on the rug and watched as Steven slowly opened the lid. The initials "P.J." had been inscribed on the underside of the lid; drawn in ink beside them was a very good rendition of a feather. The first occupant of the old relic was a wool blanket which was long overdue for the garbage. It was peppered with holes and it held the odour of years of neglect. Steven took the blanket outside and threw it across a clothesline with the faint hope of salvaging it. The next item was a newspaper which had been placed in a waxed bag to preserve it. He opened the parchment-like document carefully and looked at the heading, which revealed it to be a copy of *The Parry Sound North Star*. The date was clearly marked as October 10th, 1926. The main headline in the paper pertained to the demise of Depot Harbour and the implications this would have on its inhabitants. Steven turned the paper over and found an article relating to a manhunt which called for the capture of a man whose name was Peter James.

Shit! Steven voiced loud enough to elicit a concerned look from Rusty.

He went on to read that Peter James was the prime suspect in the death of a man named Luke Lorring. Lorring had been killed by James over an altercation between the two while attending a church service. The article claimed that over one hundred people had been deployed to find the *dangerous criminal*.

Steven placed the paper carefully on the floor and sat back against the couch. His mind was trying to put a puzzle together that had many missing pieces. His father's full name was Peter James Stiles. From the information his mother had told him, his father was born in a place known locally as Boshkung, which was a long way from Parry Sound. Steven took the next item out of the trunk. It was a curled, faded photograph of a family frozen in time. A woman holding a baby stood next to a man who wore what appeared to be a buckskin shirt. They stood next to four spruce trees with a small wood framed house in the background. Steven picked up his magnifying glass and held it over the image of his grandparents. His grandmother looked to be in her early thirties and her child, Steven's father, appeared to be one or two years old. Steven's grandfather, however, had a presence to him which was almost chilling. His facial features were angular, his hair was tied back on the sides and touched his shoulders, his stubble beard was clearly visible, and his stance was that of a man who was relaxed but ready to move at any given moment. Steven placed the picture on the ground and reached into the trunk again. He pulled out a piece of deerskin which was used to wrap a diary. The diary was that of Brenda Stiles, Steven's grandmother. She had incredibly neat handwriting which outlined, in detail, the life she had led. Rusty was beginning to make a fuss, so Steven elected to carry the diary outside where he could read it and make notes while sitting at the old picnic table. Rusty busied himself with water play while Steven delved into the life of a woman he had barely known. The sun was no longer visible when he stood up and stretched his cramped body. He had filled two pages of lined paper with notes and he felt as if he had been cheated.

Steven walked back inside and placed a meal in the microwave before he continued his journey through the trunk's contents. He laid out the final items beside the ones already on the floor. A pair of moccasins, well-worn and of no serviceable use, lay beside a deerskin vest which had been embossed with images of tracks and feathers.

Upon the vest lay a knife which had been hand-forged and set into a hilt of ironwood; its sheath contained the images of feathers and tracks. A lethal-looking flint spear point tied to a necklace of leather was placed next to the knife. The history of Steven's past played out in his mind as he stared mutely at the articles which lay before him. The timer on the microwave had long been silent when he finally got his dinner. Sitting at the kitchen table, he called Lisa.

A VERY LONG NIGHT

"Hi, you were supposed to call me when you got in?" Concern laced Lisa's voice.

"I'm sorry; I have some stuff to tell you!" Steven hoped she would be interested.

"I have a lot to tell you also; do you want to go first?"

"Can you come up for the night?" Steven hoped she was capable of driving. "I'm a little messed up, plus I miss you," he continued.

"I haven't taken a pain pill for hours, so I'm good to drive." She began packing her small knapsack.

"Great, when can you come?"

"Right now; I should be there in about an hour or so."

"Thanks. You need to see the stuff I have here from my mom's. It kind of sent me for a loop." Steven tried to keep his emotions from getting the better of him.

"Are you ok?" She wondered what it was that had upset him.

"I'm ok. I'll see you soon. I'm going to jump in the shower; I smell like an old basement."

After the two said their goodbyes, Steven got up and walked to the shower room where he removed the lingering odour of mildew from his skin. Rusty romped around in the open stall of the shower, chasing soap as it disappeared down the floor drain.

The clock showed eleven p.m. and darkness had cloaked the Highlands. Lisa and Steven sat on the floor of his room. He held her as she read the diary of Brenda Stiles. Lisa was crying by the time she placed the diary on the floor. Steven's own composure was in jeopardy as he valiantly choked back his emotions while looking at the floor and its contents.

"You had no idea about any of this, did you?" Lisa stated, gaining control of herself.

"No clue; I thought that my grandfather was just some weird guy who spent most of his time in the woods. No one told me a thing about him." Steven looked into her eyes.

"Brenda's diary is like a Harlequin Romance novel. I mean, holy shit: it has all the key components in it. A woman in need, a wild forest man coming to her aid, a battle between two men. One trying to control her and the other trying to free her. Then they end up living in a township where no one knows their history, and finally, the death of the man whom she loved to the core. Shit, it makes me cry!"

"Tell me about it. It's not every day you learn that your last name is taken from your grandmother's side and that everything up to this point in your life was a mystery, solved by cleaning out your mother's basement."

"How the hell did Peter get the name Dark Owl?"

"It's there, Lisa." Steven picked up the diary and scanned it for the explanation.

"Here, see?" He handed Lisa the book.

"My god, Brenda even explained that." Lisa looked directly at Steven.

"He was being hunted and somehow identified with the Owl, so he chose it; or, as Brenda writes, he was given the name."

"Do you know where they lived?"

"My mom told me that they lived in a farmhouse near Buckslide and Walkers line. After my grandfather died, my grandmother moved to Minden and raised my dad there," Steven answered, and then continued: "The foundation of the place is still there. I never gave the place a passing glance but now I'll have to go and check it out."

"Have you called your mom?" Lisa stood and reached for the phone.

"I guess I should, right?"

"Ya, I am pretty sure you should."

Steven dialed his mother's number.

"Steven, thank you for doing such a wonderful job down there; I can actually see the floor!" Catherine Stiles' voice filled the small room in which Steven and Lisa sat.

"Mom, I need to talk to you about the trunk; did you know what was in it?" Steven asked. There was a momentary silence which prompted Steven to ask if his mother was still on the line.

"Steven, your father wanted you to have that trunk a long time ago; I was the one who made him put it down there. I did not know how you would take the scandal of your grandparents being unmarried and having a baby, along with all the other baggage they were carrying."

"Mom, how the hell could you keep that from me? When are you going to come down off that pulpit you sit on?" Steven's voice mirrored his frustration. Lisa held onto his arm and asked him to place the phone in speaker mode.

Catherine's voice filled the room.

"My beliefs are mine. The scandalous nature of your grandparents' relationship is the reason your father took to drink. He passed away knowing that he was a bastard son, and that is something he could never overcome." Catherine was now moving into her preaching mode which Steven knew very well.

"Mom, you and I have had our differences, but shit, don't talk about Dad like that. For once, can't you cut him a break?"

"I loved your father, Steven. I tried my best to help him, but the sins of his parents haunted him."

"Mom, did you know that Grandma left a diary in the trunk with extensive information about her life?" Steven tried to get a handle on his anger.

"I never looked in that trunk; I actually would have burned it if I could have moved it. I thought you would have done the same, given its deplorable condition. How could you even bring it into your home?"

"Mom, the stuff contained within that trunk has answered a lot of questions which I had about Dad."

"I never liked your grandmother, as you are well aware. She never went to church and she always made me feel uneasy. Your father and I were respectful to her but we never visited longer than was necessary. The last time I saw her was at your father's funeral where she had the audacity to put a feather on his coffin. What kind of witchcraft is that? Do you remember the funeral?"

"Mom, I was just a little kid. But you know what? I do remember, because when you brushed the feather to the ground, she picked it up. When the service ended and you were crying in the corner surrounded by your friends, Grandma came to me and gave me the feather which I put in my scouting book; I'm looking at the book right now!" Steven said point blank, trying desperately not to explode on his mother.

"Steven Stiles, you did that behind my back after all I did to raise you? Why would you do that?"

"Mom, I was eight years old; why wouldn't I?"

His statement elicited a smile from Lisa.

"Mom, what was Dad's last name?"

"It was Stiles, of course; what kind of crazy question is that?"

"I was just wondering, that's all." He looked into Lisa's eyes.

"Steven, I don't like it when you get upset like this. You should just take that trunk to the dump and be done with it. My side of the family has no hidden past, and you should be proud of the blood flowing through your veins."

"Mom, you're right; I am proud of the blood flowing through me. Sorry if I upset you. I guess I'm tired, that's all."

"That's ok. Please get some sleep and call me tomorrow. I love you," Catherine said as only a mother can.

"Ok, Mom. Goodnight." Steven hung up the phone and punched a couch pillow which had taken up residence on the floor beside him.

"I had no idea she was like that; you are the polar opposite," Lisa said as she ran her fingers through Steven's hair.

"Why do you think I was reclusive in school? Being raised by a zealot like her would make anyone shy."

Lisa stood and busied herself in the kitchen making a meal out of the meagre contents of Steven's cupboards. Steven placed the articles from the trunk on the coffee table and hung the vest up where he could see it.

"Lisa, what was it you wanted to tell me? With all the family history stuff, I completely forgot to ask, sorry."

"It can wait. Seriously, you've had your world turned upside down tonight."

"It will be a good break. What's going on?"

The two sat down at the kitchen table where Lisa filled Steven in on the information she had gathered pertaining to Algonquin Park.

"According to my sources, there have been two bizarre incidents around the Ship-Pa-Gew Lake area. The similarities between the two incidents are incredible. The first incident occurred in early June of this year. A canoeist, camping solo, radioed for help on his satellite phone. As far as the dispatcher could make out, the canoeist felt he was being followed by a bear or something as he passed down the Pine River. Rangers were dispatched but could find no trace of the person who called in the report. A search of the area was conducted. The searchers turned up with the man's canoe and gear intact, but they found no trace of the man himself. They called off the search just one week ago."

"That guy's probably fish food."

"Steven, that's wrong and cruel!"

"Sorry, I guess I should have kept that to myself."

"Do you think?" Lisa said while smiling. Then she continued, "The second incident also happened to a lone canoeist. This time it happened in mid-July. A person called in for information pertaining to bears as he felt there was one following him as he paddled down the Pine River. His report stated that he could see a large animal slipping in and out of the bush line following his course. He also stated that he felt terrified to step on land. Rangers were once again deployed. They intercepted the man halfway along the portage trail between Ship-Pa-Gew and Blue Lake. He attacked one of the officers with a knife. The man was incoherent, babbling about huge wild animals stalking him. The man was eventually subdued, but the officer required ten stitches."

Lisa took a long breath after her narration of the events transpiring in the woods far to the north.

"The second guy, is he ok?" Steven held his pen over his notebook.

"No, he can't put a coherent sentence together; apparently, he keeps threatening anyone who comes close to him. There's been a pile of other reports ranging from campers fighting with other campers to people freaking out and leaving early because they were scared out of their minds. Does this kind of thing happen to you?"

"No, very few people tell us they are leaving early; usually they just pack up and leave." Steven's brow furrowed. "How many reports did you dig up?"

"From what I could find out, a total of twenty incidents, and get this, they all had the area around Ship-Pa-Gew and Longer Lake on their itinerary." She looked at Steven for an answer to the mystery.

"I guess that's where Agawaatesin's buddy hangs out." He tried to cover the fear building within him.

"Tomorrow I'll keep searching and find out if there have been any other anomalies in the Park. What's the plan? What has Agawaatesin told you?"

"The plan, as far as I know, is to track the creature down and remove it. Agawaatesin needs my help because according to him, this thing would know if Agawaatesin was around so he needs me to distract it." Steven held onto Lisa's arm.

"Steven, that's crap. What the fuck can you do to help? This is total bullshit! And since when did you start to refer to it as him? Has this creature suddenly become a buddy?" She stood up and glared at Steven, making him feel as if he were being arrested.

"Agawaatesin simply needs my help," he replied, standing up and approaching Lisa who was distraught at the recent revelations.

Rusty jumped up and started barking at the window which faced the lake. Steven shut off the interior light and opened the curtain. Standing to the right of a large pine tree, silhouetted by the floodlight on the boat ramp, stood Agawaatesin.

Lisa almost fell over backward at the sight of the animal which had recently blown her perception of reality to bits. It stood on two legs and its arms were hanging down beside its body with its front paws spread open. Truly, it was the image of a nightmare, obliterating any sense of security she thought she had. Steven pulled Lisa from the window. Rusty was inconsolable and scratched at the door. Steven obliged and let the exuberant canine have his freedom. Steven and Lisa watched as Rusty ran straight at the creature and then veer suddenly off.

Steven opened the window and called to Rusty. He looked toward the pine tree but could see no trace of the apparition which had just scared the hell out of Lisa and him. Fear took hold of Steven's mind and he fought to maintain composure.

"*Relax, Rusty is here with me,*" Agawaatesin pushed into the addled thoughts of Steven Stiles.

"*I showed you an image of that which we must hunt. Scary, as you have come to call him, is using fear to keep people away from that particular area of the Park. He hopes it will spread and create a widespread panic which will keep people from visiting the Park. He has lost his way and cannot see that his idea will not work. Many of the animals he is trying to protect will be slaughtered when humans move into the area to hunt down the menace. He is using your pre-conceived fears against you."*

Lisa was shaking and Steven felt his own legs quake in response to the adrenaline.

Steven helped Lisa to the couch where he wrapped her in a sleeping bag. Then he opened the door for Rusty, who was scratching at it as if he were digging a hole.

Steven walked back to the open window. *"How much time do we have?"*

"No time at all; we have to move in before the stories become part of mainstream thoughts. Your internet will provide all the evidence people need to overrun the Park and destroy the lives of many innocent ones. I have witnessed this behaviour in the past and I know that once a mob is formed, reason and sanity disappear." Agawaatesin let his words sink into Steven's mind.

"What's the plan?" Steven asked.

"I am heading to the area as soon as the sun makes itself known; I need you to book a route that will take you down the river which empties into Ship-Pa-Gew Lake. You must travel alone; the dog would be at great risk if he were to come."

"That's a two-day trip. I can make it to Little Trout in a few hours from access three, but I won't have time to move all the way down the river before dark," Steven said, trying to plan the route in his head.

"You need to be on the river after sundown, not on Ship-Pa-Gew."

"How will I be able navigate that river in the dark? Shit, I've only paddled the river once before, and it's a bitch in the daylight." Steven felt the apprehension of the journey settling in.

"You'll manage. I want you to camp at the old lumber site. There can be no witnesses to this hunt. I need you on that river at night."

"When do I leave?"

"Plan to leave midweek."

"This is messed up, but I'll plan it out tomorrow," Steven answered.

"What am I going to do?" Lisa burst out.

"Take Rusty for a lot of walks and get ready for one hell of a story when I come back. I'm sure you'll always know what's going on," Steven suggested, trying to make the situation lighter.

"I am going to come and stay at the access area; I am sure I'll be able to get clearance from the Park to do that." Lisa felt completely out of control.

"No, the Park officials have no idea what is prowling the area, nor will they ever know. This knowledge is to stay with the three of us only. That must be understood!" Agawaatesin pushed forcefully back.

Steven and Lisa looked at each other as the depth of the situation seated itself in their minds.

"The sun will soon rise and you two need to sleep. I will contact you." All communication vanished.

"It's like he pulls a plug or something!" Steven said to Lisa who was busy fumbling with her hands.

"You're right. I feel like my head's empty, like I'm drunk."

"I'll worry about the trip in the morning. I am way too tired to figure it out now; it's almost sunrise." Steven turned away from the window. This elicited an instant response from Rusty who ran over to him and demanded to be rubbed.

"What trip are you talking about?" Lisa asked in a confused tone of voice.

"I," Steven paused, "I'm going to check out the Pine River route on Wednesday. It's an ongoing joint venture between us and the Algonquin Park crew." He was amazed at the speed in which he was able to catch onto the situation.

"Did you tell me this before? I feel like you did. I guess I'm exhausted." Lisa said as she rubbed her temples.

"I'm sure I told you, but really, we need to catch some sleep. Do you want to stay over tonight?"

"As if I would drive home now. I can sleep right here on the couch."

"No, you take the bed. But what about Sue? She may be on duty tomorrow and she'll see your car."

"I think she can handle it; besides, I'm way beyond tired to give any attention to what my daughter may or may not think." Lisa walked toward the bed.

"Ok, I will see you in the morning."

"Really, you're going to stay there?"

"Is that an invitation?"

"Only if you intend on going right to sleep; otherwise, your pass is revoked."

"Yes, Officer; I understand." Steven followed Lisa into the bedroom.

IN MOTION

An unfinished dream jolted Lisa from her sleep. Steven was still unconscious, and it made her smile to see the tough outdoors man wrapped up in his blanket. She pulled herself slowly off the bed and made her way out to the living room. She walked to the window and looked out to the lake which was busy with boats and canoes. Lisa checked the parking lot and was relieved that Sue's car wasn't there. The afternoon had arrived and she was still in her pyjamas when she ventured outside. Rusty was insane as he ran in circles, trying to sniff out all the information he had missed while cooped up in the building. Lisa leaned against the wall and watched as the dog ran off the end of the dock and jumped into the water. Lisa rewound the mental tape she had of the previous night and found that pieces of the conversation had somehow vanished from her memory. There were large blocks of time which she could not readily account for. Retracing her way back to the room, she met Steven in the hallway; Rusty made a huge deal out of the situation, which resulted in the two humans trying to defend themselves from the exuberant dog who was intent on knocking them to the floor.

The sun was sitting low on the horizon when Lisa left for Minden. Steven took the Algonquin Map out of the drawer in his side table and opened it up on the floor. With pen and paper, he detailed the trip which would place him in central Algonquin Park to face a threat he could never have imagined. A dozen times he talked himself out of the trip and a dozen times he talked himself back into it. Standing, he stretched and walked to the door. Rusty bounced down the hallway like Tigger from Winnie the Pooh. The two companions moved outside where the moon was pushing long shadows from the trees. Steven walked directly to the dock. He realized it had been a very long time since he pulled his paddle through the waters of the Highlands. He thought of getting his prospector off the rack, but his ribs held him back from following through. He had no intention of pushing his luck before leaving for the tannin brown waters of Ship-Pa-Gew Lake.

Rusty swam in circles, leaving a wake which was highlighted with silver by the moon's light. After several minutes of watching the dog's antics, Steven rose and walked to the cabin. Once inside, he sat at the main desk, turned the computer on, and navigated to the site for bookings in Algonquin Park. The process was over in less than ten minutes, and within another few minutes, he had his reservation printed off and laminated. He turned off the lights and walked back to his room. His phone was ringing when he entered.

"Steven, sorry I haven't looked anything up yet pertaining to Algonquin. I will do it first thing tomorrow. Is that ok?" Lisa's voice filtered through the room. The sound made Rusty twist his head from side to side as he tried to figure out where his friend was hiding.

"No worries, let it go. I've already done some research and there were only a few minor occurrences which have already been resolved."

"I barely remember what it was that you asked me to find out, sorry."

"Relax; everything's great. Hey, I'm booked for Wednesday through to Sunday for Algonquin. Think you'll miss me?"

"Of course I will. And yes I'll take care of Rusty for you. I'm scheduled to be off work for another week. By then I hope my nose will be back to normal and I won't sound like a squeaky toy when I talk."

"It sure makes you sound like you have one hell of a serious cold. Thanks for looking after my buddy; he loves you in his canine way."

"He told you that?"

"Well, obviously not with words, but with actions."

"What about the man who takes care of him, what does he feel about me? Any ideas?"

"I have to ask him when he comes back; he stepped out for a few minutes."

"You're an ass, Steven Stiles; or should I call you Steven James Stiles?"

"Just call me whatever is appropriate at the time, Lisa. Hey, I have a question for you. Do you know anyone that drives a blue Ford Focus?"

"No. Why?"

"I had one follow me on Saturday."

"Did you get a plate?"

"Sorry, not trained like that. Canoes aren't required to have plates."

"Jerk. I'll see what I can dig up. I'm betting it's one of Mike's cronies. You could have told me before I parked in front of your place!"

"I didn't think of it. You want to hang out tomorrow?"

"Sure. You talk like you're a kid; what do you mean, hang out?"

"Maybe spend the day doing stuff, like going to my mother's and giving her something to talk about." Steven placed his sleeping bag into his pack and zipped up the cover.

"No chance, I'm not going near her place!"

"Just kidding. Maybe we could watch a movie on that flat screen of yours and you know, hang out."

"Ok, let's hang out. Did that guy who takes care of Rusty happen to come back?"

"Nope, still out wandering, I guess. I'll ask him how he feels about you and let you know tomorrow. Ok?"

"Ok, I'm going to bed. I'm exhausted. Call me in the morning."

"Ten-four, Officer. Have a good night." Steven smiled as the words left his mouth. The two talked for a few minutes longer and finally gave the phones a chance to cool down. Steven spent the rest of the evening contemplating and wandering around outside with Rusty. He was glad Agawaatesin did an Etch-A-Sketch on Lisa's memory; she would be safer not knowing what he was paddling towards.

SOME NEWS

The early morning mist rising off the lake conjured up images of spirits rising to play in the sunlight. Rusty lay on the grass and chewed relentlessly on a stick. Birds flitted about doing their part for the world as the early morning breeze swirled and danced in slight eddies across the water. Steven sat on the old brown picnic table, closed his eyes, and pondered if the events of the past few weeks were some kind of waking dream that he was unable to snap out of. The sound of a car pulling into the parking lot brought Rusty up onto the picnic table to sit beside Steven. Rusty's tail gave a cursory wag as the door of the vehicle opened.

"Stiles!" a voice broke the peace of the morning and brought Rusty to a standing position. Steven jumped off the table and turned to face the person who had called to him.

"Holy shit, what have you been up to, Mark?" Steven approached his friend.

"I'm running a trip out of here today; the bus should show up in a little while. How have you been?" Mark asked cheerfully.

"I got pounded on by a jealous asshole, but other than a few bruised ribs, I've been great." Steven wondered if the news had reached as far south as Toronto.

"I've been informed about the whole thing. Did you hear the latest, though?" Mark asked as he rubbed Rusty, who was delighted to have the free massage.

"I've been a hermit, lately; what news?"

"Mike Denton was caught driving while under suspension. Apparently, he had borrowed his friend's car and was caught doing one twenty in an eighty somewhere south of Dorset."

"Did the papers mention the type of car, Mark?"

"Ya, it was a Focus. Why?"

"The prick was following me the other day. I had a feeling it was Denton but figured no one would be that stupid." Steven felt vindicated.

"Well, he won't be driving any time soon; they pulled his license and placed him under house arrest until his hearing."

"Why house arrest? They don't do that for a suspension."

"He was spotted near his ex's place. Apparently, she has a restraining order, so they nailed him."

"Who spotted him?" Steven asked.

"Billy Hamilton ratted him out," Mark said with a smile.

"Holy shit! That sure takes a load off; thanks for the update. I guess I should listen to the news more often. What site are you on?"

"I am taking a group of urbanites to site 22 as usual. We're staying for a couple of nights and then heading back here. I see your gear's loaded; where are you headed?" Mark pointed at Steve's Chevy which had his prospector lashed to the racks.

"I'm running up to Raven and then on to Gunn. I've got a few issues up there that need some clearing up. So, you don't have to worry about me checking up on you," Steven lied to his friend and felt bad about doing it.

"Is your dog going?"

"No, he has to sit this one out, but I promised him a trip when I get back." Steven felt a lump form in his throat.

The two talked for another twenty minutes before a yellow school bus pulled into the lot. Steven watched as the group milled about, gathering up their equipment and filling the air with conversations which destroyed any semblance of quiet. He wished Mark good luck and retreated with Rusty to his room where he could complete his packing and call the one person he did want to talk to.

Lisa pulled into the parking lot just as the last canoe of Mark's crew left the dock. Steven and Rusty were waiting on the old picnic table when she turned the corner of the building. Rusty spotted her and used his barrel-like body to good advantage, almost knocking her to the ground. Steven hugged her close as Rusty barked his approval. He told Lisa the latest news that Mark had just relayed.

"Mike will lose his position on the council for sure. That kind of thing is a hard one to hide from," Lisa said in a concerned tone.

"He did it to himself."

"He is a vindictive man and this could blow up on us."

"His followers are few and far between by now; even Billy may be taking a long hard look in the mirror. You're a cop, and you're telling me you're worried?"

"No, I just don't want you to take off if he starts putting the pressure on us," Lisa replied, looking straight into Steven's eyes.

"Lisa, do you remember asking me if the guy who takes care of Rusty ever shows up, I was to ask him how he felt about you?"

"Yes, you said he was out wandering."

"Well, he stopped by to tell you he loves you," Steven smiled as he said the words. Lisa started crying and wrapped Steven in a hug which hurt his ribs.

BEGINNINGS

The sun had climbed high enough into the sky to burn off most of the mist, and the steady breeze was stirring up rivulets on the lake. Steven stood with his back against the driver's side of his pickup truck, holding Lisa in his arms. She wrapped herself around the ranger's waist and snuggled into his chest.

"Hey, what's this?" She used her right hand to push gently on the centre of Steven's chest.

"I have no idea why I put it on, but it's the spear point I found in my grandfather's trunk. I put a new piece of leather on it and figured I would wear it. Do you think it's weird?"

"No, I think it's great. Where's the leather vest you found?"

"In the truck. It fits me, but I feel like a hippie in it."

"Let me see it on you."

"Really?"

"Put it on for me; I'll tell you the truth." She reached around him to open the door. He turned his back to her and took the vest from the passenger seat where it was folded. He told Lisa to close her eyes and then he put it on.

"Ok, take a look." He hated being on display.

Lisa caught her breath when she opened her eyes and focused on Steven.

"Holy shit!" Lisa struggled for words. The vest made Steven look completely untamed and for a moment she fought off the urge to step back from him.

"What's wrong?" Steven asked.

"I was just caught off guard. It's like it was made for you; it's freaking me out!" She ran her hands over the smooth leather of the vest.

"Shit, your reaction was crazy as hell. I didn't think an old relic like this could do all that, but it does feel good."

She stepped back and took a picture.

"There, now I'll remember what you look like." She smiled as she hugged him.

Rusty waited patiently by the passenger's door of the truck. This accentuated Steven's guilt about leaving the dog behind.

"I have to get moving. Let's take Rusty inside and feed him some canned dog food. That always keeps him focused." He took the vest off and put it on the seat.

The three companions spent the rest of the morning saying goodbye.

THE JOURNEY

Steven arrived at the access point by mid-afternoon and parked in a section of the lot reserved for the movement of equipment and canoes. He released the straps holding his canoe captive to the truck, carried the boat down to the wide dock, and placed it in the water. He put his pack in the stern of the boat while placing his spare paddle against the sidewall using Velcro straps. He parked his truck in a vacant spot within the large parking area which had been carved out of the forest. As he locked the vehicle, he noticed a large raven which sat quietly on the top of a pine tree watching him. He could feel the intensity of the bird as it scrutinized his movements. The stare-off was broken by the arrival of a truck pulling a canoe trailer. Steven waited until the driver positioned the rig close to the pathway leading to the dock before he moved in that direction. Two young men busied themselves loading up rental canoes which lined the pathway to the water.

"Hey guys, is the season over or something?" Steven called out to them.

"Close to it. We'll leave a dozen canoes here until late fall, but the rest of them are getting put to bed for the winter," one of the guys stated as he hoisted the Kevlar boat over his head.

"Kind of sad when it comes to this time of year, but the Park will get a break from people for a while," Steven said as he watched the young man load the first canoe onto the truck.

"Where are you heading?"

"I'm booked on Misty for a few days." Steven felt he had to cover his tracks.

"It's a good thing you're staying there; word has it that there is some weird shit happening up at Ship-pa-gew. A couple of people have gone nuts up there. It's even freaking some locals out. I'm trying to get Alex to come with me to check it out."

"Shut up, Kev. I told you, it's a few random assholes that couldn't keep their shit together while on their own. We have been up that way at least a dozen times and nothing like that has ever happened." Alex passed Steven with a boat on his shoulders.

"Where are you two hearing this stuff?" Steven asked.

"We hear everything around here; my mom works at the Park's office in town," Kevin stated.

"Well, you're probably right. Some people figure they can handle being alone in the bush for extended periods of time and they freak out by day three or earlier."

"I told you, Kev. We will go, but shit, stop it with the spook stories!" Alex pointed his finger at Kevin to emphasize his point.

"Take it easy, guys; maybe I'll see you again in a few days, as long as I don't go nuts." Steven walked toward the dock.

"Stay away from Ship-Pa-Gew," Alex called out in a cryptic tone which elicited a laugh from his buddy Kevin.

"Stay cool, guys."

Steven pushed his canoe off the sand and walked it along the dock. When he climbed into the boat, he was instantly at home. Digging his paddle into the water of Magnetawan Lake, he pulled on his paddle and quickly closed in on the first portage of the day.

He floated off-shore at the portage while a group of people loaded their boats for the final push to the landing. He waved as they passed and quickly landed his canoe. Slinging the pack and carrying his boat, he made good time walking the one hundred and thirty-five-metre trail. Once on Hambone Lake, he got into his rhythm and crossed the water in less than fifteen minutes. Again, he shouldered his load and crossed the portage to Ralph Bice Lake. The wind pushed the waves toward the western shore; he elected to follow the southeastern shore to keep the wind at bay. As he paddled, Steven felt the tension of the past several days drain off him like the water off his paddle. The quiet peace of the lake drew him in and pushed his anxiousness back to a place where it was barely a whisper. As he crossed the mouth of a wide bay, the wind pushed at his hull and forced him to angle his canoe to keep his track. He could see the smoke of a campfire rising from a site deep within the bay.

Steven heard the raven before he saw its black outline in the sky. It soared in from the west, and he watched as it circled and grew in size as it came closer to his boat. Next, it flew a paddle's length away from Steven's port side and matched his speed exactly. Steven was astounded at the beauty of the bird which he could almost reach out and touch; it flapped its wings slightly to control the subtle nuances of air flowing across the glistening black feathers. The raven then moved to a hovering position over top of the prospector's stern and landed on the seat in a perfectly executed full stall landing. Steven was so shocked he stopped paddling. The bird turned its head to look at Steven as if to ask him why he was not moving. Steven positioned himself to take the channel between the island and the mainland, as the wind would be minimized within the confines of the channel. This allowed him to concentrate on the bird which had chosen to hitch a free ride in his canoe.

"Hello," a disembodied voice called out from a campsite on a point of land.

"How did you train him?" the voice once again called out. Steven found the owner of the voice: a middle-aged man dressed in khakis and a fleece sweater standing on a strip of sand beach. The man was soon joined by three other people: two women and another man.

"I'm pretty sure he's training me," Steven replied, feeling exposed.

"Mind if we take your picture?"

"I don't; he might, though." Steven pointed at his passenger.

He pried his blade slightly which turned the stern of the canoe closer to the campers. As he passed within twenty feet of the onlookers, the raven opened its wings and stretched them out on both sides of the gunwales.

"Crap, that's huge!" the man in the khakis yelled out. The women took a few steps back as the bird looked in their direction.

"That is the coolest thing I've ever seen!" the second man in the group said as Steven paddled past. The raven lifted from the seat and quickly moved out of eyesight.

"Did we scare him away?" a woman with short blond hair called out.

"I highly doubt it; he does it all the time." Steven pulled on his paddle and brought the canoe back up to speed. "Guess that will give them something to talk about," Steven said to the empty seat in front of him. The people's voices drifted away behind him as the prospector glided through the calm water, leaving only a trace of a wake behind her. He guided his boat around the southern point of the channel leading to the portage which would take him to Little Trout Lake.

The clouds had completely obscured the sun by the time Steven placed his prospector, belly down, into Little Trout Lake. Loading his pack in its usual position, he took his place in the bow seat and laid his map out in front of him. He had planned to camp as close as possible to the portage leading to the Pine River, but his resolve was beginning to falter. Demons crept through the corridors of his mind and his ribs hurt. He pushed off from shore and searched for a campsite.

The stillness of the lake soaked into his soul and pushed his fear aside. Placing his paddle on the gunwales of his boat, he scanned the shoreline for as far as his position on the lake allowed; nothing was moving. Reaching into his pack, Steven retrieved the monocular and scanned the shoreline. Steadying the eyepiece with both hands, he searched a campsite just west of the portage which would lead him to Little Trout Creek. Standing stoically on a log was the raven. Steven called out with his imitation of a raven; the bird lifted off the log, circled, and landed on the same log. Steven steered his boat toward a campsite he would have never chosen.

Twilight covered the forest. Fire danced in a rock-lined pit. Its flames licked the wood, causing the resin to pop and filling the campsite with sound and scent. Steven boiled water in a small pot and dropped his dehydrated dinner into the steaming liquid; the smell of the meal rejuvenated him to the point where he was totally at home in his primitive camp surrounded by miles of wilderness. He sat on the ground with his back against a log and stared at the flames.

The darkness echoed with the sounds of loons and crickets. Steven closed his eyes and rested his chin on his chest. The sound of something brushing by his nylon tent pulled him from his nap. When he looked toward the tent and turned his headlamp on, he was greeted with the unmistakable blue-green glow of nocturnal eyes. Steven's heartbeat increased to the point where he could hear it; he tried to melt into the ground in front of the fire pit. The eyes disappeared and reformed as three sets. A low guttural growl issued from the darkness followed by a soul-pounding series of howls which filled the campsite with the primordial call of wolves. Steven froze, realizing he was surrounded by the phantoms which walked unseen just beyond the reach of the firelight. Pulling the headlight off of his head, he scanned the forest. A wolf appeared out of the darkness and stalked toward him. Stopping twenty feet from Steven, it stood with head lowered and legs spread. A short, muffled growl issued from the predator, and then it turned around and lay down on the ground in a curled but attentive position. Steven was transfixed watching the impossible. The reality of the situation took hold in his mind. He was glad he had heeded Agawaatesin's advice to leave Rusty at home. Steven stood; the wolf raised its head. Talking as he would to

Rusty, Steven walked slowly to his tent, unzipped the door, climbed inside, and zippered the door closed. Wrapped in his sleeping bag, the ranger listened to the subtle breathing of the predator which lay just outside the thin nylon walls. The loons' voices mixed with the sound of gentle soft rain hitting the tent formed an enchanting lullaby to coax Steven into a much-needed sleep.

INTERRUPTION

The mid-morning sun streamed through the forest and cast shadows on Little Trout Lake. Steven sat by the fire pit with his map and studied the next leg of his journey. Again, a feeling of foreboding overtook him. The river twisted and turned and was narrow, which would make the job easy should a predator choose to place a lone canoeist on its menu. He began to conjure up scenarios which weren't in the best interest of his nerves.

Realizing he had to move or lose his mind, Steven broke down his camp and pushed off onto Little Trout Lake. The sense of foreboding left him as he paddled toward the portage to Queer Lake. He was watching several loons chase each other with much wing flapping and splashing when he noticed two occupants in a white canoe paddle out from the bay where he was heading. He decided to hug the south shoreline so as to avoid a conversation with the couple. They, however; had a different idea and paddled directly toward him.

"Good morning. I'm Rebecca and this is David," the female in the bow called out to Steven.

"Hello, how are you?" *Shit.* Steven cursed his luck.

"We're ok; we got a little freaked out last night though. Did you hear the wolves howling?"

"Yes, I did; it didn't last long though. It seemed to be coming from this shoreline." Steven pointed to the shoreline he was attempting to hug.

"They were close enough to scare the living shit out of us!" David said as he adjusted the trajectory of the boat to parallel Steven's.

"They won't do you any harm." Steven had lowered his voice.

"I doubt that. We were going to cruise down the Pine River to the take out for Shah Lake, but now we think we will hang out on Little Trout," David stated with presumed authority.

"If the wolves wanted you, we wouldn't be conversing right now. That's quite the change in plans; were you doing a loop?" Steven tried to cover his rising anger.

"We were going to drop into Shah Lake from the Pine River, then move on through to Misty Lake, and back to Magnetawan," Rebecca answered while David gripped his paddle tighter.

"I'm not sure I would change my plans that much just because wolves were howling, but if you're sure, I think the wardens would understand. Just say you're feeling ill and I'm positive no one would question it." Steven knew that was the truth.

"Really, how do you know?" she asked.

"Same way I know the wolves won't bother you," Steven blurted out before thinking about what he was saying. "I just left a site which is all cleaned up and ready to go; it's behind me on that point." He used his paddle as a pointing stick.

"Thanks. Two full nights and days not having to portage sound great to me. Right hon?" The woman turned to look at her partner.

"I think we should just continue on Magnetawan and get out of here. You're nuts, mister; and those wolves, they are killers, plain and simple. The Park should take care of them so we wouldn't have to change our plans," David's anger erupted.

"David!" Rebecca's face was flushed with embarrassment.

"It's fine; I'm not offended." Steven stared at Rebecca. She averted her gaze.

The raven dove directly at David, its body hurtling down in a controlled dive topping forty kilometres per hour. It opened his wings and swooped over the man. David flung his arms up in a vain attempt to ward off the ebony dive bomber. Rebecca screamed just as their canoe capsized and sent the occupants into the cold dark water of Little Trout Lake.

For a few seconds, Steven sat mute in his canoe trying to process the recent events. Then he laughed, unable to control himself.

"I'm sorry, man; that was crazy. What the hell?" Steven blurted out.

"You could at least help us!" David yelled.

Steven grabbed a rope from his pack and tied it to a backpack that was beginning to sink. He tied the free end of the rope to his centre thwart and then he collected other items that were still floating. He paddled alongside the couple who were holding onto their submerged canoe.

"Flip your canoe over, belly up; we have to get the water out of it."

"Fuck you!" David replied.

"Really!" Steven said with clenched teeth.

Steven paddled to shore, untied the couple's pack, and threw it on a rock. He left the rest of the items beside the pack.

"Your stuff is here; have a great day."

"You're leaving us?" Rebecca asked, clearly confused and scared.

"David seems to know everything; you should be just fine."

"Half of our gear is at the bottom of the lake and you're just going to leave!" David yelled out.

"Tie your stuff down and it won't drown. Just saying. But you're right, I don't know anything. Catch you later." Steven didn't hide his disdain.

As he rounded the point and entered the bay, Steven struggled with his decision.

What the hell am I doing? The realization that they were all being manipulated hit him like a brick. Steven turned his canoe around and paddled hard toward David and Rebecca.

Steven found the couple on shore; Rebecca was crying and David was close to exhaustion. Steven retrieved their canoe, drained the water from it, and then loaded their remaining gear.

"I don't know why we got into that cock fight, but I apologize," Steven said as he held the canoe for them.

"What the fuck was that bird doing?" David asked.

"I wish I knew. Here, take these, they should help." Steven handed David four protein bars.

"Thanks, I was a bit of a jerk. I don't know what came over me. Are you sure you didn't train that bird?"

"Positive. You have a five-hour paddle to get to the landing. You should get moving." Steven shook David's hand.

"Thanks for the bars. I guess we have one hell of a story to tell when we get home."

"Yes, you do. Take it easy and try to stay in the canoe." Steven smiled as he spoke.

"We will." David pushed off from shore, raised his paddle in a gesture of goodbye, and then moved off around a point of land.

Steven pointed his canoe toward the bay and plunged his paddle into the water.

THE RIVER

The trail rolled beneath his burdened feet as Steven balanced the canoe on his shoulders and a fifty-pound canoe pack on his back. The sound of his feet hitting the ground was accentuated by the echo effect of the upside-down hull. He trudged on until his shoulders began to complain and his ribs started rebelling. He leaned the bow of his canoe in the fork of a tree and put his pack on the ground. Sitting on a small log he scanned the immediate area. A raven called out, very close to his position, yet Steven could not discern where the call was coming from as it seemed to resonate from everywhere at once.

He surmised that the part of the trail where he presently rested was often used by other canoeists as a rest stop. Testing a theory, he opened his ration pack and tossed a piece of granola onto the ground. Then, from a perfectly round vertical hole just off the travelled portion of the trail, a chipmunk poked his head out and surveyed the situation. Steven watched and smiled as the little fellow scampered over to the piece of granola, sniffed it, and stuffed it into his cheek pouch. The chipmunk stood on his hind legs and begged for more. Steven tossed another piece of food toward the cute panhandler. The little guy grabbed the offering and then turned and scampered back to his side of the trail to disappear down the hole.

"You sure know how to pick a good spot to call home, little buddy," Steven said to the chipmunk as it reappeared from its hole.

The ranger stood up to collect his gear and saw the ventriloquist standing stoically on the raised end of his prospector. The raven lowered its head and stared at him; he could see his reflection in the mirror blackness of the bird's eyes. The two beings stood unmoving for a few heartbeats before the bird lifted off and flew down the trail in the direction Steven was heading.

"I guess I've been told," he said to the chipmunk who was staring at him from the safety of his drop hole. Picking up the pack and securing it to his body, he placed the yoke of the boat on his shoulders, tossed another piece of granola to the panhandler, grabbed the balance rope, and followed the raven to the end of the portage.

The water level of the river was low but canoe worthy. This was a concern which had been weighing on Steven's mind. Placing the prospector into the water and putting the pack in the stern felt immensely satisfying. He boarded the canoe and pushed off, following the current. The sun had dropped from view and twilight was beginning to engulf the region; this made the forest surrounding the river look like a wall.

Steven forced himself to think only about the task of navigating the river; fear was constantly stalking his mind. The silence of the forest was a sound in itself as Steven moved deeper into the convoluted twists and turns that the river had carved out for itself. Several times he had to get out and pull his canoe over downed logs and debris dams, making him feel incredibly vulnerable. He took his camera from his waist and placed it in voice mode.

The river is quiet and seems as if it is pulling me into itself; I'm not sure why I feel safer in this sixty-pound canoe then out of it. Does he want me to move faster? Is he controlling my mind or is it the other one? Maybe I am not being influenced by either. I can't even think of why I ever decided to do this, but I guess I'll soon find out. I'm nervous as hell and I miss my dog. The light is gone and I know I'm being watched.

After his last words were spoken, he put the unit back into its waterproof bag and pulled on his paddle. The canoe shot forward and soon he was moving at a speed which he felt was fast enough to force him to concentrate on the river rather than on the fear which hunted him through the encroaching darkness.

The stars were starting to group in large numbers, reflecting off the water and creating the feeling of travelling through space. The darkness was so complete that Steven had to turn on and direct the beam of his headlight toward the south bank of the river to look for clues as to where he was. Checking his map, he had covered seven kilometres in two hours; he calculated he would make it to the old Pine River Farm site within an hour or two given his slow rate of progress. At one point, the river tricked him and he took the bait. He inadvertently followed a side route which led him into a marsh area. Steven paddled, unaware of his mistake until he was forced to leave his boat to pull it over a beaver dam. When he placed his feet on the debris of the dam, a howl arose from the surrounding forest. Steven crouched beside his canoe. Reaching up to his forehead, he pressed the button on his headlight which instantly flooded the area with light. The trees stood frozen as if they were trying to avoid detection. Steven panned his light in a shallow arc, concentrating on the tree line. Somewhere, just beyond the light's reach, Steven heard a low growl. Shadows moved among the trees. Steven froze in place, unsure how to proceed. A long-drawn-out howl echoed from the forest, joined by other howls. The wolves had formed a semi-circle, and this blocked his forward direction. Steven checked his map and realized his mistake. Breathing for what seemed the first time in minutes, he turned his canoe around and made his way back to the main river. His body shook as adrenaline worked its way through his muscles, and once again the reality of the situation was pressed deep into his core.

Time stood still as the steady current of the river flowed beneath him; he scanned the banks on both sides, hoping to catch sight of the predators which he knew were following. The faint sound of a snapping twig or branch would make Steven turn his attention in the direction of the sound, but the progenitor of the noise never allowed its identity to be known. The moon showed its crescent face just as he was approaching the take out for the portage which would lead him through the old Pine River Farm site and onto his appointed camping spot. Steven turned his headlight on and unloaded the boat. The engulfing silence was so intense he could hear his heart as it responded to his nerves which were well on their way to a full-out revolt.

THE WALL

Shouldering his load, he started the first portion of the two-hundred-and-seventy-five-metre portage. His headlight cast a white glow which filled the upside-down canoe and flooded the ground beneath. Steven could discern nothing but the trail directly in front of him, so he shut the light off. Somewhere far to his left, a great horned owl called out into the darkness. Its call filled the forest and echoed off the trees.

Steven felt a slight push. It came in faintly, just after the owl's call, but then intensified. He felt the usual tingling sensation in his scalp as the unspoken words entered his thoughts. Images of bears stalking him crept out of his subconscious as he fought hard to maintain his control. The push became stronger.

He could plainly see his mother's basement door. Though it was closed, there was a faint light spilling from underneath it. He felt as if something within the dark corners of the subterranean room was beckoning him to take a chance, turn the pitted doorknob, and descend the timeworn wooden steps. Steven could taste the fear as it crept through his body. He started to falter in his steps as the pressure within his skull increased. His thoughts became darker and he envisioned grabbing Mike Denton by the neck, strangling him. He saw himself as a young man, walking through the halls at school. Lisa made cruel intentional jests and taunted him with a disdainful laugh while the jocks of the school jeered. Steven fought hard to regain control. The power that possessed him was becoming insurmountable. He watched as his father stumbled up the front stairs of his house and yelled for help because the door would not open. He saw himself opening the door for his father who then pushed Steven to the floor for not being fast enough. Tears channelled through the dirt on his face and dripped to the ground. His body shook with emotion as the images continued to cascade through his suffocating mind. He saw Rusty with Lisa outside at the cabin. She was talking to a man and was so engrossed in conversation that she failed to see Rusty getting close to the highway. Rusty ran after a red squirrel which pulled him onto the busy two-lane road. Steven physically yelled out into the blackness of Algonquin Park for the dog to stop as Rusty ran straight into the path of a vehicle which hit him and sent the lifeless dog skidding across the pavement. Steven dropped the canoe, fell to the ground, and curled up in a ball as Rusty came to a sliding stop on the gravel shoulder of the highway.

Steven's body heaved with the uncontrollable spasms of anguish which tore into his soul. He was held captive on the dirt, unable to move and unable to fight the images which were woven deep into the maze of his mind.

Teeth clamped down on Steven's neck; he felt his skin yield and rip as the predator closed its jaws. He could feel the hot breath pass across his exposed flesh. Blood and saliva flowed, following the dictates of gravity. Unable to move or even know if anything was real, he simply raised his hands in submission to the death which was pressing its muzzle into his neck. A deep, long growl vibrated through Steven's body and the pressure of the jaws holding him increased. He instinctively reached out to defend himself and grabbed a handful of fur. The realization that he was being physically attacked forced him to open his eyes; he found himself staring straight into the eyes of a wolf.

The animal pinned him to the ground; he was unable to move. The thought of death released his mind from the tortuous pressure which had enveloped it. A second growl issued from the animal and coursed through his body. Steven replied with a growl of his own which emanated from deep inside his core. With strength building back into his body, the ranger dug his fingers into the throat of his assailant. The animal responded by releasing Steven and backing up a few paces. Kneeling, he faced the wolf which stood with lowered head and spread front legs. Its eyes bored a hole into Steven's mind. He reached for his knife which hung from its sheath on the right side of his belt; the wolf responded by taking a step toward the ranger. The knife stayed in its sheath. Steven's addled mind began to function again.

"Back off!"

The words left his mouth and left him wondering if sanity had truly escaped him. The wolf responded by issuing a sound he had heard Rusty make when he was curious about something. It was a soft sound, a cross between a growl and a bark. The animal then turned and vanished into the underbrush. Within moments, the spine-tingling sound of wolves howling filled the darkness.

Steven stood; the image of Rusty's lifeless body had entwined itself deeply in his mind and weakened his legs. Tears flowed unabated where they dripped onto his shirt joining the blood and sweat which already adorned the garment; however, the altercation had released the grip of insanity which had enveloped him. He wrapped his wound with his bandanna, picked the canoe up from where it had fallen, and continued along the trail while listening to the sounds of the wolves as they paced him.

The campsite lay close to the trail beside a waterfall which lay unseen in the darkness. Steven placed the canoe on the ground and made a mental note to check the hull in the light of day. He scrounged up enough firewood to lay a small fire in the existing pit. The light from the burning wood danced across the ground and escaped into the surrounding forest, making it hard to discern if the movements of the shadows were not indeed creatures of the forest. He busied himself by setting up camp and boiling water in a small pot which blackened as the flames licked at its belly. He contemplated the psychological attack he experienced on the trail and realized he had absolutely no chance of dealing with the creature which stalked him.

Steven nervously scanned the area; the faint moonlight frustrated his ability to focus. Sitting with his back against the remains of a camboose cabin, pressure once again pushed into his mind. This time it crept in with no preamble. Steven stood and prepared himself for the inevitable onslaught. He walked to his pack and put the buckskin vest on. Using a length of cordage, he fastened the spearhead to a staff of ironwood.

The intensity of the push increased. Thoughts coalesced within his mind which pressed upon him his inferiority and his uselessness. He resisted, forcing his brain to reverse direction. He drew power from the memory of the animal which had recently held him in its jaws. He widened his stance and lowered his head slightly; firelight cast his shadow far from his feet where it stood in defiance to the energy attempting to consume it.

"You are different than the others who have passed this way; you have help."

Steven felt the words as they meshed into his mind. He tried to get a fix on his antagonist but his head felt as if it were going to explode. The energy coursing toward him was palpable; he collapsed to his knees as he tried to negate its power.

"Come on, you bastard; I can take it!" Steven cried out.

His mind reeled from the next assault which forced his temples to throb and his eyes to close. Steven fell to the ground. His tortured mind reached out into the darkness, calling for help. He could feel the wolves moving around the clearing. The connection brought relief to the unbearable pain in his head.

The ranger knelt up and searched for his antagonist. A shadow entered the dim light; it drifted in and out of his vision. Watching the wraith was terrifying. Steven stood and leaned against the log wall of the camboose cabin, knowing full well that running was not an option.

"You have the ability to face me; I'm curious how you have managed that?"

The shadow materialized into something which was impossible. A searing pain coursed through Steven's head, causing him to hold onto his temples with his hands. Blood dripped from his nose and his ears pounded as he faced the menace which was determined to remove him from the Earth. He held the spear out and braced himself against the logs for the charge that would surely come. Silence engulfed the area; nothing moved. He could feel his heart jumping and he was aware that the thing facing him could feel it also.

The energy came at him like a wave, hitting him square in the chest and knocking him back against the rotting wall. The animal attacked from his right side. It hit him like a freight train and threw him against the trunk of a tree. He lay as he fell: crumpled, broken, and bleeding.

Standing in front of him, faintly bathed in moonlight, was a nightmare which glared at him with eyes that dissected his very soul. The animal dropped to all fours; it pulled the shaft of Steven's spear from its leg and advanced on the helpless man. The ranger raised his torn arm as a last gesture of defiance.

A large body hurtled through the air and smashed into the animal as it closed in on him. Steven watched as two impossible beings fought. They swiftly moved in on one another, committing their existence into the attack. They rolled on the ground, embraced in a fight which filled the air with devastating sound. The energy emanating from them drove wedges into the ranger's fragmented mind, and he cried out in terror to the surrounding wilderness.

The ranger desperately clung to consciousness as he watched the battle unfold before him. Trees snapped like twigs, ground debris was tossed into the air, and the sound emanating from the combatants was primal. The smell of blood permeated the air. Darkness stalked in on his mind; the ranger lost control and slipped into oblivion.

RELEASE

The wolves approached in a semicircle, moving in unison and eventually encircling the area. The leader stalked toward the combatants who lay locked together and unmoving. It circled them once and then chose its target. The wolf clamped down on the fur of one of the animals and pulled backwards. The animal responded and grabbed onto the wolf with its arms. Agawaatesin rolled onto the wolf, bit its neck, and then released it. The wolf ran in circles. The rest of the pack joined in and pounced on each another in a celebration of living.

The ranger's eyes opened.

"Ranger, it's done."

The words entered Steven's head like gentle rain.

"One of us is dead; he has travelled many lifetimes to this conclusion. I'm not proud of what had to be done, yet I'm relieved at the same time." Agawaatesin lay down in front of Steven. *"You were brave; it was your defiance which altered the outcome."*

"He kicked my ass. I think I'm done. I'm freezing cold and I can't feel my arms or legs." Steven tried to hold his tears in check.

"You are dying, my friend."

"What does that mean?"

"You will pass, soon."

"*I can't, not now.*" Steven broke down, tears rained from his eyes as he thought of all the things he would never touch again.

Agawaatesin closed in on the fallen man.

"*This will hurt.*"

Agawaatesin plunged four of his claws into Steven's side. Steven screamed out in pain. This set off a chorus of howls from the wolves. The last thing Steven remembered was a searing flow of pain coursing through his body; he succumbed to the power of it and left his consciousness behind.

QUESTIONS
ANSWERED

He awoke beside the fire pit. Sunlight was streaming through the trees and the river flowed by the site as it had always done. Birds flitted about, doing whatever chores they chose. He examined his body but could find no trace of trauma. Slowly sitting, and then carefully standing, he felt the stiffness that accompanies a night spent on hard ground in cold temperatures. Steven took off his vest and shirt. Four distinct claw marks decorated his right abdominal area, yet the wounds looked as if they had healed a long time ago. Steven paced around the campsite taking mental inventory, trying to understand the reality of the situation.

"You'll be fine."

Agawaatesin's voice entered Steven's head. His last memory was of Agawaatesin plunging his dagger-like claws into his side. Steven touched the scars which coincided with that memory.

"What the hell happened; how is this possible?"

"You have attained a gift, Ranger; don't ask the question how."

Agawaatesin drifted into the campsite from the east side.

Steven watched as the creature closed the distance. The power emanating from it was so intense that he had to put up a mental block to stop it from overpowering him.

"You have learned well, brother."

"How close was I to dying?"

"You were right on the edge, my friend. That is why I had to plunge my claws into your flesh; I had to take your life in order to give it back."

"What are you talking about?"

"Don't ask."

"I knew you would say that," Steven pushed back as he followed Agawaatesin to the clearing where his life had irrevocably changed. A huge patch of ground was torn up and blood painted the area.

"Where's the body?"

"The wolves ate while you slept."

"Holy shit, they ate it?" Steven pictured the predators ripping into the creature's meat.

"The wolves were hungry and the cycle continues." Agawaatesin lay down and asked, *"Where did you obtain that arrowhead?"*

"I got it from a trunk I found in my mother's basement."

"The vest was also in there."

"How the hell did you know that?" Steven asked, perplexed.

"Look on the ground to your left." Agawaatesin motioned to Steven's side.

Steven looked to his left and saw the makeshift spear on the ground.

"Man, I thought this was gone!"

Agawaatesin moved closer.

"Do you know who your grandfather was?"

"Only what I read about him from my grandmother's journal."

"The spear and the vest were both made by your grandfather; I know this because I was there."

Steven was completely stunned.

"He was a man of great courage and empathy; he loved the world as deeply as anyone possibly could. He walked the Earth with reverence, the likes of which I have not witnessed until recently. Dark Owl carried the burden of correcting the transgressions of others toward

the land. He festered at people's lack of compassion. He was a man who wanted peace but found himself constantly embroiled in conflict due to his convictions."

"How did he die?"

"Dark Owl – your grandfather, was tending to a wolf; it had been crippled by a bullet. The man who shot the wolf approached Dark Owl and told him to move aside so he could kill it. Dark Owl lunged at the person who in turn shot him in the leg. The man ran off while Dark Owl lay bleeding. As his life's blood soaked into the forest's floor, he crawled to the side of the wolf and plunged his knife into its heart. He killed the animal out of compassion. Had the animal still been alive when the people returned, they would have dragged it out of the forest by its feet while it still held breath in its lungs. Such was the attitude of humans in the past and still is to this day."

Steven literally saw the event unfold through the eyes of the only witness. He watched as his grandfather held onto life long enough for Brenda and their son to come to his side. He watched as they held onto Dark Owl in a desperate attempt to coax life back into him. Steven could feel the pain of his father and of his grandmother as they sat helplessly beside the man they loved.

"You were there; why didn't you save him as you did me?" Steven yelled at Agawaatesin as tears dripped off his chin.

"It wasn't my call; do not press me on it. I saved you for reasons you do not need to know at this time. Your grandfather had chosen that moment, and I was not going to take it from him."

Steven looked at the bloodstained ground which marked the events of the previous night.

"I wish I had met him."

"You did, last night."

"What are you saying?" Steven's confusion was painted on his face.

"I'm saying that there are individuals who are allowed to manifest themselves as something other than human. The individual we locked claws with last night was Dark Owl."

"What the fuck! Why the hell didn't you tell me this from the start? The outcome of this trip would have been significantly different!" Steven continued while feeling the onset of collapse.

"I had no knowledge of whom or what that individual had once been until I took on his energy. At that moment I was able to see him as he was in the past, and I recognized my old friend. I passed with him to a place where he is free of his anguish. I have been granted the privilege of welcoming him back here when he chooses to return. I have shed much emotion over the outcome of last night as you lay recovering. What had to be done, was accomplished." Agawaatesin averted his gaze from Steven to look at the ground where the battle's conclusion took place.

Steven looked at the spearhead which Dark Owl himself had created many years ago.

"He wanted out. His struggle to accept humanity will never end, yet next time he may succeed in understanding his anger and protect what is left of the wilderness so that other people may understand it," Agawaatesin said as he stood up and shook his fur.

"How can all of this be understood? None of it makes sense; I have no idea if I'm stuck in a really wicked dream or if this is all somehow impossibly real."

"There are things which exist far beyond what your mind can fathom; I'm a living example. Don't ask the question, just accept the answer."

"How do I accept something that is not possible?"

"You have accepted me, have you not? Our journey together is never going to end, so I would suggest you stop asking questions." Agawaatesin moved closer to the tree line.

"Hey, is this all over? Can I get out of here and bury my dog?" Steven asked while tears rolled down his face and his throat constricted.

"Head for Longer Lake and stay tonight on the campsite next to the waterfall. I will see you soon, my brother."

Steven was alone; the area had become quiet and sombre. Walking to the spot where the other creature had died, he knelt down on one knee.

"I'm sorry — I'm having a hard time coping with all of this, but please forgive me." He spoke quietly as tears rolled, unchecked, toward the ground. A deep chortling croak lifted Steven's eyes from the earth. Directly in front of him was the raven; it looked straight into his eyes and called out. Then it jumped into the air and took flight; the ebony mystery lifted over the northern tree line. Steven thought momentarily of burying the spearhead where the creature had died, but then he placed it in his pocket.

Walking back to the campsite, he shouldered his gear, picked up his canoe, and followed the remaining leg of the portage to the river. Looking around one last time, he climbed into his boat and pushed off to follow the river's current to Ship-Pa-Gew Lake.

A NEW LONGING

A PREDATOR MUST HUNT FOR SOMETHING IF IT IS TO STAY TRUE TO ITS HEART.

S teven reached Ship-Pa-Gew Lake by late afternoon under a warm sun and deep blue sky. The effort he used to navigate the river greatly improved his perspective. He felt a deeply profound connection to the wilderness; it coursed through his bloodstream and attached itself to his very soul. Agawaatesin had told him to head for Longer Lake which would take him at least another two, possibly three hours. He was mentally drained and physically exhausted, yet somehow completely invigorated. He hesitated as he passed one of the two campsites on the lake. He eddied just offshore for several minutes before he felt the need to follow his friend's advice.

Reaching the trail head, he unloaded his boat and stood silently by the rushing water of the falls which cascaded over the rock-strewn base of the river. He drank the sound of the falls deep into his body, trying to mitigate the pain encapsulating his heart. Balancing his canoe on his shoulders, he set off for the lower end of the river which spilled into Longer Lake.

The trail taxed his physical reserves, forcing him to rest slightly more than halfway along its length. A white birch tree had succumbed to the push of heavy winds and provided a perfect canoe stand. Dropping his pack, he sat and closed his eyes to feel the forest around him. A slight rustle brought his attention to the direction from which he had come. Standing silently in the centre of the narrow trail stood a lynx, its grey-black fur ruffling slightly in the breeze. Steven held his breath. It scented the air and then moved silently toward him. He closed his eyes and pushed a thought gently toward it. The silent predator brushed Steven's outstretched hand and purred quietly as it passed. The ranger opened his eyes and watched as the lynx vanished from the trail not one metre from him. He touched the ground and smiled. He donned his pack, hoisted his canoe, and continued to the end of the portage.

Longer Lake was quiet and calm as Steven paddled out of the bay in which the portage resided. He scanned the eastern shoreline for the campsite by the waterfalls. Three canoes were beached on the rocky shore. Steven stopped paddling; he was unsure what to do as Agawaatesin had told him specifically to aim for that site. As his boat drifted, he heard a chorus of yells issuing from the site. The noise of the waterfalls obliterated any understanding of the words. He instinctively wanted to retreat, but curiosity forced him to slowly move out of the bay and into the open water of the lake. As he closed the distance to the site, he noted five people, all of whom were yelling in his direction. Steven realized something must be wrong, so he kneeled up in the canoe and pulled hard for the camp. An animal was in the water coming toward him; the distinctive outline of a dog's head formed as the distance shrank. The realization that it was Rusty dawned on Steven and he burst into tears at the sight of the crazy animal. Rusty sounded like an old two-stroke motor as he coughed and choked his way across the lake. Steven brought his canoe up alongside the Lab and kissed his head. He slowed his paddling so the dog could keep pace with him and manoeuvred his canoe toward shore. Within a few minutes of strained longing, he side-slipped into the rocks and jumped into the water where he and Rusty collided with each other. The dog cried loudly and jumped all over Steven who in turn held onto the Lab as if he was never going to let him go. Steven sobbed as Rusty licked his face. He lifted Rusty into the boat where the dog took up his usual position and thumped the side of the water craft with his tail, telling everyone he had found his leader.

Steven turned the boat and paddled for the campsite where the people were laughing and calling out to him. As he approached, he saw the familiar faces of Ralph, Tom, Larry, Bill, and Lisa. All of them were lined up on the steep shore and yelling for him to paddle harder. He jumped out of the canoe and grabbed the rope on the stern. He pulled the boat behind him as he waded through the rock-strewn landing, followed by Rusty, who shook his fur while still in the lake. Five bodies collided on the steep bank while Rusty ran in circles soaking everyone with well-timed shakes.

Lisa kissed Steven hard, which elicited a response from Tom who mentioned that he had wanted to be the first to do that. Steven lifted his canoe up onto the shoreline and turned it over. Grabbing his pack, he followed his friends up the incline to the warmth of a well-made fire.

"What the hell did you drag us out here for, Steven? Do you realize we haven't had a beer in two days?" Tom said as he threw a cigarette butt into the fire.

"Lisa called us the day you left and planned this whole thing out. Cool, eh!" Larry said while adjusting his camp chair to fit the contours of the ground.

Ralph grabbed the ranger and hugged him close.

"Rusty's all yours, my friend; he clearly loves the shit out of you, and I'm not coming between that."

Tom made suggestions that Lisa should keep Steven on a shorter leash.

"You almost missed dinner. Tonight's special is dehydrated chicken teriyaki served in a collapsible bowl." Tom made a face which spoke volumes about his real feelings.

"Camping on this site makes me want to pee all the time," Larry informed the gang as he stood up from his chair and walked to the back of the camp to relieve himself.

"I almost didn't come, but I figured someone had to look after these idiots," Bill stated which incited the men to hurl comments and pine cones at him.

Ralph smiled as he busied himself tending to the needs of the fire.

"You look like hell; how hard was that river?" Lisa was concerned.

"I'm ok; I can't believe you came all the way out here. How did you make it so fast?"

"Those portages were brutal; I'm worn out," Bill interjected.

Lisa looked at Bill and shook her head. "I pulled some strings and got the Park to drop us off by float plane on Big Trout. We just arrived today and I've had a hell of a time trying to understand your buddies." Lisa pointed in the general direction of the men.

"Who said they were my buddies? I should have busted them when I first met them. Why would anyone agree to fly these bums in?" Steven tried to control his smile.

"I actually have no idea how it happened. When you told me about your trip, I thought it would be great to get out and meet you, so I called a friend who works here in the Park. She called me back a few hours later, and before I knew it, the plan was set."

"The thought just crept up on you, huh?" Steven questioned Lisa.

"Weird, I know; but here I am, and those guys are like the four stooges in real life," Lisa said as she passed her fingers through Steven's hair.

"Hey, you're lucky Bill could make it; he rounds us out. Get it?" Tom volleyed back.

"If I knew there was a plane involved, I would have backed out. I'm not that adventurous, you know," Bill commented.

"No shit, Bill; your definition of adventure comes with a couch and a blanket," Tom volleyed back.

"Ha, Ha, Tom's hilarious." Bill made a face and pretended to laugh. The men crumpled in laughter. Lisa looked confused.

Steven watched as the group settled into the routine of camp. He knew that the chances of getting access to the Park via plane were next to impossible, but then so was the existence of Agawaatesin. The fire shot orange sparks up into the air as if it were celebrating the group's reunion with a miniature fireworks display. Steven stared deeply into the coals and listened while the men told Lisa stories of their adventures. He struggled to subdue the memory of the prior night. His hands trembled as images of the fight poked and prodded his mind. The group fell silent, and the sounds of the waterfalls and the crackling of burning wood filled in the hollow spots and worked its magic.

Wolves howling to the west captured the attention of everyone, including Rusty, who lifted and tilted his head.

"Shit, now I have to deal with wolves!" Bill commented as he sank lower into his chair.

"Imagine meeting them on a trail in this darkness?" Larry whispered.

"I wouldn't be on a trail at this time of night; you would have to be an idiot to try it," Tom replied.

Lisa snuggled closer to Steven. She felt the tension within him which concerned her. "Have you ever been portaging at this time of night?"

"Yes, I have." Steven tried to control the effects of the adrenaline pumping through his veins.

"Are you ok? You're shaking," Lisa said with concern.

"Something about their voices; is it that noticeable?"

Lisa placed both her hands on Steven's scalp and massaged his head.

"Hey, Larry, can you do that to me, buddy?" Tom asked.

"Screw off; I would have to be really lonely to put my hands on your scalp." Larry leaned back in his chair trying to get some distance from Tom.

"Hey, how about you, Ralph?"

"Oh man, don't you ever stop?" Ralph laughed.

"I've got it: we'll form a circle and everyone can run their hands through the hair of the person in front. Are we all in?" Bill chimed in while everyone else found something to throw at him.

"Tom, I wouldn't want to touch your hair in case the rest of it fell out," Larry laughed as the words left his mouth.

Ralph started singing a song which he had thought of that moment. "I left my hair on Longer Lake, now it's gone, I must move on."

"What the hell?" Tom replied while the others burst into laughter which drifted out across the dark water.

Agawaatesin stood quietly in the shadows of the trees, watching Steven closely.

"*Ranger, meet with me.*"

Steven got up from his spot and told the group he had to relieve himself. Walking away from the fire felt good to him somehow. Rusty ran past him and disappeared into the darkness of the forest. Crouched on the ground beside a large boulder, he spotted Agawaatesin. Rusty was lying on his back while Agawaatesin ran his paw over the belly of the dog.

"*I'm having a rough time of it,*" Steven pushed.

"*You carry strong medicine; it runs through your veins as it did your grandfather. It will take time. I will teach you.*"

Tears formed in the corners of Steven's eyes and trickled down his cheeks. The words Agawaatesin spoke broke through barriers around his heart and worked deep into his soul.

"*I would love that.*"

"*You undervalue yourself; humility is always the strongest pole in a lodge. You have earned this and a name which I will call you from now on.*" Agawaatesin stood and approached Steven, who crouched on the ground, struggling to gain control of his emotions.

"*The wolves that followed you last night were tracking you because of what you carry. They protected you as one of their own. Their kinship with you runs deep, as it did with Dark Owl. You will always be able to run with them. However, you have to suppress your energy around humans; they will feel it and repel you. I will teach you to mask it, yet harness it when you feel the need.*" Agawaatesin stood close to Steven.

Steven looked into the impossible face of the being in front of him.

"*I'm going to call you Ranger from now on.*" Agawaatesin grinned.

"*I thought you were going to call me Running Wolf or something cool.*"

"*Ranger is a good name for you. By definition, it means one who travels far from home yet is at home wherever they find themselves. I'm not changing it; get used to it.*"

Steven punched Agawaatesin on his shoulder which precipitated Agawaatesin to push the ranger and pin him to the ground.

"Shit!" Steven yelled out as he struggled futilely under the power of Agawaatesin's arm.

"What the hell is he doing over there?" Tom said loud enough for Steven to hear.

Lisa turned on her headlight and walked in the direction of the commotion, followed by the four men.

"That must be one hell of a shit he's having," Tom stated while Larry and Ralph laughed.

Steven lay on the ground, with Rusty straddling him and chewing on his arm.

"Is this normal, or has he been on his own too long?" Bill asked, trying to keep a straight face.

"Should I be worried?" Lisa added.

Rusty jumped off Steven and raced through the surrounding trees as if he had gone mad. Steven stood and brushed the dirt off his clothes.

"Rusty tackled me as I was coming back to the fire, so we had a play fight. I think he won."

"Well, it's your story. Who are we to judge?" Ralph said as he tried to follow the antics of the crazy dog. The group made its way back to the fire pit which invited them with its promise of light and warmth.

Agawaatesin rose from where he had hidden and followed the group. Staying in the shadows, he lay down and watched the interactions of the people who shared his friend's life. Lisa's mind was conflicted; he could feel her concern and confusion. He would watch her closely.

Agawaatesin then focused on Ralph, for his disease was spreading. The ranger would need this man's companionship as he struggled with his metamorphosis. Agawaatesin closed his eyes.

"Fuck!" Ralph jumped off his chair and fell to the ground.

"Ralph! What the hell!" Bill shouted out.

Ralph rolled over, stood up, and pulled his pants off. "Something just took a chunk out of me! Fucking hell, that hurt!"

"God, I love camping. Put your pants on, Ralph; your legs glow in the dark, dude," Tom said as he doubled over laughing.

"Holy shit, what the hell bit you, Ralph!" Bill said as he doused himself in bug spray. "I hate camping!"

Steven and his friends laughed until their sides hurt and breathing became a chore.

Agawaatesin smiled and moved deeper into the shadows.

The moon travelled its path westward, threw its light into the forest, and covered the lake with twinkling diamonds. Loons called out with their plaintive haunting sound as they scouted for food and talked of their upcoming flight south.

Steven sat quietly listening to the group as they conversed about bugs and any other given topic which came to mind. Eventually, the strain to keep his eyes open won the battle and he told the gang he was heading to sleep.

"Ya, no worries, Steve; goodnight buddy," Ralph said as he placed another log on the fire.

Steven thanked the men once more and headed to the tent Lisa had claimed, followed closely by Rusty. Lisa brushed her teeth and said a goodnight to the boys, and then she climbed into the tent with Steven.

"What went on out there? Something is bothering you; I know it," Lisa whispered.

"I had a hard time on the river. My ribs hurt like hell and it scared me that a small injury like a fractured rib could put me out of commission. I'm totally wiped out."

"Ok, I was just worried something had happened to you. I felt anxious as hell last night." She held onto Steven's arm.

"I am alright, Lisa; it was a tough night and I missed you like crazy," Steven said as he stroked her hair.

Rusty pushed his way between them and sprawled out as if he deserved the entire sleeping area. Steven placed his head on his backpack and listened to the quiet chatter of his friends whose silhouettes flickered off the tent walls.

Closing his eyes, he pushed his energy out into the surrounding darkness. Within a few heartbeats, he was running with the wolves. They ran in almost complete darkness down paths unseen by humans and they ran for the sheer joy of it. Steven released his connection and opened his eyes; Rusty stood over him and licked his face. Pushing the Lab off of him, Steven took advantage of the situation and cuddled up beside Lisa. Rusty surveyed the situation for a few minutes, and then he lay down. He let out a big groan as he dropped his head to the mattress, clearly upset about the arrangement. Steven lay on his side with his eyes open; firelight flickered on the nylon walls of the tent and created a kaleidoscope of images which seemed to dance to an inaudible melody. Lisa's and Rusty's breathing filled the shelter with reassuring comfort, but Steven's mind was a blender of unanswered questions and unrelenting emotions.

"Sleep, Ranger; your answers will come in time. I will teach you the art of camouflaging yourself in the open; you are no longer what you were."

Steven felt the reassuring push from Agawaatesin which organized the confusion in his head.

"I feel stronger, yet weaker; sad, yet elated; tired yet awake."

"You are all of those and always will be. You will get used to it."

"What do I tell Lisa?"

"Nothing."

"Why did she go through all the trouble of coming here to meet me?"

"She loves you and I asked her to. I persuaded her associates to facilitate her arrival here. The encounter last night is not to be taken lightly; it has changed you in ways that you cannot comprehend. Lisa and your friends will keep you safe. Embrace and enjoy their lives; lead and follow; hide in plain sight. This is the way of your life now."

"Thanks, brother; don't let me drown," Steven pushed back as a tear creased his cheek.

"Close your eyes so you can run, my friend; tomorrow and all the days that follow will be filled with the answers you need."

"I bet they will."

"I will see you soon."

Agawaatesin's final statement acted as a tonic for him, and the last thing the ranger felt was Rusty's paw pushing into his face.

Agawaatesin used the rushing water cascading over the rocks beside the campsite to cover his sound as he left the group. Travelling southward, he joined up with the portage trail to Big Trout Lake and followed it to the end. He looked across the large body of water and spotted the flickering glow of many ebbing campfires. Standing on the sandy soil of the shoreline, Agawaatesin raised his head and let out a powerful primordial howl which echoed off the rock faces and hills for several minutes.

People responded by turning on every light they had at their disposal. Fear drifted on the slight breeze across the lake to Agawaatesin. He called out into the blackness of the night pushing the primal energy of the wilderness deep into the hearts of the humans cowering within their civilized brains. Wolves, not far to the west, howled their approval. Fires sprung to life as the humans huddled closely together, looking apprehensively into the darkness of the forest surrounding them.

R.G. Wright ©

CPSIA information can be obtained
at www.ICGtesting.com
Printed in the USA
LVHW012255240619
622265LV00001B/92/P

9 780228 808169